# THE THIRD BANANA

## A REX & EDDIE MYSTERY

### SEAN CAMERON

D1264118

**DAPPER FOX
PUBLISHING**

Cover Design: Anthony S. Hales

ISBN-13: 978-1-946215-04-8

# ONE

A battered old Morris Minor pulled up alongside the River Invicta, a winding waterway that branched off the Thames estuary. When it passed through the town of Cloisterham, the water became decidedly brown and murky. Some locals claimed the colour came from its rich minerals, but even they daren't swim in its waters.

The car engine petered out with an asthmatic wheeze. Inside, Eddie and his private detective partner watched their target walk down the poorly lit street. The young man approached The Barge Inn, a sizeable brown-bricked pub and one of the few buildings next to this part of the river; an area that flooded regularly.

Rex Milton, a tall man in his late twenties, straightened his round glasses and brushed his dark shaggy hair away from his ears.

"What came first, the chicken or the egg?"

Although the watching investigators had only parked ten seconds ago, the windows had already fogged from Rex's excessive body heat. Eddie sighed as he cranked the driver's door window ajar.

Eddie Miles, a slightly shorter than average man who held himself like a rather short man, buttoned up his crumpled beige suit jacket.

"The egg," he said.

Rex pursed his lips. "What makes you so sure?"

Eddie straightened his already straight neat hair and scratched the slight stubble on his chin. Usually a daily shaver, he wasn't happy with his messy appearance. "Because dinosaurs laid eggs millions of years before chickens ever did."

Outside was cold and the ground wet. Specks of water filled the air, meaning you'd never quite notice you were being rained on, but Eddie felt his right side progressively dampen from the open window.

He wiped the water droplets from his notepad, a meticulous list detailing time, locations, and the activities of their target — Daryl Archer.

Rex chewed on a Red Vine, his fourth of the evening. He furrowed his brow at Eddie's excessive note writing. "Is a badger more like a bear or a dog?"

"Please, Rex. No more animal questions." Eddie scribbled on the pad furiously. "I need to focus on documenting Daryl Archer's behaviour. Note taking is the most important part of an investigation."

"Not if we lose him." Rex wiped the windscreen condensation so he could see their target.

Daryl Archer was in his early twenties, tall and slender, with a mop of mousy brown hair and a tidy goatee. He turned up the collar of his green puffer jacket as he walked into the pub.

Rex unbuckled his seatbelt. "I'm gonna follow him."

"No, wait." Eddie cranked his window closed as he wrote. "I'll be a second."

Rex gave the passenger door a solid shove to lodge it

open. Once outside he rammed it closed as Eddie continued to plead.

"Not without me, I'll just be—"

With the door closed, Rex's window reflection smiled back at himself, overlaying Eddie's disapproving stare.

Eddie rushed out of the lime green Morris Minor Traveller 1000. As he wiggled the key into the lock, he noticed a loose splinter poke out from the car's wooden frame. He pulled the splinter as he locked the door.

"We're going in there together," Eddie said.

With a grin, Rex did up the buttons of his dark brown corduroy jacket. "Maybe we can get a pint too."

---

Inside The Barge Inn, framed paintings of boats and ships covered the walls. A U-shaped bar filled the middle of the room, rammed with a youthful crowd covering the floor space.

Using a tall wall mirror, Eddie adjusted his tie. He leaned towards Rex so he could talk over the music.

"I'm gonna look for Archer. You—"

"Get the drinks in?" Rex wiped the rain from his round frame glasses with the bottom of his untucked shirt.

"This isn't a Friday night pub crawl, Rex. We're on a case."

"Got to look the part though. Everyone else has a drink."

Eddie glanced at the people around him; each one was holding a glass.

"I suppose we can claim it as an expense."

Rex smiled and held out his hand.

Eddie tightened his upper lip and handed over a ten-pound note. "I want change."

As Rex rushed towards the bar, Eddie squeezed through a group of half-drunk students arguing over who had the most selective taste in music.

Frustrated, he pushed his way through the crowd until a pint of beer hovered into his view. He turned to see Rex holding the drink.

"Seen him?" Rex asked between sips of his pint.

Eddie took the beer while eyeballing Rex's drink. He'd been handed the flatter of the two.

Being slightly over six foot, Rex glanced over most of the crowd. He saw Archer laughing with a blue-haired young man.

"What's he doing?" Eddie asked.

Archer's right foot bounced up and down as his knee jittered.

"He's nervous."

A pale man with platinum dreads approached Daryl Archer with a knowing nod.

"There's a guy with blond dreads now."

"Get a photo." Eddie handed his phone to Rex.

Archer talked into the dreadlocked man's ear. He handed the dreadlocked man a computer disc with handwriting on it too small to read.

Rex raised the phone above the nearby people to get a good shot of Daryl. As he took a photo the phone flashed.

Alerted, the nearby crowd turned to Rex and Eddie. Both detectives spun around one hundred and eighty degrees. The duo slurped their beers as they mimed searching for the mysterious flash.

"He handed over a disc," Rex whispered. "What do you think's on it? Is he a hacker? Maybe he's got government information."

"Oh, please. Don't get carried away."

Rex grinned. "We're going up in the world of private investigation, Eddie."

"We follow Archer, not the disc." Eddie wrote the details in his notebook. "Let's get a clear photo of the guy with the dreads; we'll see if the client can ID him." He held Rex's arm. "Try to be a bit more subtle this time."

A space in the crowd briefly emerged, and the pair darted towards the dreadlocked man. Rex raised the phone as Eddie posed to give the impression he was the subject of the photo. As Rex took a flashless photo, the dreadlocked man placed the disc in his inner jacket pocket, downed his drink, and approached the bar.

Eddie gulped his beer as he took his phone. "Where's my change?"

Rex handed over a few silver coins. "Archer's leaving."

"Nine quid for two beers? What do they think this is? London?"

Rex tipped his head back to finish off his pint. He walked towards the exit. "Come on, Eddie."

Having drunk only a third, Eddie took a desperate gulp of his beer. "Hold on."

Archer headed out the door with his blue-haired friend. Through the windows, Eddie watched the pair walk down the road. He forced his drink down his throat in a few hard swallows. He shuddered and his neck muscles tensed.

Rex placed his empty glass on the bar. "Come on, Eddie. Let's go."

Eddie took another gulp. "I paid almost five quid for this drink. I intend to finish it."

He washed down more of the beer as they approached the front door. After swallowing, Eddie involuntarily stuck out his tongue. "How'd you do yours so easily?"

Through the front door's glass panels, Rex saw a black van pull up next to Archer. Two men in matching grey hoodies jumped out of the car, their faces obscured by the hoods.

"Uh, Eddie," Rex said.

With his head tipped back slurping beer, Eddie raised a finger hinting he'd be done soon.

"Eddie!"

He swallowed and looked out the window. "What is it?"

Outside the two hoodies surrounded Archer. He tried to dodge them, but the pair grabbed him and pulled him into the van. The blue-haired friend ran off down an alleyway.

"Oh," Rex said.

Eddie swallowed, leaving one inch of beer in the glass. "Ah."

The van sped off down the road. Rex and Eddie's target was gone.

# TWO

Eddie let his pint glass slip from his hand. The glass crashed against the floor, releasing a small puddle of his leftover beer.

The crowd gave a sarcastic cheer at the sound of the smash.

Eddie spun around to the bar. "Sorry." He turned back to Rex. "We, uh, have to chase them? Right?"

Rex nodded. "Yes, please."

As the black van drove away, Rex and Eddie bolted out the pub door towards the Morris Minor. Eddie felt his pint of beer swish around in his stomach. His abdomen sounded like a shaken hot water bottle.

The pavement was so wet that when Rex attempted to stop at the car, he skidded into the Morris Minor's passenger door.

Eddie unlocked his door. Once inside, he kicked the passenger door repeatedly until it popped open.

Rex climbed in and buckled up while Eddie turned the key, but the engine merely whimpered.

"You can do it, Eddie."

"It's not a matter of me doing it. The car doesn't like the damp weather."

"Or hills," Rex added. "Or cold mornings, or cold nights, or cold in general." He cocked his head. "Doesn't like the heat much either—"

"Yes, thanks, Rex."

Eddie cranked the key again. The car turned on. He slapped the dashboard with pride and the engine sound tailed off.

"No, I'm sorry. Please, don't." The engine rolled along louder again. Eddie kissed his hand and gently placed it on the dashboard. "Thank you."

Another dark van whooshed by the Morris Minor, causing the parked vehicle to sway left and right.

Eddie forced his foot on the accelerator. "There's two of them."

The two vans drove through the cross junction as the traffic lights turned amber. Eddie floored the accelerator and zipped through before the light turned red. Buzzed from his rushed beer, Eddie felt dizziness as the car turned into the street. He'd run through a red light, but he didn't have time to feel guilty about it.

"This is a kidnapping, right?" Eddie said.

Rex gave a toothy grin. "I think so."

The pair of vans took a hard right into a side road. The Morris Minor continued straight missing the vans' route.

Rex's smile dropped. "What are you doing?"

Eddie gripped the steering wheel. "Their street becomes a one-way road in a minute. If we go up here, they'll be sent straight towards us."

The Morris Minor took a right and glided along the road. Eddie turned the vehicle to the side to block the one-way street. The two vans came at the Morris Minor.

He smiled. "We've got them now."

The first van honked and pulled onto the pavement. It rattled along the paving slabs as a pedestrian dodged them. The van drove off the kerb back to the street and zoomed off. Eddie drove the Morris Minor forward to block the second van.

The second van barrelled down the street as the Morris Minor crept forward. Eddie held on to the gear stick, ready to move forward or reverse to get in the van's way.

Without hesitation, the van sped straight down the centre.

Rex swallowed. "Uh, Eddie."

Eddie revved the engine. The van continued to approach. Fearing getting T-boned, Eddie chickened out at the last second. He reversed over the kerb, clearing the street, and terrifying the confused pedestrian. As the second van drove by, the side of the vehicle scraped along the nose of the Morris Minor.

Rex's head jerked to the right, watching the van. On the left side, towards the back, he noticed a small bulbous round window. "Cool. That van's got a porthole window. We should get a van with a porthole."

The pedestrian stomped up to Rex's door. "What do you think you're playing at?"

Rex shrugged.

Eddie put his foot down and beelined after the vans. Thanks to a downhill slant, the Morris Minor caught up to the black van with the porthole window.

"You're doing it, Eddie," Rex said.

"This is more gravity than me."

The Morris Minor's nose bumped the back of the van. In the van's side mirror, the driver leaned forward allowing a sliver of street light over his eyes. He gave Eddie a deathly stare.

Uncomfortable, Eddie took his foot off the accelerator. After slowing for a brief second, Eddie shook it off and hit the foot pedal. The Morris Minor sped up and rammed their target's bumper.

The van wobbled, jumped the kerb, and hit a road sign. Eddie braked hard to avoid colliding with the crashed van. With the wheels locked, the car screeched along the tarmac. The front bumper tapped the van, and the engine sputtered out. While the Morris Minor rocked back and forth, Rex and Eddie opened their eyes.

Rex let out a sigh. "We did it?"

"We did what, exactly?"

"We caught him. Right?"

The driver stormed out of his damaged van. He was a tall man with slicked-back hair and a face shaped by chiselled straight lines. Under his stubble hid a defined dimple in his chin. A long brown wool coat hung from his broad shoulders.

"Shall we go interrogate him?" Rex asked.

"Be my guest," Eddie replied.

The man trudged towards the Morris Minor and pulled out a small knife. His open coat flapped in the wind, revealing a sharp, black suit.

Rex tucked in his chin. "Maybe just a chat?"

Both Rex and Eddie pushed their nearby door locks in and skulked in their seats. The man bent down and stabbed their front right tyre. Air escaped with a loud hiss as Eddie's side sank forward.

Standing tall, the man stared at the pair, his grip on the knife tightened.

Rex raised his right hand to shoulder height and waved his fingers timidly. Eddie slapped Rex's hand down.

The man marched back to his van. The van reversed, pushing the Morris Minor back. He steered back to the road and sped off in the direction of the van containing Daryl Archer.

Eddie's jaw dropped. "He stabbed our car?" He noticed a glint in Rex's eyes. "What are you so happy about?"

"Don't you get what that means?"

Eddie shook his head while scratching the fuzz on his unshaven chin.

"He thinks we're a genuine threat. He had to take us out."

"I think it was more like swatting a fly."

"You can't fight it, Eddie. We had him worried. We're, like, real detectives. We're going up in the world."

# THREE

Rex and Eddie stepped over puddles reflecting the orange hue of the street lights. The Morris Minor stayed at the crash site. Even if they knew how to change a tyre, the engine was unlikely to start in the damp air.

Eddie stopped and tugged the sleeve of Rex's corduroy jacket. He pointed ahead to the young man with blue hair walking along the road.

"Hey, you," Rex called out.

The blue-haired boy saw them and sprinted off.

Rex clenched his neck muscles. "Sorry, Eddie."

Both detectives raced after their new target. He ran under the railway bridge that crossed the street. Once the detectives had passed through the bridge's dark underpass, the blue-haired man was no longer in sight.

Eddie bent down with his hands on his thighs. Following Daryl Archer all evening had meant his dinner had been nothing but a downed pint. He was lightheaded and wobbly-kneed.

"That beer ruined me. My stomach is a mess."

"You need a kebab."

Eddie furrowed his brow, relaxed, and nodded. "Yeah, all right." He checked his wallet. "I have a twenty."

They walked back under the bridge and turned into a little alleyway that cut two minutes off their journey.

"Oi," came a voice from the darkness.

"Hello?" Rex called out.

"Ignore them," Eddie muttered.

Out stepped four teenagers. They were decked out in white tracksuits and gold chains. Three had their hoods up while one wore a baseball cap.

"I'm talking to you," the baseball cap wearing leader said. "You got a ciggie?"

He had a blond step haircut, pointy chin, and thin teeth.

"We don't smoke," Eddie said. He held his breath to stop himself from sharing health statistics.

The leader stepped into the pair's personal space and glared at Rex. "What about you?"

"Nope. Have you tried the shop?" Rex said.

"You saying I'm some sort of freeloader?"

Eddie stepped in front of Rex and smiled at the leader. "This is his form of help. He didn't mean anything."

"You hear that, lads? He's trying to be helpful. You just want to do me a solid?"

Rex leaned to the side to look over Eddie's shoulder. "I try."

Eddie shook his head. "Don't engage," he whispered through his teeth.

The four teens circled Rex and Eddie.

The young ringleader cocked his head and narrowed his eyes. "Look at Corduroy and Bumfluff, so happy to help."

Eddie raised a finger. "I'm not happy to— Who's

Bumfluff?" Eddie turned to Rex and examined his brown corduroy blazer.

Rex shrugged his shoulders apologetically.

"This is stubble."

"Yeah, a bit patchy though innit, mate?"

"It's designer stubble."

The ringleader sniggered. "Designer patches. You boys got any money?"

Rex and Eddie shifted.

The leader got uncomfortably close to Rex. "Well, do you?"

"Eddie has a twenty."

Eddie's eye twitched. "That's not true."

Rex nodded. "I forgot the change from the round. Eddie has twenty pounds and seventy pence."

The three other teens stepped forward. One was lanky with shoulder length hair, the second had bug-eyes and a button nose, the third teen was podgy with a thick brow.

The leader tweaked his cap. He pointed to Rex, "Corduroy," then Eddie, "Bumfluff." He waved his fingers at their hips. "Empty your pockets."

Eddie's jaw tightened. "Oh come on now. Are you serious?"

The lankier teen's head cocked, pointing to a bulge in the right hoodie pocket.

Eddie observed the bump. "What, you got a gun? Bit much, isn't it? What happened to Britain's knife crime epidemic? We're supposed to be afraid of everyone having a gun now as well?"

"Nah." The leader put his hand on the shoulder of the bug-eyed teen. "You gonna be afraid because of this one. Whatever it is you're scared of, he takes pills to stop him doing much worse. Ask him if he's taken his pills."

The bug-eyed teen smiled with enthusiasm, ready to answer.

Eddie winced. "This is all a bit theatrical, don't you think?"

"Ask him!" The leader's spit sprayed across Eddie's face.

Rex raised a hand. "Did you take your pills?"

Bug-eyes shook his head with menacing glee.

The leader offered his hands out. "Give us your wallets."

Eddie stepped back and attempted to walk around them, but he stepped on the toe of the podgy boy who'd snuck up behind the pair. Feeling light-headed, Eddie was utterly helpless against the teens.

"Empty your pockets now."

Rex's hands searched around his deep pockets.

Eddie elbowed him. "Let me do the talking," he whispered. "I can see you guys might be having some kind of nicotine withdrawal. How about we all go to the nicely lit shop around the corner, and I'll get you a box of ten?"

"Packs of ten aren't legal no more," the podgy teen said.

"Okay, fine. Twenty."

The cap-wearing leader wiped his nose with his hand. "Mate, you two are long."

The lanky teen sniggered. "Well long."

Eddie turned up the corner of his mouth, confused by the slang.

"We ain't got time for this," the leader said. "Empty. Your. Pockets." He took a step with each word. Rex and Eddie shuffled back until they bumped into the alley wall behind them.

"Bloody hell. Fine, here, my wallet. You happy?"

The leader took the twenty-pound note from Eddie's

wallet and examined what Rex gave him: a bunch of supermarket membership cards held together in a bulldog clip.

"My nan likes me to collect points for her. The Nectar card has at least two thousand points."

The leader scoffed. "And your mobiles."

Rex and Eddie handed over their phones. Eddie had an older smartphone with a cracked screen. Rex handed over an old brick of a phone with a grayscale display.

The leader sneered. "What are these?"

"Phones," Eddie said.

"Mate, these are ancient."

Eddie set his teeth. "Mine is only four years old."

The teen leader tipped his head. "Like I said, ancient."

He chucked Rex's phone and membership cards to the wet ground sending ripples across a thin puddle.

"Let's do one, boys."

The teens ran off into the night. The bug-eyed teen howled as the others cackled.

Rex and Eddie stood in the alleyway, shaken and confused.

"Well, that was embarrassing," Eddie said.

Rex lifted his stuff out of the puddle. "It's fine. They had a gun. What were you supposed to do?"

"I'm not sure if they did have a gun actually." Eddie narrowed his eyes. "What do you mean, what was I supposed to do? They mugged you too."

Rex wiped the dirty water from his phone with his corduroy jacket sleeve. "I've still got my stuff."

"They still mugged you, they just left it behind. And they insulted us both. Corduroy and Bumfluff."

"Corduroy isn't an insult." Rex stroked his jacket. "What do we do now?"

"I'm going home for a shave. We'll meet with the client

tomorrow, tell her everything that happened. See what she makes of it. The blue-haired friend, the guy with the dreads—"

"You getting mugged by teenagers."

"No, not that."

"How we stood and watched the vans snatch him?"

"Well, maybe not everything."

# FOUR

After his kebabless walk home, Eddie woke up starving. He remembered Rex's attempt to convince the kebab shop owner to accept Nectar card points as tender and grinned. Following a bowl of cereal, Eddie took a bus to the Morris Minor where he met Rex and had the tyre replaced.

They drove to 369 High Street, a row of pink Georgian houses turned into offices with shops at the ground floor. A few months ago, the two friends began renting a small office unit there when they first decided to become detectives.

After parking in the back, close to the brown river, the pair entered the building and climbed the stairs.

Outside the Milton Miles Investigations office door stood Maude Archer, their client. She cocked her pretty, round face and forced a smile. Maude was a petite brunette in her mid-twenties with big blue eyes and one freckled iris of brown-orange. The duo had met her a couple of times, on each occasion, she had a different colour of tights; today they were a bold red.

Maude's eyes welled as they darted between the pair. "Daryl's been kidnapped."

Eddie's false smile switched to panic. "Let's go inside and sit down shall we."

They passed the empty reception and entered the office. Three mismatching office chairs were placed around a large wooden desk with an old bulky computer on top. A rusty and dented filing cabinet stood next to a little kitchenette. Although the walls appeared newly painted, a ring of damp brown patches had taken over the corner by the window.

Maude sat at the desk. Rex and Eddie raced to the other side to get the better chair, the one with the least amount of duct tape holding it together. Rex won.

"How are you?" Rex said.

She swallowed. "Not good. Last night my parents got a call saying they'd kidnapped my brother. If only you saw it, you'd have saved him."

Eddie shuffled in his dodgy office chair.

"I hired you to find out why my brother's been acting so weird. I thought he was being paranoid, but maybe it wasn't paranoia after all."

Eddie leaned back slowly to make sure the chair wouldn't collapse. "Tell us what happened."

"The phone rang. The man had a deep voice like he was using one of those voice changer machines."

Rex leaned forward placing his chin on his hand. "Classic stuff."

Maude held back tears. "What?"

"The voice changer. Classic kidnapper move."

Eddie cleared his throat. "Ignore him. He means that... they follow basic etiquette. Which is good, because they will follow other rules, like keep him well fed, respect his personal space. This is a very... reassuring sign."

Maude calmed a little. "It is?"

Eddie nodded at her in a rapid panic and then eyeballed Rex.

"Oh, yes. Very promising," Rex said. "I'm sure they'll respect the code."

"The code?" she asked.

"Guidelines." Rex bared his teeth in confusion. "Rules. Whatever Eddie said, that's the one."

Maude took a deep breath and wiped her eyes with her hands. "Do you have any tissues?"

Eddie gave a sunken headshake.

Rex put a hand on her shoulder. "I can get some toilet paper from the bogs."

Maude wrinkled her nose. "No, thanks."

He sat back in his chair while Maude composed herself.

Eddie checked a desk drawer and found a soft white napkin with some plastic cutlery. He passed her the napkin. She accepted it with a fleeting smile.

"What did the kidnappers say?" Eddie said with a pen and paper in hand.

"They told my parents they want four hundred thousand pounds. We have five days to come up with the money."

"Do they have that kind of money?"

"They're trying to work something out."

"You told the police?"

"No. Absolutely not. They said if the police find out then they'll kill him." She soaked the napkin with her tears. "You must promise not to tell the police."

The pair nodded.

Eddie opened his drawer of leftover takeout utensils. He opened a plastic packet of a spork and knife to get to the paper napkin.

"Thank you." Maude took the thin napkin. "You've been following him for a week. If something suspicious were happening, you'd have seen it, right?"

Eddie pursed his lips. "We'd like to confirm a positive ID on one of Daryl's acquaintances."

"Did you take a photo?" she asked.

"Yes."

"Can I see it?"

Rex and Eddie looked at each other, nervous. The phone had been stolen in the mugging.

Eddie turned away from their client. "No."

"Why not?"

Rex took a deep breath, ready to give a long explanation, but Eddie cut him off before he could talk.

"That's not important right now. It was a man in his thirties. He had blond dreads down past his shoulder blades. A bit pale looking. Ring any bells?"

She shook her head.

"Daryl handed the man a disc," Rex said. "Do you know anything about that?"

She shook her head faster.

Eddie entwined his fingers. "What about a friend with electric blue hair? You ever met him?"

Maude sunk into her chair and swallowed hard. "I don't know anything about his friends. Did they do anything shady?"

Eddie pinched his lips. "Nothing to be alarmed about."

"Did he mention any government secrets?" Rex asked.

She buried her head in her hands and cried.

"Not now, Rex." Eddie opened the last utensil pack to get the napkin and handed it over.

Maude looked up, her eyes were glossy from the tears. "Government secrets?"

"It's a lead we're following," Rex said sheepishly.

Eddie drew in a sharp breath. "It's nothing. Ignore him. We could continue to investigate his friends if you think it's relevant to his kidnapping?"

Maude took another deep breath and sat up straight. Her hands resting on her knees. "I need you to find the kidnappers and help bring back my brother."

Rex smiled.

Eddie winced. "No-one else reported anything to the police? None of his friends?"

She brushed her hair away from her drying face. "No."

Rex gave a guilty look. "Not even the blue-haired one?"

"Say you'll find him," Maude pleaded.

Eddie hesitated. Maude's eyes refilled with tears as she covered her mouth with her hand.

"We... will..."

"Find him," Rex said, jumping to his feet. "We'll find him. Right, Eddie?"

Maude calmed but her lips quivered.

Eddie hesitated. "We'll speak to his friends, acquaintances, whoever they are. We'll see what information we can dig up."

Maude leapt from her seat and hugged Rex. "Thank you."

Every part of Rex's face smiled.

She moved to Eddie and wrapped her arms around him. Halfway through an out breath, the sudden hug squeezed out the rest of his air.

"Thank you," she repeated.

After her grip loosened, Eddie took a deep breath and noticed Maude smelled like cherries.

Maude stared at him with her blue eyes. The orange freckles in her iris looked like tiny islands on a beautiful ocean.

He swallowed. "I'm not sure where to find his friends."

"When he's drunk too much he sometimes sleeps on the floor at a friend's place in the student halls of residence. He must have a friend or two there."

"Do you know the friend?" Eddie said, distracted by her eyes in close up.

"No, but I'm sure you can find out. Say you'll go."

"We'll, uh, do our best."

# FIVE

The Morris Minor rolled along Station Road, passing the alleyway from last night. Eddie felt palpitations in his chest as they drove by.

Rex leaned into Eddie's view. "You all right, Eddie?"

He snapped out of it. "Fine. Fine."

Under the railway bridge, the Morris Minor pulled to the kerb and parked.

"Where do you buy a voice changer from anyway?" Rex said.

Eddie turned off the engine. "What are you talking about?"

"Why do people buy voice changers, other than for kidnapper ransom calls? The police should go to the shop that sells them, look up credit card details of previous purchases, and arrest the buyer."

Eddie scrunched his nose. "We'll call that Plan B."

The pair exited the car and looked across the street. Between the railway bridge and a Victorian warehouse converted into luxury flats, were two almost identical buildings. One was a halfway house filled with young teens, some trying to get to grips with society, but others bunking up while they continued with illegal activities. The other building was the student halls of residence for the Cloisterham College of Art and Design. No one knew who came up with the idea of building a halls of residence next to a halfway house, but it created a strange ecosystem.

At the beginning of each year, the senior residents advised the students to stay away from the half-way house, as they were drug dealers; which meant the students knew exactly were to get their drugs from. It also meant the half-way house residents could easily find an unlocked window of a naive, or stoned, student to steal from.

"That's how we lost blue-hair," Eddie said. "He snuck in here."

The pair approached the halls of residence's front door. To the right was an intercom with three call buttons indicating each of the floors: G, 1, and 2.

"We'll buzz the door, and see if we can get someone to talk to us. We just want to talk."

Eddie pushed the ground floor button. After a series of rings, they were connected to an answer phone message.

Rex scratched his head, confused.

"It's hooked up to the flat's phone but no one's in, or interested in picking up."

"It is eleven a.m.," Rex said. "A little early for students."

Rex pressed the first-floor button. The call box crackled to life.

"What?" a crackly voice said.

"Hi, uh." Rex squirmed, unsure of himself. "Can we come in?"

"Who are you?"

"Friends of… the guy with the blue hair?"

Eddie winced.

"What's his name?" the voice asked.

Rex curled his top lip.

Eddie leaned towards the call box. "We're more friends of friends. Do you know Daryl? Daryl Archer."

"Maybe."

The awning window above them opened a crack. A forehead poked out for a brief second. The window slammed shut.

"You're TV licence inspectors!"

Eddie frowned. "No, we're not."

"Two old guys in suits, you're TV licence inspectors."

Rex's jaw dropped. "We're only twenty-eight."

The call disconnected. With a sigh, Eddie pushed the buzzer for the top floor.

After two rings, the call box made a click sound. "What, man?" a stuffy voice asked.

"Hey, It's Daryl," Eddie said.

"Who you want?"

"Uh…"

The middle floor awning window opened again. Water poured out and splashed over their heads.

Soaked and freezing, the two stepped back from the door. The young man with the crackly voice stood at the window.

"Everyone, the TV licence inspectors are here. You don't have to let them in, and they can't fine you."

Eddie palmed his head to squeeze the water out of his head. "We're not TV licence inspectors."

"Yeah, right. You've got a van and everything, probably trying to pick up TV signals right now."

"We don't own a van." Eddie paused.

The detective duo checked the vehicles parked on the street. Half-tucked under the railway bridge was the black van with the porthole window. They ran to their car as the van's engine started. With a loud hum, the van drove off while Rex and Eddie fought with the Morris Minor's faulty lock and dodgy doors.

Once they managed to get into the car, they buckled their seat belts. Eddie turned the key. The car's engine did little more than a whimper.

"Come on," Eddie yelled.

He tried again but nothing. Eddie thumped the dashboard. Rex's attention wandered back out of the passenger window. He noticed their blue-haired target poke his head out of the halls of residence door. The young man bit his bottom lip as he peered outside. With Rex and Eddie hidden in their eyesore of a vehicle, he shrugged off this justified paranoia. He stepped out wearing a combo of green army surplus clothing.

Rex tapped Eddie's shoulder. "Code blue!"

Eddie batted Rex's hand away. "What on Earth is a code blue?"

Tapping on the window glass, Rex pointed towards the blue-haired young man across the street.

He headed along the street towards the hill, likely to Cloisterham College of Art & Design, a brown-bricked blocky building on top of Elizabeth Gardens Park, which overlooked the town centre and river.

Eddie turned the key hard, and the engine came to life. With a gap in the traffic, the Morris Minor pulled out of the spot and crawled forward towards their unsuspecting target.

They hung back to avoid being noticed, Eddie changed gears which caused a grinding sound, as if a giant robot had cleared its throat.

Alerted by the noise, the blue-haired student turned back and saw the Morris Minor hobbling along. Eddie pulled up to the kerb to appear like they were parking.

"Shouldn't we maybe do this on foot?" Rex whispered.

"I just got the engine to work, I'm not turning it off now."

Their target shook it off and walked under the railway bridge.

Rex leaned out of the passenger window.

"Don't, Rex. It's too obvious."

"Sorry, but I think that's the black van parked up ahead."

Eddie leaned over the steering wheel and perused the underpass. The van with the porthole was parked on the other side of the railway bridge.

In the darkest, wettest corner of the railway underpass, where mildew grew on the Victorian bricks, stood the man in the long coat. His face was covered in shadow.

"That's him, the other kidnapper," Eddie said.

Rex straightened his neck. "He's come to kidnap blue-hair, he's here to finish the job."

Eddie dropped back into the seat. "We can't watch another kidnapping, we have to do something this time."

"Let's go save him."

"I can't leave the car. If we turn it off it might not start, if we leave the keys in it might get stolen."

Rex tucked his chin in. "Really? You think someone might steal this?"

"We could follow the black van?" Eddie said. "Then we'd get to wherever they're keeping Daryl Archer."

"You think we'd keep up in this?"

Eddie rolled his eyes. "What do you want to do?"

Rex peered out the window as their blue-haired target stepped closer to the kidnapper.

He turned back to Eddie. "Keep the car running."

Rex unbuckled and opened the door.

"What? What are you doing?"

He tackled the door closed and sprinted down the street. The blue-haired student turned around after hearing Rex's echoing footsteps reverberate around the underpass.

In a panic, the young man ran. Rex lunged forward and caught him in a bear hug.

From the car, Eddie gave a desperate sigh.

Rex's arms squeezed the boy's chest, he fought back by kicking Rex in the knees. Rex fell to the ground, pulling his captive down with him. The blue-haired young man continued to elbow and kick Rex, but he wouldn't let go.

Out of the shadows, the man in the long coat marched through the underpass. His bright blue eyes pierced through Rex.

Eddie waited for the traffic to pass, and pulled the Morris Minor out into the street. The Morris Minor rattled along under the bridge. He reached the fighting pair and double parked alongside other stationary cars.

"Rex, he's coming!"

Rex glanced up at his partner. The blue-haired student threw a punch square into Rex's face.

Unmoved, Rex blinked; confused as to what had happened.

The sound of the kidnapper's stomping boots thumped against the pavement.

Rex grabbed their target and brought him to his feet. The student continued to kick away at Rex's shins, making it difficult for Rex to get closer.

"What'd you think you're doing?" the student shouted.

"Come with me if you want to live." Rex offered his hand.

The young man's lips stretched and tensed. "You threatening me?"

"Uh, no."

"You said come with you or you'll kill me."

Rex raised his top lip. "I didn't mean it like that."

Stepping backwards, the blue-haired man tripped on a wonky paving slab. "Just back off, yeah."

Rex nodded as he raised his hands. The blue-haired student calmed down. Seeing the man march through the underpass, Rex stepped forward. The young student turned to escape. To stop him from running away, Rex jumped on his back to weigh him down.

Eddie put his foot on the accelerator to coast by the fighting pair but the car stalled. He restarted the engine and attempted to find the clutch biting point. The vehicle kangarooed forward.

The man in the long coat had almost reached his blue-haired target. Rex was shaken off by the student, launching him into the long coated man's torso. Rex raised his eyebrows, shocked at how rigid the man's stomach was.

"Excuse me," Rex said in a higher tone than usual.

The blue-haired student stepped back from Rex and the tall man. His eyes darted between the pair. He ran across the road at the same time as Eddie raised the clutch. At the biting point, the Morris Minor lunged forward knocking the student to the ground.

Eddie stepped out of the car and looked over the bonnet; their target was unconscious in the road. He glowered at Rex. "This is your fault."

"How is that my fault?"

A car pulled up behind the Morris Minor and beeped the horn.

"You're blocking the lane," the man shouted.

The honking echoed under the bridge causing neighbours, pedestrians and other drivers to pay attention to the underpass.

A pedestrian walking his dog made a call on his mobile, possibly to the police.

The man in the long coat stepped back and walked to his black van at a fast pace.

In a panic, Eddie picked up the blue-haired student by his arms. "Grab his legs."

The blue-haired student groaned and moaned in a haze.

"He seems okay. He's okay, right?" Eddie asked.

Rex shrugged his shoulders. He dropped a leg and opened the Morris Minor's backdoors.

Several cars were backed up behind them, and the other lane had slowed as they watched with concern. From the other side of the railway bridge, the black van drove off at a steady speed.

Eddie raised the corner of his lip. "We should take him, right?"

Rex nodded. "I think so. For his protection."

They lowered the blue haired student into the back of the car and closed the doors. The pair got in the front and buckled their seat belts.

"We did it, Eddie. We saved the day."

Eddie straightened the rear-view mirror, a handful of potential witnesses reflected back at him. If they were lucky, the underpass was too dark for them to be identified.

"Eddie, we saved the day, right?"

"I'm not sure, but I think we might've performed a kidnapping."

# SIX

Standing over their victim, Eddie wondered what to do. Parking in the back, they had snuck the unconscious blue-haired young man out of the car and into the office building. Rex had even scoped out the stairs and hallway to make sure no other tenants were about when they dragged him into their office.

Eddie hadn't said anything since they arrived. Rex had tried to offer words of encouragement like "We did save him," and "He'll be thanking us when he's awake," but Eddie had remained silent.

The blue-haired student was slumped in a rolling chair. Rex wrapped some electrical tape they'd found in the maintenance cupboard around their captive's torso and the backrest. His arms were taped behind his back, and his feet were individually taped to the chair base, using the last of the sellotape.

Rex bit the tape to break off the almost finished roll. "That's secure, I think. I found some packing tape if you want me to go over him once more."

Eddie frowned.

"What?"

"I know we aren't kidnappers, but tying him up does look bad."

"He's not tied up, he's taped up."

"I'm not sure that makes a difference."

"If we were kidnappers, we'd have intent, right?"

"I guess so."

"So, we'd have some rope or handcuffs if we intended to do this."

Eddie crossed his arms tight. "*This?*"

Rex nodded. "Kid— Kidnapping."

"So this is a kidnapping?"

"Oh, I don't know, Eddie. I thought it wasn't, but you've confused me now."

"When he wakes up, let me talk to him. He needs to be persuaded to open up." Eddie straightened his tie. "I can get him to talk."

A rummage through the student's backpack led Eddie to a tatty nylon wallet. Inside, a clear plastic pocket displayed the young man's student ID, which included a photo of him with orange hair.

"Karl Burke," Eddie read.

Their captive shook his head awake. "What?" He opened his eyes.

"Uh, hello," Eddie said.

Terror filled Karl's face. "What do you want from me?"

Eddie put on a forced smile. "I know this looks bad, but we aren't kidnappers. Okay?"

"What did you do with Daryl?"

Rex raised a finger. "That wasn't us."

"He said two guys were following him."

Rex lowered his finger. "That *might* have been us."

Karl shifted in the chair, noticing he was restrained by electrical tape. "What the hell?"

"I know you've been restrained," Eddie said, "but we really aren't kidnappers. I want to make that clear."

"You better let me go, or I'll scream."

Eddie winced. "Please don't."

Rex leaned into Eddie's view. "I could gag him?"

Eddie raised his palms. "No, that won't be necessary, because we aren't kidnappers. Right? So calm down. Take a deep breath."

As much as the tape across his chest would allow, Karl breathed in until his chest puffed out.

Eddie's shoulders relaxed, he was getting through to their witness. "Good, and breath out."

Karl narrowed his eyes and let out a scream. "Ahhh!"

"Shhh." Eddie crouched down and held a finger to Karl's lips.

Karl attempted to bite it.

He turned to Rex. "How do we gag him? Have you got a cloth?"

Rex's eyes sparkled as he had an idea. He ripped off his shoe and took off his sock.

Eddie grimaced. "Really?"

"It's all we've got."

"Ahhh!" Karl continued.

"Fine, go on then."

Rex rolled up the dirty sock and stuffed it into Karl's mouth. The loud screams had become a tiny mumble.

"This is your doing," Eddie told Karl. "We don't want to do this."

Karl's eyes narrowed at the pair. His throat bounced up and down as he tried to shove the sock out with his tongue.

Eddie huffed. "Tape his mouth shut."

Rex took the packaging tape and wrapped it over Karl's mouth. Karl's face turned red as he mumbled, jiggling about on the seat. Since the wood floor wasn't quite straight and he was on a rolling office chair, he moved the chair around a couple of inches.

Eddie grabbed the armrests. "I know we took you in the car, and tied you up, and gagged you. But we really, really, aren't kidnappers."

The mumbles went from a subdued scream to a rolling grumble. Although his words were obscured, Karl's sarcasm came across perfectly.

Eddie raised his hands. "Look, we didn't kidnap Daryl."

Rex perked up. "And he means it this time, we *really* didn't kidnap Daryl."

Eddie's eyebrows drew together. "As in we weren't the ones to pull him into a van. We don't have Daryl. We're detectives hired by his sister to try and find him."

Karl gave a restricted, "Ha."

"We saw them take Daryl while you ran," Eddie said. "That man under the bridge was there too. We think he was trying to capture you. That's why we—"

"Humhapped hee?" Karl mumbled through the tape, an obvious attempt at saying "Kidnapped me?" through a sock.

Eddie pursed his lips. "Rescued you."

Karl narrowed his eyes, sizing up the pair.

"Is there anything you can tell us about Daryl that will help us find him?"

Their captive sighed out of his nose. He mumbled something. Rex and Eddie looked confused. Eddie removed the tape from Karl's mouth and pulled out the sock.

Karl gagged on the taste of Rex's foot. "Daryl was mixed up in something, some kind of deal."

Eddie cocked his head. "In what?"

"No idea, but I'm pretty sure it was illegal."

"The disc," Rex said.

"You know the man with blond dreads?" Eddie asked.

"Not personally, but Daryl knew him enough to talk to him."

"Tell us where we can find him."

"He's at The Barge Inn every Friday."

Eddie huffed. "We can't wait that long. Any reason to think the dreadlocked man could have organised the kidnapping?"

"Daryl was cagey about the details. He asked if he could stay on my floor for a few days because someone was after him."

"He suspected getting kidnapped?"

"I think he thought he'd get a beating, but nothing like this."

Eddie pursed his lips. "Why didn't you report it to the police?"

"I don't know, man. Whatever Daryl's mixed in I didn't want to make it worse."

Rex crouched down to Karl's eye level. "What's on the disc?"

"What disc?"

"Government documents?"

Karl shrugged.

"Trade secrets? Photos of a high ranking official cheating on his wife?"

"I didn't see no disc."

Rex backed away, with a suspicious eye.

Eddie huffed. "You don't know anything else about white-dreads?"

"Nothing. I mean, I heard someone call him Spin Doctor, like once."

Rex folded his arms. "Spin Doctor? Like government

PR stuff?" He bounced as he spoke. "It's a secret. A government secret."

Eddie waved him off. "Calm down, will you?"

Rex stood still.

"We'll go back to The Barge Inn and see if we can learn about this Spin Doctor."

Karl sat up. "So, am I free to go?"

"Of course, because we *aren't* kidnappers."

Rex leaned in. "So, I should release him, then?"

Eddie clasped his hands over the back of his head. "Yes."

# SEVEN

R ex and Eddie spent the better part of the day in The Barge Inn nursing their beers.

They'd managed to make their pints last a full three hours before the barmaid passed by carrying empties.

"You fell out with your drink?" she said

Eddie checked his wallet for cash before approaching the bar.

"Two more."

The place was dead quiet when they arrived, but the wall benches and side tables had slowly filled with students as the night approached.

Eddie returned with the fresh pints.

Rex took a sip. "Quite a few people here now. Maybe we could go ask questions."

"Let's keep an eye out for this Spin Doctor chap, if we ask around he might rumble that we're on to him."

The second round of beers was drunk with ease. Both needed food to slow down the alcohol. Since The Barge Inn didn't offer hot meals, they settled for packets of crisps, peanuts, and pork scratchings to accompany a third and fourth beer. The snacks had little effect on the pair who stumbled to the bar.

"Same again?" the barmaid asked.

Eddie put on a friendly smile. "Do you know Spin Doctor?"

"You're looking for a doctor?"

"Spin. Spin Doctor," he slurred.

"You've been a doctor?"

Eddie's jaw tightened as he realised he'd drunk too much to successfully investigate.

Looking for an out, he shrugged. "Where's the men's room?"

She pointed to the right. Eddie nodded and headed back to Rex.

"Grab your jacket, we're leaving."

"You got a lead?"

"She said… come back tomorrow."

"Oh, great." Rex stood up a little too fast and held the table for balance. "Do you want to ask any of the other people?"

"I think we should get some rest. Last night was a little intense."

"With you getting mugged?"

"With *us* getting mugged."

Rex screwed his face in disagreement.

Too drunk to drive, the duo headed home on foot. They walked 200 feet down Canal Lane to the High Street.

As they exited Canal Lane, Rex and Eddie passed a working girl standing on the side of the road. She had jet black hair in a bob which contrasted with her youthful, milky skin. The young woman wore a short zebra print dress with black boots.

She cracked a half-hearted smile. "You looking for

business?"

The embarrassment of talking to a prostitute had the odd effect of doubling their drunkenness.

"Sorry?" Eddie said.

"Are you looking for business?"

Which Eddie heard as "Our who ooh kin four business."

Rex heard, "Are you starting a business?"

Rex turned to Eddie, "How does she know we started a business?"

The prostitute rolled her eyes and shouted like she was explaining something to an old deaf relative. "Are. You. Looking. For. Business!"

The pair turned to each other with furrowed brows. They understood, smiled back at her, and shook their heads.

"No, thank you," Rex said. He was flattered, not realising her only standard was cash, which Rex didn't have much of, making him far below her standards.

Eddie put on a serious face, to make up for being condescended to by a prostitute. "Sorry, no. We're—"

"Together?"

"Yes, I mean, no. Not like that. But we are together, physically. That doesn't sound right either."

Rex hiccuped. "We're partners."

She looked past the pair, ignoring them, but they didn't move on.

The prostitute sighed. "What do you want?"

"Nothing," Eddie said. "Actually, are you here often?"

"I don't do reservations."

"I meant last night. Did you see a man dragged into a black van outside The Barge Inn yesterday evening?"

"Like a kidnapping?"

"Nooooo," Rex said.

Eddie shook his head. "Absolutely nothing like a kidnapping."

She curled the corner of her top lip. "What's it worth to you?"

Eddie pulled Rex aside. "Okay, we have a potential informant. We have to build a connection, find some common ground, and she'll be more forthcoming. It's like a negotiation, understand?"

"Gotcha,' Rex replied.

They both turned to their new tipster.

"What's your name?" Eddie asked.

"Ruby."

"Hi Ruby, I'm Eddie."

"I'm Rex. His partner—"

"Business partner," Eddie added. "Ruby, I can see you're a hard-working young lady. You want to work on a safe street, and that's what we're here to do; make the street safer."

"Yeah," Rex said. "We'll protect you."

She gave a hearty laugh. "Out of the goodness of your heart, I'm sure."

"Well, we get paid," Eddie said.

She nodded. "So information is worth somethin' to you, yeah?"

Eddie pulled a face. "Fine, ten quid?"

"Fifty."

"Twenty-five?"

"Thirty."

Eddie huffed. "Come on, you said fifty I said ten, I met you in the middle with twenty-five."

"Twenty-five is the middle of fifty. Thirty is the middle of ten and fifty."

Rex and Eddie paused to do the maths in their sloshed heads.

"Okay fine. Thirty." Eddie handed her thirty quid in cash.

She smiled for the first time. "I didn't see anyone dragged into a van. I did see a black van parked outside the pub about one in the morning. What's it to you?"

"Did they have anything?"

"You mean, the briefcase?"

Rex and Eddie gave each other a look.

"What briefcase?" Rex asked.

"Never mind," Ruby said. She looked past them again, as if they were invisible.

"Didn't Daryl sometimes carry a briefcase?" Rex said.

Eddie opened his notepad. "It's true, he walked to the pub with a briefcase. I noted it last night, but I stopped writing about it after we got to the pub."

"He did a drop-off." Rex bobbed up and down in excitement. "Right in front of our noses."

"Faces," Ruby said.

"What?"

"It's either in front of your faces or under your noses." She had a sneer that ensured everything she said made the pair feel stupid. "Just forget about the briefcase, I bet it's nothing."

Eddie sighed. "If we had my phone we could check the photos."

Ruby cocked her head.

"He got mugged," Rex said.

"We got mugged."

"Where, here?"

Eddie waved off in a general direction. "An alleyway close to the train station."

She tsked. "You shouldn't use alleyways at night. It's not safe."

Eddie narrowed his eyebrows as he checked his notes.

"So, when Daryl walked to the Barge Inn he had a briefcase, but inside he didn't."

Rex's eyes bulged "Maybe it's a drug thing!"

Eddie scoffed. "How do you know that?"

"Because of the shoes hanging from the telegraph pole." He pointed up at the telephone wire close to the pub, a pair of Adidas running shoes with the laces tied together dangled above.

Eddie's nose crinkled. "What's that got to do with anything?"

"That's what gangs do to indicate drop-offs."

"It's not." Eddie turned to Ruby. "Is it?"

She shrugged. "Not my industry."

Eddie nodded. "I didn't mean to imply you take drugs. I thought maybe your pimp might be involved?"

"My pimp wouldn't be seen dead near them shoes."

Rex leaned in. "Because it's a rival drug dealer's sign?"

Ruby curled her lip. "He wears Nike."

"I'm sure it's just some teens playing around with old shoes."

Rex scoffed. "It's a gang sign."

"Who drove the black van?" Eddie asked. "Did you see a tall man, not in a grey hoodie."

"He was a bit over six foot," Rex added. "Slick hair, cool coat, confident walk. He had an angry face."

"I think he was making that face at us, he's probably not always angry."

Ruby waved the pair off. "If you two don't mind, take this someplace else. You're scaring away the punters."

The pair nodded apologetically as they headed to the pub. They searched outside the pub looking for a drop off spot. Rex tapped the wood of the fuse box door.

"What about in here?"

Eddie nodded. "Open it."

He shoved the bolt to the side and opened the fuse box. Inside they found nothing out of the ordinary. Just the electrics, a timer for the outdoor lights, and a few cobwebs.

Eddie sighed.

"It's big enough, though," Rex said. "This is where I'd hide a briefcase."

"Come on, this is a dead end."

When they returned to the opening of Canal Lane, Ruby had gone. They strolled back into the town centre.

A little over a mile from The Barge Inn, Rex and Eddie walked past their office building. Rex noticed the front door that led to all the office units was ajar. The lock had been broken.

They made their way up the thin stairs, stumbling and shushing each other as they did. In the hallway, their office door was open a crack. The lock was scratched and picked at.

Eddie turned to Rex. "Someone's in there."

# EIGHT

Eddie pushed the office door wider. Rex popped his head inside. Files were opened and tipped, the chairs pushed over, and the rubbish from the knocked over bin scattered on the floor.

"We've been burgled." Eddie picked up the client chair and placed it on its wheels.

Rex refilled the bin. "Did they take the valuables?"

Eddie curled his lip. "What valuables?"

"I'm surprised they didn't take the computer." Rex gestured to the clunky, yellowed PC tower and heavy, square monitor with 'Property of Cloisterham Council' branded on the side.

"Yeah," Eddie said. "They might have got a whole ten quid for it."

"It's good that, it runs Windows XP."

There was a knock at the door. Still ajar, it was pushed an inch with each knock.

"Come." Eddie cleared his squeaky voice. "Come in."

The door creaked wide open and in stepped the man

with slicked-back hair and a long brown coat — the driver of the black van.

"Hi," Eddie said, bluffing confidence. Between the beers, the mean prostitute, and the muggers, he felt a nervous wreck. His chest constricted.

The man stepped forward. He passed Eddie and punched Rex in the eye.

Rex stumbled backwards with his hand covering his face.

Eddie hunched his shoulders and raised his palms. "What was that?"

"It was a tap," the man said in a deep, calm voice. He pointed at them. "Which one of you is Rex Milton?"

In a flash, Eddie pointed to an oblivious Rex, who was too busy rubbing his eye. The man pointed a finger at Eddie. His hand was rough but clean.

"That makes you Edward Miles."

"Ah, no. My name is... Jim Jams."

"That's not a real name, you need to think a little faster. Try fish oil supplements."

Eddie rolled his shoulders back, to mimic the man's stance. "I'll give them a go." He frowned. It wasn't the witty comeback he had hoped for.

Rex blinked continually as his teary eyes adjusted to the pain.

As Rex and Eddie shuffled back to their shared desk, the man stepped closer.

He lifted his chin. "I'm not here to talk about your health."

"No?"

"No." He sat on the client chair with a forceful plonk. "Take a seat, the pair of you."

The duo picked up their toppled chairs and sat behind

the desk. Rex rummaged through the plastic utensil drawer for a napkin to dry his weeping red eye.

Eddie held his breath as the man reached into his jacket pocket. He pulled out a packet of tissues and offered them to Rex. The man's arm stretched out, exposing his wrist from his shirt sleeve. Eddie noticed a thick bracelet of entwined nylon rope.

Eddie wrinkled his nose. "Is that a friendship bracelet?"

The man glanced at his wrist. "It's a paracord survival bracelet. You never know when eight feet of rope will come in handy."

As he took a tissue, Rex's eyes widened, the punched one opening a little less than the other. "Were you in the military?"

The man scanned the office. "I have training. So, Edward."

Eddie scratched his nose. "There's no Edward here."

"You're lying." He glanced at Rex, who waved, and back to Eddie. "You know how I know you're lying?"

Eddie swallowed. "Because I'm Eddie," he replied with a squeaking mumble.

"When a person lies, your stressed brain sends blood to the capillaries at the end of your nose and you scratch it unconsciously. You give yourself away, Mr Miles."

"Sorry?"

"No need to apologise, you make my job easier."

Eddie cocked his head. "Kidnapper?"

The man threw a business card with a twirl, it landed on the table between them with a spin. The card stopped the right way up. Rex grabbed it before Eddie could get near.

"Cool, we should get business cards." Rex read aloud: "Jason Cole, Private Detective."

Eddie straightened. "You're a sleuth too?"

"Too?"

"We're detectives," Eddie said. "You didn't notice?"

Rex sniggered. "What kind of a detective are you?"

"Oh, I noticed plenty. You can sit in your car all day and play picture taking with your friend here, but that doesn't make you a detective. What is this? Your first case?"

"Fourth." Rex bobbed his head with pride.

Cole glared. "My mistake. I see I'm dealing with seasoned professionals."

Rex's bottom lip lowered. "Alright, take it easy."

Eddie folded his arms. "I think you should leave."

"I understand, fear is a natural reaction."

"I'm not scared." Eddie swallowed again.

"You're defensive. You're worried. Your folded arms show me you feel unsafe."

Rex and Eddie uncrossed their arms. Wherever they placed them felt awkward, so they held them at their side, which now felt unnatural.

Eddie sneered. "Oh yeah, and how worried are you?"

Cole stood and put his hands on his hips. "Do I look worried to you?"

"No," Rex said. "You look like a superhero."

He wagged his finger within inches of their noses. "Stay away from my case. If I see you near the Archer family, or you interfere in any way, I will make it my mission to end you. Understood?"

Rex cocked his head. "You gonna beat us up?"

*Don't give him ideas*, Eddie thought.

Cole leaned towards Rex. "You wish."

Jason Cole spun one hundred and eighty degrees and stepped out into the corridor.

"Why'd you punch him?" Eddie said.

Cole turned to them. "In my line of work, I find things

go much better for me when I hit the biggest one of the group. Puts everyone in check."

He walked down the corridor and out of sight.

Rex sat up with a grin. His drying tears slid down to the corners of his smile. "You know who he is, don't you?"

"Of course I do. He's the man who will end us."

"A few months ago when I said we should be detectives, I showed you the private investigator ad in the paper. That's him. He inspired us."

"Perfect." Eddie recrossed his arms. "What a role model."

———

Eddie approached his flat's building, a four-storey grey building with rusty fixtures and a flickering entryway light. He huffed.

*What a day*, Eddie thought.

A hot shower in the quiet solitude of his own home was what Eddie needed. Not that the shower would be hot, or even warm. The shower would dribble out tepid water thanks to low pressure, which meant at least half of him would be exposed to the coldness of the bathroom air at all times. He slowed as he approached his front door, thinking about the practicalities of a half-relaxing, half-tortuous shower.

*Solitude*, he thought. *At least I'll have some peace in my own space.*

Eddie climbed the last step to his flat and found an envelope taped to the door handle. He opened it up and glanced through the letter until he reached the word 'Eviction'. Eddie dashed through the notice in a panic. It was a writ of execution, explaining that after repeatedly failing to pay his rent he had been evicted. A High Court

Enforcement Officer had changed the locks. The letter informed him he would be allowed to collect his possessions within seven days at a mutually agreed upon time.

Eddie pulled his old phone from his pocket, a beaten and scratched up Nokia 3310 he'd found in his electronics drawer this morning. He rang the number at the bottom of the letter. An answer message told him to speak after the tone.

"Hello, this is Eddie Miles. I've received an upsetting letter. There has been some kind of mistake, and you've evicted me from my home. I want to fix this right away. Please call me back as soon as possible."

Eddie hung up as his breath became shallow. After a few deep breaths, he called a second time.

"Hi, Eddie Miles, again. Calling about the eviction mix-up, again. I want to clear up this whole mess. I think you've got the wrong person. I mean, I am a little behind on rent, and my name is Edward Miles, but I know it's a mistake. I'd like to apologise for the confusion. Not saying it's my fault. Not saying it's your fault either." He hesitated. "I'm not saying it's 'not' not your fault. In fact, I didn't receive any other notice, so I think it's someone's fault. A middleman, or middlewoman. Going forward, I think—"

Beep. The answer phone message timed out. His breath sank a little shallower. He crouched down.

*Perfect*, he thought. *A panic attack.*

He dialled again.

"What I'm saying is, you can't jump to an eviction notice. There are laws. I should have access to my flat. If you think I'm going to walk away, well you're wrong. I have squatter's rights. I'll wait out here until one of you comes by. I'm not going to walk away, you hear me?" He calmed. "This is Eddie Miles by the way." He raised his voice again. "And I know my rights. Well, I know I have rights and as soon as I find out what they are—"

Beep.

Eddie growled at his phone.

Out of ideas, he knocked on his door. Unsurprisingly, no one answered. He thought about knocking down the door, but without a door, he wouldn't be able to protect his stuff from other people. Eddie imagined a well-practised burglar could easily break the door in. So his home was no safer with or without a door.

*Oh God*, he thought. *I'm gonna get robbed while I'm not even home to protect my stuff.*

Not that he'd be any good at protecting his stuff, last night proved that. He would be better off being robbed while he was out.

Eddie took a deep breath. *No one is robbing you*, he thought. *You're just homeless. Oh God. I'm homeless.*

"Sod it," Eddie said. He rammed the door. His shoulder took a pounding while the door seemed unaffected.

Eddie stomped down the stairs, barged through the entryway doors, and stood wondering where to go.

He walked the half mile back to the Morris Minor on Canal Lane. Inside, he lowered the driver's seat to make it as bed-like as possible. Eddie tried to settle down for the night, but his head dropped back. The Morris Minor seats did not include headrests. He pulled his head back up and scooted down the reclined seat until his knees bumped against the steering wheel.

Eddie slept on and off all night. At one point he managed to get a full hour of sleep, until a homeless man woke him up. The tramp streaked his fingers across the glass of every misty car window as he passed by.

The squeak of the glass panicked Eddie into a full

upright position until the seatbelt locked and yanked him back down with a yelp.

The homeless man screamed as he ran away.

*At least I have my solitude*, Eddie thought.

He crawled to the back seats and curled up into a foetal position, something he found himself doing more regularly as his detective career progressed.

# NINE

Outside a small terraced council house on a street full of cracked pavement, Eddie parked the Morris Minor. Rex exited the house and closed the front door with an excited slam. Peeled paint hanging from the bedroom windows broke away and dropped like falling leaves.

A voice from inside cried out, "Don't slam the door!"

"Sorry, Nan!"

Rex ran to the Morris Minor. As he got inside, he turned to Eddie revealing bruising under his right eye and smiled.

"You've got a black eye."

"I know, we should go to the pub tonight. I want everyone to see."

Eddie shifted into first gear and drove towards the halls of residence. Once parked Eddie immediately unbuckled, having spent the night in the car, he was sick of being inside it.

Rex screwed up his face. "Does the car smell musty to you?"

Eddie narrowed his eyebrows. "No."

"It's got a slight tramp smell."

"I don't smell tramp."

Rex shifted in his seat. "Maybe it's more of a vibe."

"I'll buy a pine-scented air freshener. Will you focus?" Eddie snapped his fingers until Rex made eye contact. "Our mission is to find Karl and see if he's heard of Jason Cole. We need to know how Cole ties into all this, and find out who his client is."

The pair exited the car and approached the yellow brick building with a blue roof. Rex pointed up at the telephone lines that ran between the halfway house and the halls of residence. A pair of tied together shoes hung from the wire.

"Drug dealers," Rex said.

Eddie approached the front door, pretending he didn't hear Rex. "Here we go again."

Rex opened an umbrella to avoid water being thrown at him.

Eddie pushed the ground floor buzzer button. After three rings the intercom connected. A dial tone beeped and the door buzzed.

Eddie pulled the door open. "They're gonna let us up without question?"

Inside, the painted breeze block walls had graffiti tags on them. Eddie peered up the staircase. He stopped himself from resting his hand on the sticky railing.

Rex relaxed, leaning his back on the bricks.

"Don't touch the wall," Eddie said. "It's filthy."

Rex lunged forward. Eddie approached the ground floor flat's front door and knocked. A pale young man with a sharp chin and a gold chain opened the door. He stepped out using one foot to keep the door from closing.

"Yeah, what?" he said in a gravelly voice.

Rex smiled. "Is Karl home?"

"Don't know no Karl."

Eddie nodded. "This must be the wrong floor. You know a Karl on any other floor?"

"Don't know no Karl. You deafo or what?"

"Deafo?" Eddie asked.

The pale young man scoffed. "Yeah, deaf."

Eddie shook his head. "No."

"You blind?"

"No."

The young man widened his eyes. "You see a Karl?"

"Come on, Rex," Eddie said.

The pair headed to the staircase and walked up the first few steps.

"Oi, you fellas like to paint?"

Eddie turned back. "Um, no."

"How about some party favours, or ASAP."

Rex crinkled his nose. "ASAP? What's that?"

"It's wicked, bruv. Gets you high as soon as possible."

Eddie examined the graffiti and litter throughout the foyer. "Is this the halfway house?"

The boy glared at Eddie. "It's called Approved Premises."

"You've not seen a tall guy with a fop of hair called Daryl around here, have you? We think he sometimes stays in the halls of residence."

"Nah, bruv. Daryl, you say?" He kicked the door wide open and called down the hall. "Oi, Jamie, you know anyone called Karl or Daryl from next door?"

From behind the half-closed door stepped a short boy. A bright white baseball cap partially covered his blond step haircut.

The blond boy sucked his teeth. "Nah, mate."

Eddie held his breath. It was their mugger, the leader of the group.

Jamie appeared relaxed until he saw Eddie's red face. His eyes darted between Rex and Eddie. He pushed the pale boy inside and shoved the door closed as Eddie ran down the steps towards them.

"You give me back my stuff," Eddie shouted, as he thumped on the door.

Rex caught up and put his hand on Eddie's shoulder to calm him down.

"Easy, Eddie."

"He's lucky he closed that door in time, or I'd have had to…"

"What?"

Eddie rubbed his jaw. "I don't know. I guess I'm lucky as well, now I think of it."

"Well, do we go to the student halls now?"

"Rex, our attacker is in there. Don't you want justice?"

"Actually, that's him there." Rex pointed through the hallway's wired glass window as Jamie ran by on the other side.

Eddie burst out of the halfway house entrance with Rex close behind. Jamie ran across the road, stopping traffic, and up into the alleyway. The detective pair ran a few steps before Rex skidded to a stop, blocking Eddie with his hand. He pointed to the halls of residence entrance where Jason Cole pushed the buzzer.

Eddie grimaced. "Perfect."

The pair snuck behind the halfway house and watched from the corner. A blonde girl dressed all in black passed the duo. She approached a ground floor awning window hidden from the street's view. After checking her surroundings, the girl dismissed the detectives with a sneer and knocked. The window opened. She raised a banknote through the gap. A hand took the note and swapped it for a tiny package in a clear plastic baggie.

Eddie split his attention between the window transaction and Jason Cole at the halls of residence entrance.

Rex pointed at the girl with his eyes.

Eddie shrugged. "We should follow Cole. Find out what he knows."

The girl walked past the pair, avoiding eye contact.

"Excuse me," Rex said. "Do you live in the halls?"

She curled her lip. "Why?"

"We're Daryl and Karl's friends."

She looked them up and down. "No way. What are you? Debt collectors? Salesmen? Jehovah's Witnesses?"

"Detectives," Rex said.

She laughed. "Nice one."

"We are. Aren't we, Eddie?"

"Daryl Archer is in trouble. We heard he stays here sometimes."

The girl looked at him, emotionless. "You get me party favours, and I'll talk."

Eddie pursed his lips. "I'm guessing that's a drug, right? I can't. If I have kids I'd want to say I've never bought drugs."

"Twenty quid?"

At the halls of residence entrance, Karl opened the door to Cole. The two spoke in a civil manner, but the detective pair could not make out the conversation.

Eddie pulled out the twenty. "You won't buy drugs with it, will you?"

She snatched the note and rolled her eyes. "Karl lives in the flat above me. His mate Daryl sleeps on the floor sometimes. He graduated last year, but he comes and hangs out with us."

"Karl and Daryl met at college?"

"School. They're the same age, but Karl took a year out and travelled."

"Did he ever mention being worried or stressed about something?"

"Nah, Daryl's chill."

"What about computer hacking?" Rex said. "Did he ever talk about cracking government documents?"

"Nah, nothing like that."

From the corner, they witnessed Cole shake Karl's hand and give him a business card.

Eddie: "He ever buy from the window?"

She nodded. "Him and Karl like to paint."

Rex and Eddie looked confused.

"Is that slang?" Eddie asked. "Are you saying yes to them using the window?"

"Yeah." She blew air. "You guys are old."

"You ever see someone called Jamie at the halfway house?"

Rex pointed. "Cole is leaving. We've got to go."

"Jamie, what can you tell me about him?"

"You paid me to talk about Karl and Daryl."

"Eddie, let's go!"

Eddie narrowed his eyes at the girl. He turned to see Cole across the street, entering his black van. "Fine. Let's go."

---

Rex and Eddie followed Cole's van until it pulled up by a dirty, grey office building. The pair sat in the Morris Minor, parked a few spaces back.

Cole entered the office grounds and waited at a bench. A young brunette in bold orange tights approached him.

Eddie leaned over the steering wheel. "Maude Archer?"

"What's her game?"

"Is she working for him? Or do we both work for her? Is this some kind of set up?"

Rex bit his lip. "She's a femme fatale."

Eddie massaged his neck. "She'd better not be. For once, can't we work on a straightforward case?"

"You okay, Eddie?"

"At least, give us a chance to be the hired guys that follow the tricked detective."

Rex gave a tiny nod. "Always the bridesmaid, never the bride."

"Bloody Cole. Thinks he's smart with his experience and practical knowledge. Well, he hasn't got one thing that we've got."

Rex grinned. "A partner?"

Eddie paused. "Well, yes, I'm sure that's an advantage somehow."

"Because?" Rex raised his eyebrows, fishing for a compliment.

"That's not the point. One thing he's not got that we've got is the hunger."

Rex nodded. "I am hungry."

"Exactly, he's complacent, that's how we've been able to follow him. His guard is down. But not us, we have the hunger for—"

"Doughnuts."

"And—"

"Scotch eggs."

"Always, but he hasn't got the hunger for—"

"A bottle of coke."

"That's thirst. I mean hungry for the kill, for the reward, for the acclaim, for justice. To prove ourselves."

"I'm fully on board, Eddie. Can we also go to Tesco's Extra and pick up the things I'm hungry for?"

Eddie sighed. "Take a photo, will you."

Rex took a scratched digital camera with a dented corner from the glove compartment. He took a flash photo of Eddie.

Eddie bared his bottom teeth. "You're gonna give us away. Take a photo of Cole without the flash."

"I'm trying." Rex held out the camera, and the monitor went white. He checked the front of the screen. "It's fogged up. Stupid cold weather." Rex breathed on the lens.

"That makes it worse."

"Sorry."

Rex attempted to snap a photo, but Cole passed by some trees and got back in the van. "He's gone. I couldn't get a shot."

"Take Maude's photo."

Rex pointed the camera back to the bench, but Maude had left. Moving the camera right, he focused on Maude's back. He snapped a shot as she entered the office building.

Rex turned the camera back towards the black van and zoomed in. He wobbled to the left, and the monitor was filled with Cole's face. Lowering the camera out of view, he could see Cole marching right at them.

"He's headed this way. I think he's coming to end us."

Eddie started the engine. It didn't quite roar to life so much as squeak along, as if a hamster turning a wheel kept the car going.

As they drove, Eddie kept glancing at the rear-view mirror to make sure Cole wasn't following. A schoolboy ran across the street. Eddie slammed his foot down on the brake, stopping a half foot short of the boy. Rex, unsure the car even had airbags, reached his hands out on the dashboard. A tailgater behind them braked hard. Eddie gave an evil eye to the driver in the rear-view mirror. He was used to staring competitions with tailgaters as he refused to flirt with the speed limit.

In the rear mirror, as the other cars all stopped, Eddie noticed the black van a few cars behind. They were being followed by Cole.

Eddie straightened the mirror. "I've found Cole."

Rex perked up. "Where?"

"He's behind us, four cars back."

Eddie gave a wave to the boy to let him know he was safe to cross. The boy gave Eddie the finger and ran to the kerb.

Rex turned to the rear. "So what do we do now?"

Eddie's heartbeat quickened. "We carry on. We don't let his intimidation tactics work. They can threaten us, they can scare us off, they can mug us. But we will beat them all."

Rex curled his top lip. "I don't think the muggers have anything to do with this."

Eddie took a deep breath. "Of course not. I mean, we gotta prove ourselves to them all."

"Maybe Cole can help. We could team up before that disc gets into the wrong hands."

"Forget about the disc. I'm not playing second banana to your antics, Rex. I'm taking charge. You hear me?"

"I'm right next to you, so, yeah."

"Good. We're gonna get information from Cole."

Rex sat up. "You mean team up?"

"No, I mean interrogate."

"Interrogate him? How do you suppose we do that?"

"We turn the tables. We need to capture Cole."

# TEN

The Morris Minor sat parked at the kerb as the two detectives discussed their options. Following their previous engine troubles, Eddie chose to keep the car running. He left the windows slightly ajar, as the exhaust fumes seemed to emanate from beneath and fill the vehicle.

Cole continued to watch the pair from his van, parked down the street, almost out of view.

"We're not going to torture him or anything," Eddie said.

"No," Rex nodded in agreement. "We're just gonna ask questions. How we gonna get him to talk to us?"

"We tie him up or something."

Rex flinched. "Tie him up?"

Eddie shrugged his shoulders. "Or something?"

"This is grim, Eddie. I don't want to be a serial kidnapper. I'm a nice boy."

"I'm a nice boy. I mean, I'm a man. A nice man, but not one to be taken advantage of. He followed us, he's the instigator. We capture him, tie him up if we have to, and get some answers."

"How do we do that? He keeps hinting at his military history." Rex folded his arms. "What have we got? I got two swimming badges and you passed your cycling proficiency first time."

"Which is why he's overly confident. He has such little confidence in us we only have to do one half-smart thing, and we'll trap him."

"Great, we're a least half-smart. So, what's the plan?"

Eddie's smile faded. "I've got a few ideas, but why don't you go first."

Rex nodded. "Right. Um, I got a laser pen keyring. We shine it in his eyes and…"

"Yes?"

"That's all I've got."

Eddie squeezed the steering wheel. "Is your nan's garage available?"

"Yeah. Why?"

"I'm gonna drop you off near your nan's house. You head to the back of the garden, unlock the garage door and wait there."

"In the alleyway?" Rex gave a sour expression. "On my own?"

"He'll follow me, then I'll drive through the alleyway to the garages. I'll speed up, he'll need to follow. I do a quick ninety degree turn into the row of garages and zip into your nan's garage. He'll be speeding, do the turn, and see we aren't there. It's a dead end, so it'll be like we disappeared."

"I see, the alleyway is so narrow he won't even be able to open his doors. You sure you can make the turn into the garage? It's a bit tight."

"Yeah, I'll be fine. Then I'll reverse out of the garage and block him in. He'll be trapped in his van until he answers our questions."

With a full grin, Eddie drove towards Rex's nan's house. Cole's van followed from a distance. At a red light, Rex gave a satisfied nod and slipped out of the Morris Minor. He crawled behind a parked car.

After the light turned green, Eddie drove. Cole's van passed the car Rex hid behind, pleased his trap was set. Eddie's smile soon dropped when he took a wrong turn. He made a full loop on a mini roundabout to get back on track. Cole's van followed, and they both drove towards an unsuspecting Rex on his way to the garage. Rex saw Eddie waving and waved back. He realised it was a hand gesture to duck. He dropped before Cole's van passed.

Eddie led Cole on by driving around the neighbourhood for a few minutes. He guessed Rex would have unlocked the garage by now. The Morris Minor pulled into a thin alleyway. Cole's van hesitated, purring at the mouth of the alley.

Eddie slowed, staring in the rear-view mirror. "Come on, follow me."

Cole's van drove into the alleyway. With a quickened breath, Eddie put his foot down. The van matched Eddie's pace. Eddie turned into the tiny side alley with a row of garages. The Morris Minor completely missed the open garage door on the right. A black alley cat watched with disapproval.

Rex stood at the corner waving his hands. "Abort. The garage is full."

Eddie peeked through the rear passenger window at the garage. It was filled with stacks of water damaged cardboard boxes.

"You mean, we've trapped ourselves in a dead end? Cole is headed this way."

Rex hunched his shoulders. "Nan asked me to clear it out last month, but I forgot."

Eddie yanked the gear stick into reverse. The engine sputtered out. He turned the key. When the engine started, the car sprung back, scaring the alley cat. It jumped and ran into the main alleyway as Cole's van reached the side alley. The van swerved to avoid the feline and crashed into a wooden telephone pole against a garden fence.

A rolling squeak from Cole's engine rose in volume and cut out. The van rolled back a foot and settled.

Eddie rushed out of the car as Rex approached the van's passenger door. Inside, Cole was unconscious at the wheel.

"He knocked himself out."

Eddie sneered. "I guess we should tie him up."

"You mean kidnap him?"

"Well, he can't answer any questions like this. Do we have any rope?"

Rex opened the door. He pointed his laser pen at Cole's limp right hand. Around his wrist was the paracord survival bracelet.

"Cole does."

# ELEVEN

R ex and Eddie waited in their office with an unconscious Jason Cole tied up to one of their chairs. The paracord rope had been used to wrap his wrists to the armrests and his chest to the backrest.

"This rope Cole brought is great," Rex said.

"He's gonna be annoyed when he finds out we used it on him."

Rex tilted his head and studied their sleeping captive. "Do you think we should offer to buy him a new one?"

Eddie tugged at the rope around Cole's chest. "Are you sure that's how you tie a knot?"

"It's a knot. I don't know which one, but it's pretty solid."

Eddie folded his arms.

"I could go over him with the packing tape as well, to be safe."

"No, it's fine. Just secure his feet as well."

Rex gave a mock salute. He crawled under the chair and taped each foot to the wheelie legs.

Eddie went through Cole's black suede wallet. He sifted

through a few credit cards, a driving licence, business cards, and stopped at a photo. The dog-eared picture featured twin blonde girls aged about four, sitting on some grass.

He showed the photo to Rex. "He's got two kids."

"We kidnapped someone's dad?" Rex ran both his hands through his hair.

"Calm down. We're not kidnappers."

"Are you sure?" Rex's voice rose. "We already kidnapped two people."

Eddie waved his hands down. "Shhh, the neighbours will hear. We don't want them to think we're—"

"Kidnappers. What are those two little girls gonna do without a dad?"

"They still have a dad. He's here. We're just gonna ask a few questions and let him go, but don't tell him that."

Rex and Eddie stood over the unconscious Cole, waiting. Eddie checked his watch while Rex crossed his arms.

Rex huffed. "They don't show this bit in the films."

Eddie furrowed his brow. "What do you mean?"

"Well, the hero gets knocked out and wakes up in a new place. I never thought about the amount of waiting the other parties have to do. What's it been, half an hour?"

Eddie scoffed. "He's not the hero. They must multitask while they wait. Pay bills and stuff."

"Should we be doing that?"

"Pay bills? We'd need money to do that." Eddie leaned in and examined Cole. "He has been out a long time. Maybe we should take him to the hospital."

"I'm sure he's fine. This is Jason Cole. He's Cloisterham's number one detective. He might even be the best in Kent."

"He can't be that good. His van is rubbish."

"That's so it doesn't draw attention."

Eddie leaned in to examine Cole's face. "What about his flip phone? That's as old as yours."

Cole's eyes flashed open. "It's a burner."

Eddie jumped back with a scream. Startled by Eddie, Rex screamed too.

Cole rattled the armrests his arms were tied to. He examined the rope and tape securing him to the chair. With a knowing smile, he shook his head.

"I told you to stay away. Who hired you and why do they want my case sabotaged?"

Rex stuck out his chin. "You're the tied up one, we're meant to ask the questions."

Cole jumped, shunting his chair forward. The pair flinched.

"Don't do that," Eddie said. "You'll break the chair."

He relaxed back into the seat. "Are you working with the kidnappers?"

Rex's jaw dropped. "No, we'd never do something like that."

"You kidnapped me."

Eddie's upper lip tightened. "Oh, for goodness sake. Technically, we haven't kidnapped you. It's not like we put out a ransom, we just want to ask you some questions. If we're satisfied with the answers, we'll consider letting you go."

Cole let out a sigh through his nostrils. He shook his head. "So torture, is it?"

Eddie hesitated. "If that's what it's got to be."

Rex's forehead wrinkled. "He's got kids."

Eddie leaned to Rex and whispered, "We're not actually gonna torture him."

Cole laughed. "So why should I talk?"

Eddie glared at Rex, passing the blame. Rex shrugged.

Eddie bobbed his head, "We might move up to questioning under duress."

"I have a confidentiality agreement with my client."

Rex stepped forward. "Maude?"

Cole smiled.

Eddie sat down. "So the only way we can get you to talk is with torture?"

"Even then, I've been trained to withstand stress beyond what you can comprehend."

"Like military training?" Rex stammered.

Cole smiled.

"Oh really?" Eddie stood and offered the chair to his partner. "Rex."

"Yes, Eddie."

"Tell Cole here about your issue with badgers."

Rex pulled up a chair, dragged it in front of Cole, and placed it backwards. He sat using the back as an armrest and stared Cole square in the eyes.

"So, the badger, is it a bear or a dog?"

Cole's eyebrows tensed. "It's a badger?"

"But what is a badger?"

"It's a woodland animal."

Rex cocked his head. "Like a woodland bear or like a woodland dog?"

"I don't know." Cole shrugged. "It's kind of a rodent, isn't it?"

"I see, like a heavy-set weasel."

"No, like a badger." Cole's lips pressed into a thin line.

Rex raised a finger. "Or are they the otter of the woods?"

Cole's eyes darted between Rex and Eddie. "What?"

Eddie grinned.

"A land otter?" Rex straightened his neck like he'd had an epiphany. "Or is the otter a sea-badger?"

Eddie leaned in. "My friend Rex's questions go beyond what you can comprehend."

"And why is a group of goose called geese, but a group of moose aren't called meese?"

Cole huffed. "Maude Archer. She's your client, isn't she?"

Eddie's eyebrows raised. "What makes you think that?"

"You mentioned her first. I was hired by the boy's parents."

Eddie settled into a chair and pulled out his notepad. "Daryl's parents?"

"They were threatened by a gang of hooligans. They've been using intimidation tactics ever since. Last week they came home and found Mrs Archer's car vandalised. Mr Archer wanted me to find out what it was about."

"Maude never told us that," Rex said.

"When we interviewed her," Eddie added. "Because she may, or may not be, our client."

"A few weeks ago, Daryl paid off his student loans with a suspicious sum of money. His father refused to pay for his college. Since graduating, he regularly scolded Daryl for getting into debt. I believe the funds came from the gang and now they want their money back."

"So they're blackmailing the parents?" Eddie said.

"No. Vandalising was a scare tactic to rile up the family. To incentivise Daryl."

There was a knock at the door. Rex and Eddie's heads swung to the door and back to Cole.

"You boys should untie me."

Eddie grimaced. "We can't do that yet."

Rex frowned. "We can't?"

"We need more information first."

"Then we untie him?"

"Then we talk about it."

Rex cocked his head.

"I'm all for untying him, but I don't want him to beat us up when we do."

"How about one of us does it? Then he can only beat up one of us."

Eddie placed a hand on Rex's shoulder. "You can let me know how it goes."

The door knocks became louder.

Cole jiggled the loose armrests. "If whoever's behind that door sees me, you'll go to jail. Time to let me go."

The door knocked faster.

Eddie pointed at Cole as he headed to the door. "Tape his mouth."

Rex pulled the duct tape from the roll. "Sorry, about all this." He covered Cole's mouth. "You think someday we'll laugh about all this?"

Cole jumped, sliding the chair forward. Rex's arms snapped up to protect his upper body and head. He looked over his forearms at Cole.

The man puffed his chest out, as much as the rope would allow. His eyebrows lowered. His fists clenched.

Rex slowly returned to a relaxed posture. "Yeah, you can keep fighting it, but one of these days, you and me are gonna be friends."

---

The detective duo entered their small, empty reception room. Rex closed the office door and moved side to side to see if Cole's shadow was noticeable in the door's clouded glass. They'd just about get away with it.

Eddie approached the hallway door and opened it a crack. In the corridor stood Guy Sumner, a slender man with a short quiff made from the remains of his receding brown hair. He had a long friendly face, which currently sported a put-upon smile. Although the pair had only ever seen him in his police uniform, today he wore a brown suit.

"Officer Sumner," Rex and Eddie said in a joyful, unified greeting. Rex with excitement and Eddie with a nervous dread.

"Detective Inspector Sumner," he said in a friendly tone. "I got a promotion."

Eddie nodded. "Good for you. What brings you to Cloisterham?"

"Got transferred here after the Terry Palmer case."

Rex nodded. "Wow, that's cool. Must be a bit different."

Sumner chuckled. "Quite a bit different I can tell you. A couple of other countryside bobbies have joined me, and we're being trained on urban policing. We even did some terrorism training."

Rex's jaw went slack as his eyebrows raised. "You think terrorists would want to attack Cloisterham?" He put his hand on his chest, flattered.

Eddie frowned. "Terrorists don't even know about Cloisterham."

"It's simply a precaution. With London only forty miles away we can offer support if needed. It's been tremendously interesting. If anything were suspected in Cloisterham we'd be pretty busy, I can tell you. The very mention of a terrorist attack would bring every case to a standstill. Anyway, I'm not here to chat shop. My real role here in Cloisterham is serving and protecting the likes of you." Sumner's smile mellowed. "Unless that is," he lowered his tone, "I'm here to serve and protect people from the likes of you."

"What's that supposed to mean?" Eddie said.

"Well, I came to pay you a professional courtesy, on account of you helping the force out in the past. You see, we've had numerous witnesses say they saw two young men run over a blue-haired man and put him in their vehicle."

Eddie covered his mouth. "How horrible."

"You see, the vehicle has been identified as an old green car made with wooden posts."

"Uh-huh."

"And one of them identified it as a Morris Minor. So I thought it best if I came and checked up on you."

Eddie laughed. "You think we kidnapped someone?" He tapped Rex on the shoulder playfully.

Rex grinned. "Ha, that's silly. We didn't kidnap Karl."

Sumner paused. "Who's Karl?"

"Uh…"

Eddie put on a fake grin. "A Karl, you know it's lingo for a… an art student."

Sumner looked over their shoulders at the main office door. "Why would you say an art student?"

"Well, no-one but the students at Cloisterham College of Art & Design, have bright hair colours, usually. They're all a bunch of Karls. Right, Rex?"

Rex put on a laugh. "What a bunch of Karls."

Sumner cocked his head. "How'd you get that black eye, Rex?"

"Fightin'." Rex gave a proud smile.

"Right," Sumner said in a hushed tone. He lightened up. "Can I come in and see your office?"

Rex swallowed. "Do you have a warrant?"

Sumner leaned in. "Should I get a warrant?"

"He's joking." Eddie pursed his lips. "It's a bit of a mess that's all. We're not taking guests at the moment."

A thud came from the office.

Sumner peeked at the clouded glass of the door behind

the pair. A slight, blurred silhouette bobbed left and right. "No guests, eh?"

Rex and Eddie gave big goofy smiles.

"Earthquake?" Eddie offered. "Must have knocked something over."

"In England?" Sumner said.

"We still get the occasional one, but people forget," Eddie said. "There was that four-point-three in 2007 that cracked Rex's nan's kitchen window."

Rex nodded. "She was well annoyed."

"I didn't feel anything. Wouldn't the hallway have shaken?"

"It was a little earthquake," Eddie said. "This is England after all."

"Come on, lads. I'm on your side, but I've got to do my job. I need to cross you off my list. I've been down to the car park and inspected your car for signs of a collision."

Rex's eyes widened while Eddie held his breath.

"All fine, of course." Sumner peaked over their shoulders. "Now, show me your office, and I can leave you alone."

"Otherwise you'll get a warrant?"

"I can arrest you for obstructing a police officer in the course of carrying out his duties. Unless you want to spend your evening at the station, show me your office, and I'll have done my duty."

Eddie sighed.

"I get it, you're private investigators, you've got private information on your desk, an open file case. I promise whatever I see…" He mimed zipping his lips. "Mum's the word."

Eddie bit his inner cheek. "You promise?"

"I'll turn a blind eye."

"So as long as we haven't got a blue-haired hostage in there, you'll look away?"

Sumner smiled. "I promise."

Rex and Eddie exchanged glances. Rex shrugged. Eddie nodded. The pair stepped back, and Sumner entered the reception.

"After you two."

Eddie held the office door handle for a brief second. After a sigh, he opened the door.

Inside the office, Cole's chair lay on its side with one of the armrests broken off. A pile of rope lay on the floor. The window was open.

Rex and Eddie paled as they studied the office, checking each corner.

Sumner patted them on the back. "It's not that messy at all. In fact, I'd go as far as saying it's rather tidy." He furrowed his brow at the sight of the rope. "Been practising your knots?"

"Yes," Rex said, confused.

Eddie swallowed. "We really need to practise our knots."

Sumner crouched to the floor. He pointed at the rolling chair's base. "What's that about?"

Cole's shoes were still duct taped to the plastic legs of the chair base. The duo exchanged glances.

Eddie hunched his shoulders. "Those are my... chair shoes."

Sumner tilted his head. "Chair shoes?"

"Yes, I have a nervous tick. My feet bob up and down. To break the habit, I have those shoes to keep them in place."

Rex drew a smile through gritted teeth. He had nothing to add.

Sumner blew out his cheeks. "Huh, clever." He stood.

"It's been an absolute pleasure catching up, lads. I'll see myself out."

Sumner headed along the hallway and down the stairs with a jolly whistle. Rex and Eddie stood in the doorway watching the office.

"He went out the window, right?"

"I'd imagine so?" Eddie stepped in and straightened the chair, revealing a pair of scissors on the floor. "Rex, did you leave the scissors on the desk when you cut the rope to size?"

He bit his lip. "Sorry."

Eddie sighed. "At least next time we know to put the scissors away. We should probably avoid tying anyone to the rolling chair too. That should keep them from travelling to the stationery in the first place."

# TWELVE

E ddie turned the Morris Minor into the driveway of a mock Tudor detached house; his parents' home.

Rex glimpsed at the passenger wing mirror for any signs they'd been followed. He tapped his fingers on the door window ridge.

"Will you stop that," Eddie said.

Rex turned around, peering out the back window. "Aren't you worried?"

"It's my family's weekly dinner. I can't cancel on the night."

"But what if he ends us?"

"Don't get me wrong. I'm concerned about Cole, and what a revenge-seeking ex-military man could do to us. It's just—"

"You're more scared of your mum."

Eddie furrowed his brows. "That's ridiculous. I like to stick to my plans and be punctual and—"

"And you're scared of your mum."

Eddie clenched his jaw. "My mum is a saint."

They got out of the car and approached the front door. Rex walked backwards, his eyes on the street.

Eddie pushed the doorbell. "And remember, don't mention the whole detective thing. As far as she is concerned, I have a normal office job."

"Because you're *not* scared of her?"

"I don't want her to worry."

Eddie's mother answered the door. She was a small woman wearing oversized tortoiseshell glasses. Her shoulder length hair was straight with streaks of grey, white, and black.

"Come in, come in."

She ushered them inside and closed the door. "Are you okay dear, you seem a bit frazzled?"

"I'm fine, Mum."

"You've got dirt on your face." She spat on her fingers and wiped it off.

Eddie took the wash. "Thanks for that."

Rex continued to check over his shoulder. "Mrs Miles, have you seen a tall man around here? In a long brown coat? Chiselled good looks?"

She peered over her glasses, up at Rex. "What are you drivelling on about? Is that a black eye?"

"Forget it, Mum. Rex is playing. Right, Rex?"

Eddie and his Mum waited for an answer. They had the same disapproving expression.

"That's a no then?" Rex said, failing to pick up the social cues.

She walked them through the house. The dining room was packed with a large mahogany table and a cabinet filled with Egyptian and Mediterranean trinkets. A grandfather clock struck seven o'clock, letting everyone know dinner was officially late. Eddie's brother and father were seated.

Eddie's father sat at the end of the table, his tired eyes looked down at his leather placemat. He swished his wine glumly.

Rex and Eddie squeezed against the wall lined with mounted Greek masks and sat at the table. It was the usual spot when Rex attended since the masks tended to distract him.

Mrs Miles brought out bacon wrapped chicken breasts with potatoes and buttered asparagus; neatly served on floral print china.

"Sorry if it's a little cold," she said. "I was expecting you to be a few minutes early."

"If you're not ten minutes early, you're late." Eddie's brother Andy smiled as he took his plate. He looked like a lankier, taller Eddie, but with a pointed nose like his mother.

Mrs Miles headed back to the kitchen. "Indeed, Andrew. Like I've always said. How was work, dear?"

"It was good. Made lots of money. You plant the seed, water the seed, and it grows into a beautiful tree. Actually, you don't even have to water it, you pay someone else to do that."

Eddie sneered. "So you just bury the seed?"

"Beautiful trees, every time."

"What about last time?"

Rex and Eddie's plates arrived, and Mrs Miles took a seat.

"Edward, don't pick on your brother."

"I wanted to know—"

"You should be nice to Andrew. He could get you a job in finance."

Andy gave a superior half smile.

"I'm fine, Mum."

During a brief pause in the conversation, the Miles

family ate from their plates with a methodical approach. Rex artfully knifed and stirred everything into a food mountain and shovelled the mix into his mouth.

"Anyway," Mrs Miles began. "How's your job?"

Andy smirked. "Yeah, whose underling are you nowadays?"

Eddie glared. "Actually, I'm in a superficial role."

"Superficial?" Eddie's father looked up from his glass of wine for the first time.

"Uh, supervisory role," Eddie said. "Rex is my assistant. Can we talk about something else?"

Rex grimaced at Eddie.

"Did you hear about the kidnapping in town?" Andy asked.

"Oh, Andrew, not at the table."

"A blue-haired boy got grabbed near the High Street. You heard about it?"

Eddie swallowed his bite. "I heard he wasn't kidnapped. He was helped by friends after an accident."

"Oh right," Andy said. "You were there were you?"

Rex nodded. Eddie shook his head. They were in perfect sync as if controlled by clockwork.

"This isn't good for digestion," Mrs Miles said. "Tell them, Harold."

Mr Miles nibbled his asparagus and swallowed. "Now, boys. You heard your mother."

"I saw it while working," Rex said. "They were in a hurry, 'cause the friend needed medical attention. That's why it looked like a kidnapping."

Andy cut his chicken. "The police called it a kidnapping."

Mrs Miles dabbed her mouth with a cloth napkin. "Eddie, were you near a kidnapping? That sort of thing is too much for you. You know that. Why can't you get a job with Andrew?"

Andy narrowed his eyes. "I thought you worked in the town centre. The kidnapping happened a mile away."

Eddie let go of his cutlery, which tapped against the china plate.

Mrs Miles placed a hand on Eddie's arm. "Careful with the silverware, dear."

"Rex saw it," Eddie said, "at his other job. He's part-time with me."

Rex nodded, his mouth full.

"I'm a private detective."

"You're not a detective," Andy said, giggling.

Eddie's parents laughed. Rex joined in.

"What are you laughing at?" Andy asked.

"I don't know," Rex said.

"What nonsense." Mrs Miles cut into her meat. "I'm glad Eddie's smart enough to stay away from your endeavour." She looked across at her husband. "Could you imagine such a thing? Edward Miles P.I."

Eddie clenched his jaw. "I could be a detective if I wanted to be," he mumbled.

Mrs Miles tapped his arm. "Don't be a silly boy."

Eddie's eyes darted around the table. His mother, father and brother were all in a fit of giggles. Rex hunched over his plate and ate faster.

*I'm a man*, Eddie thought. *Not a boy. I can fight crime, I can win cases. I'm a proper manly man.*

He sat up straight. "I'm a male man," he said with conviction.

Andy tucked his chin. "A postman?"

"No, a male, as in the gender, man. I'm a bloody male manly man."

The Miles laughter calmed down to a titter, stopping as each of them took a bite of food.

"Can I grab a sleeping bag?" Eddie asked.

Mrs Miles cut her asparagus. "What on earth would you want a sleeping bag for?"

Eddie winced. "Uh, well, Rex and I are gonna take a camping trip."

Rex's spine straightened. "We are?"

"Camping, dear? With your allergies?"

"I've got my antihistamine tablets. I'll be fine."

"What if your asthma flares up again? Will you be camping near a hospital?"

"Mum, that's not happened in years. I just want a sleeping bag."

"And the rest of the camping gear," Rex said. "For the trip."

Eddie nodded at Rex with a forced grin.

Mrs Miles cut vigorously at her chicken. "Fine, go if you *think* you can *handle* yourself. It's upstairs in your old bedroom cupboard."

"Old?" Eddie asked.

"Yes, I tried to keep your room for you, hoping you'd have the sense to stay here and save up for a house deposit like your brother."

Andy raised his glass with a smile. "Cheers, Mum."

"But since you insist on living in that squalid flat, I've turned it into your father's office. Because he needed it. Isn't that right, Harold?"

"Yes, dear," Mr Miles said in a mumble, eyes on his food.

"So take the camping stuff for all I care, if you must endanger yourself unnecessarily in the wild."

"It's the British countryside," Eddie said, defending his imaginary trip. "There aren't any predators, nothing's going to come after me. The worst that could happen is a fox will make a mess going through my rubbish. They do that at any address in Cloisterham."

Rex's shoulders pulled back. He searched his pockets and pulled out Cole's business card. Under the table, he pointed at the printed office address.

"Address. We have his address," Rex whispered, but everyone could still hear.

Mrs Miles leaned forward. "Whose address? What are you two blathering on about?"

Rex and Eddie stood. The heavy mahogany dining chairs screeched along the wood floor. The backs tapped the decorative wall moulding close behind.

"Thanks for dinner, Mum," Eddie said with his mouth half full. "It was delicious."

"Very nice." Rex scooped the rest of his food into the napkin; a makeshift to-go container.

"You've hardly eaten," Mrs Miles said, "you only just got here."

Eddie ran to the door, followed by Rex. Andy shrugged and went back to eating his dinner.

Mr Miles rose from his chair. "Let me get you that sleeping bag before you go."

# THIRTEEN

The Morris Minor drove at the strict speed limit of thirty miles per hour. It wobbled a little from side to side as Eddie's eyes darted left and right, checking the wing mirrors for Cole.

Rex leaned forward in the passenger seat. "Eddie, are you okay?"

"Fine."

"Because you're driving a little erratically. Well, erratic for you, and your neck is doing this weird clenching thing."

"What is my neck doing?" Eddie turned around before he remembered he couldn't possibly see his own neck. "I'm fine, I slept in a funny position so I'm a little bit stiff."

The Morris Minor whizzed past an amber traffic light.

Rex bit his lip. "Do we have a plan?"

"Go to Cole's and... I don't know... investigate him."

"You're stressed because we kidnapped him and tied him up, and you think he might hold it against you?"

Eddie widened his jaw to release tension, it clicked. He grimaced at Rex's black eye. "How's your eye? Does it still hurt?"

"My eye's fine, it's a fashion statement at this point."

Eddie's neck muscles tensed. "He's going to kill us, isn't he?"

"He said end us; that could mean any number of things."

Eddie glared at Rex. "Is that meant to calm me down?"

Rex shrugged. "It's not a yes."

As a pedestrian walked across a zebra crossing ahead, Eddie slowed the Morris Minor to a stop. The engine rumbled as the windscreen wipers shoved off the spitting rain. While waiting, Eddie gnawed on his teeth.

"What's the address number again?"

Rex held up the business card. "78B Orange Hill. Cole's card is pretty cool, see the 'o' in Cole is a magnifying glass. Did you notice that?"

"Wouldn't the handle make it a 'q' or a 'p'?"

Rex gave the card a closer examination. "I think it works."

The pedestrian reached the traffic island, and Eddie put his foot down. The sunset disappeared behind the row of buildings to their right.

Eddie swallowed. "Okay, I've got a plan. We go to Cole's. If he's in we apologise, maybe take him out for a drink. We'll promise to pool our resources, and never upset him again."

Rex nodded then paused. "And if he's not in?"

Eddie cleared his throat. "We break in, steal his case file, and go through his stuff."

Rex pointed out the window. "That's the address."

On the corner of a busy intersection, in a thin, brown-bricked Victorian building, Cole Investigations sat unmarked in the floor above a kebab shop.

With no parking spots nearby, Eddie continued up the

hill and into the neighbourhood. They ended up a quarter of a mile away from the office before they found street parking. The pair speed-walked back down the hill in a fluster.

Rex and Eddie passed the front of the kebab shop, which had a white painted entrance with big glass windows. On the side of the building, the kebab shop's wheelie bin stood by a poorly lit doorway with a rusted intercom. Eddie pushed the call button. After a few rings, the buzzer connected.

"Hello," Cole's voice said in a monotone fashion.

Eddie frowned.

"You've reached the office of Jason Cole Investigations. I'm unable to answer your call right now, so please leave a message, and I'll get back to you."

"The buzzer's connected to his office phone." Rex threaded a hand through his hair. "We can leave a message. Say we're sorry and move on."

Eddie narrowed his eyes at the door. "We're men, right?"

"Yes."

"We're detectives."

"Yes!" Rex's eyes lit up.

"We've got a case to solve and the ability to solve it."

"Of course."

"For Maude, and Daryl, of course."

"Exactly."

"So we have a duty to them and ourselves to go in there and collect evidence."

"I'm with you, Eddie. Every step of the way."

"I mean this is real detective work. It's what we signed up for."

"Always game for some real detective work."

Eddie took a deep breath. "How about we do it after a kebab?"

Rex's jaw jerked to the side. "If you're hungry."

Eddie sighed. "I'm not." He turned to the side door. "Sod it. Let's do this."

He attempted to shove the door open, no luck. Eddie thumped his foot against the door. With his face twisted, Eddie hobbled in a circle, walking off the pain.

Eddie leaned a hand on the wheelie bin flush against the brick wall. He shook his foot.

"Rex, it's your turn."

Rex ran at the door but bounced back, hitting his bottom against the cold, damp pavement.

Eddie peered into a crack in the wheelie bin's plastic, warped lid. "Maybe there's information in Cole's rubbish. You still game for some real detective work?"

"Ah, really?" Rex lifted the cover and peered in. "We're not sure if Cole even uses this one."

Eddie pulled the lid open as wide as he could. "One way to find out."

Rex's lips drew in tight and turned down.

"It's what any real detective would be doing."

Rex removed his corduroy blazer and handed it to Eddie. He pushed his glasses up on his nose and climbed in.

Inside, Rex kicked around. "I think I found some shredded documents." He grabbed them and lifted it. "Ah no. It's lettuce."

He rummaged around some more. "More lettuce, no wait, that's shredded paper in…" He gave it a smell. "Burger sauce."

Eddie rolled his eyes. "I bet he shreds everything. We should get a shredder."

"For when someone goes through our rubbish?"

"Exactly." Eddie's eyes widened. He realised Cole would be going through their rubbish. "Exactly!"

Eddie yanked Rex out of the wheelie bin. With his foot caught on the lip of the container, Rex tumbled to the concrete floor. A patch of red on the side of his shirt alarmed Eddie.

"Rex, are you bleeding?"

Rex wiped the red with his finger and licked it. "Nah, it's ketchup."

"Uh, disgusting." Eddie did a mini-retch, reserved for mild disgust. "Must you put everything in your mouth?"

"A good detective should use all five of his senses."

Their office was a quarter of a mile down the High Street. The car was about the same distance in the opposite direction. Rex and Eddie ran straight along the High Street to the back of their office building. The floodlight switched on as they approached the wheelie bin.

"Well, Eddie, it's your turn to jump in this time."

Eddie rested his hands on his bent knees, gasping for air. "Not necessarily. Wait here."

He marched to the corner shop and returned with a box of matches.

"You want to burn it? Are you sure we put anything Cole would want in there?"

"It doesn't matter, Rex. I won't give him the satisfaction."

Rex screwed up his face. "Of going through our bins?"

Eddie lit a match and threw it in the bin. The tiny flame fizzled out in the damp rubbish. He lit a second match, but the wind blew it out. Eddie grabbed the driest paper from the bin and held it out towards Rex.

"Light a match, will you."

Rex struck another one and held the flame to the paper.

Eddie waved his arm, alarmed by the growing fire. He threw the burning paper into the wheelie bin. The fire spread along to the black bags. Loose Styrofoam melted. Eddie offered Rex a high five but failed the landing. Cole's black van pulled up behind them.

The pair turned to the vehicle. Rex bit his lip while Eddie raised an eyebrow.

"You lose, Cole," Eddie said.

Jason Cole stormed up to the pair, his face emotionless. Rex and Eddie slowed their victory dance and hunched together.

The fire burning behind them lit Cole's face in a flickering orange. Black shadows danced along his chiselled features. As he approached, the pair noticed he was a good deal taller than either of them. Fire reflected in his eyes.

"You— You don't have anything on us now," Eddie said with a slight squeak to his voice. "We burnt our rubbish."

"Yeah, we're a mystery." Rex stuck his neck out. "Watcha gonna do now?"

Cole furrowed his brow. "I've already been through your office. I've collected records from all over town."

"Pffft," Eddie said. "What do you know?"

"Edward Miles. Twenty-eight years old. You have a two-two in Media Studies. You did an internship placement at the Kent Gazette and bounced around from dead-end job to dead-end job. Until this week you lived at 171 Fort Newman Street, flat eight, but were evicted. I'd imagine you must be staying with your parents at this point, Bertha and Harold. Or you've chosen to bunk up with this nitwit, Rex Milton."

The pair exchanged glances.

"Look at me!"

They snapped back to Cole.

"You two met in primary school. A couple of months ago you became business partners." He pointed at Rex. "You finished school at seventeen after attempting A-levels but dropped out. According to your school records you were invited to leave to avoid lowering the school's national rating by one place. It's probably not your fault. At seventeen-years-old, your parents died in a car accident. You live with your maternal grandmother and your twelve-year-old sister. Did I miss anything?"

"You read our school records?" Eddie asked. "Like, our permanent record?"

Rex's jaw dropped. "No way, those aren't real."

Cole continued, "Eddie received two detentions in his entire school time, the second was for forgetting to attend the first. Rex received twenty-one detentions in total, along with a stern talking to after sneaking a Big Mac into food economics, and claiming to have prepared it in class himself."

"He's messing with us."

Rex's jaw dropped. "Permanent records are real?"

"Maude Archer hired you to investigate the suspicious behaviour of her brother, Daryl Archer. You've been impeding my investigation ever since and jeopardised the welfare of Mr Archer."

Eddie folded his arms. "Our investigation has just as much value as yours."

Cole narrowed his eyes. "I am not interested in arguing with you. There is a young man out there who has been kidnapped. Every hour counts. Now you'd better cough up whatever information you have before Daryl is found dead in the River Invicta."

The detective pair gave each other a look.

"Yes, well." Eddie straightened his tie. "If you were a bit more forthcoming, we could help you out."

"The parents were threatened. I asked local gang members that owe me favours for information; lots of people owe me favours. Last month, Daryl drunkenly walked home after a night at the Monte Carlo nightclub. On the way, he found a dead gang member in a bush. Daryl took the dead man's bag of drugs. Later, he sold it to The Cloisterham Massive to pay off his student loans. They decided they needed an unsuspecting, wealthy hipster to do deliveries for them. He did it for a bit but wanted to quit. Since The Massive were on to a good thing, they didn't accept his resignation."

Eddie raised an eyebrow and crinkled his nose. "So they kidnapped him instead?"

"It's a possibility."

"What else could it be?" Rex asked.

"The drugs Daryl stole from the dead body belonged to a gang called The Cloister Posse. If they think he killed their man found in the bush, they'd want revenge. Killing Daryl would send a message to the criminal community to not mess with their members. They could have captured him."

Rex tilted his head. "But not for ransom money?"

"No. They want Daryl dead. If that's the case, it's my job to buy out his death penalty on behalf of the Archer family. Unfortunately, I lost the kidnappers because you crashed into me and stopped me from identifying them."

The two detectives avoided eye contact with Cole.

"Look at me! I believe the van went straight to the chop shop and we won't see it again. According to DVLA records, the licence didn't match the vehicle type anyway."

Eddie's forehead wrinkled. "You can get information from the DVLA?"

"I need to know what you saw. Faces, markings,

anything? Any descriptors could help identify them and secure Daryl Archer's safety."

Eddie shrugged. "They wore hoodies. We didn't see their faces."

"We know someone who might have," Rex said. "She was a bit withholding with us, but I'm sure she'll cooperate with you. We can go see her together."

Cole considered it and nodded. "Fine."

"Partners?" Rex offered his hand.

"This isn't partnering up. You're my informants."

"You're our informant," Eddie said.

Cole shook his head. "No."

Rex put his hands on his hips. "Who's the one giving all the information?"

After marching to his van, Cole pulled the back doors open. "I'm not arguing with either of you. Get in the van."

# FOURTEEN

Cole drove the van towards Canal Lane. Rex and Eddie sat in the cargo area filled with surveillance gear, computer tech, and a plastic crate of disguises. All of it was secured to the van's sides.

Rex leaned towards the corner. "Is that a mini-fridge?"

Cole waved a finger but kept his eyes on the road. "Don't touch anything."

Rex tapped a monitor. "What's this hooked up to?" He froze in excitement. "Do you have spy cameras?"

"I said don't touch. It's Gucci."

Rex sneered. "Gucci makes surveillance gear?"

"No. It's expensive. Gucci means expensive."

Eddie furrowed his brow. "Where on Earth does it mean that?"

Cole shook his head as he changed gears. "Sorry, Bootneck slang."

"Oh, right," Eddie said, feigning understanding.

Rex sat back down. "What's Bootneck? Some kind of elite force?"

Eddie shrugged.

Rex raided a snack box and helped himself to a packet of trail mix. He offered one to Eddie.

Eddie shook his head and tightened his crossed arms. He lowered his voice to a whisper. "Telling Cole about Ruby is risky. What if she mentions the briefcase?"

Rex picked at the trail mix, only eating the dried fruit. "So what? We can't do anything with the information. Let him do the legwork, and we can swoop in and save the day at the end." Rex softened. "Is it true that you've been kicked out of your flat?"

Eddie pursed his lips and nodded.

"What happened?"

"I was behind on rent."

"When I don't have enough money Nan lets me do chores, like take out the rubbish bins. You could do that for your flat?"

"I did do that for my flat."

"Rent and chores? You're getting conned."

The van slowed to a stop. Cole stepped out of the front, walked around, and opened the back of the vehicle. "Where's the witness?"

"She'll be here," Eddie said. "She must be, uh, working."

"And I can trust her?"

Rex nodded. "Yeah, she's a no-nonsense lady. Can I ask a question?"

Cole gave an irritated nod.

"How come you got all this stuff but no guns or anything?"

"A weapon being carried by you can be used against you in an unarmed attack."

"What about in an armed attack?" Eddie asked.

Cole gave a reserved grin. "A weapon used against you can be used by you."

Rex smiled. Eddie looked around to prove his disinterest.

"It avoids prosecution for intent as well. If I have a gun, I have an intention to use it. You want your weapons to have a primary purpose. For instance, a Maglite, it's solid, strong, and quick to deploy."

He pulled the aluminium torch from his belt and flashed them in the eyes. The pair blinked and scrunched their faces.

"Even a distraction buys you a few seconds."

"You got a spare?" Rex said.

Cole shook his head. "Sorry, you'll need your own. You got loose change?"

Rex nodded. "It's the only kind of money we have."

"Projectile weapons. Surprises the attacker and delays their advance."

Rex's smile grew. Eddie cocked his head.

"If you're desperate even a set of car keys help."

"Car keys?" Eddie scoffed.

"An improvised knuckle duster."

Eddie sneered. "You're having a laugh. What good are keys against a gun?"

Rex nudged him. "I'll carry the keys if you like."

Eddie paused, his hand over his pocket feeling the keys. "No, I'll carry them," he said sheepishly.

"If you can't take the attacker's gun, it's best to run, preferably in a zig-zag pattern."

"Outrun bullets?" Eddie folded his arms.

"Most people are terrible shots," Cole said. "It's always worth running. What's the alternative?"

Eddie grimaced. The pair climbed out of the van as Ruby strumbled on spiked high heels to her street corner. Cole approached her with Rex and Eddie in tow.

"You looking for business?"

"Hi Ruby," Rex said.

She dropped the smile. "What'd you want now?" She looked Cole up and down with approving eyes.

"My name is Jason Cole, I believe you've met my associates."

"We're his partners," Rex said.

"They are not," Cole responded.

Eddie gave a firm nod. "Couldn't be further from the truth."

Rex pointed between him and Eddie. "Well, me and him are partners."

"Business partners," Eddie insisted.

Ruby raised her hands to the pair, then eyeballed Cole. She gave a satisfied smile. "Hello, Mister."

"He's not a John," Eddie said.

Rex nodded. "He's a detective, like us. Are you looking for a John? We can help you find him."

Cole smiled. "We're after information. My associates tell me you witnessed the kidnapping of Daryl Archer."

She cocked her head. "What's it to you?"

With a sigh, Cole lowered his voice. "His family hired me to help him. They're anxious. What's your name?"

Her eyes twinkled. "Ruby."

"Pleased to meet you, Ruby."

"Pleasure's all mine."

"Daryl needs our help." He raised a photo of Daryl looking fresh-faced and innocent. "Dangerous people have him. His parents are terrified. Do you think you could describe the men that took him? Had you seen them before?"

"Yeah. I did."

Rex put his hands on his hips. "You're helping him for nothing?"

Cole turned to Rex with a furrowed brow.

"What? She charged us. It's not fair."

"Twenty quid," Ruby suggested with an apologetic look.

Cole handed over the cash.

"What did you see?"

"This guy." She pointed at the photo. "He hides a suitcase in the pub's electric meter. Then another van shows up, picks it up and leaves."

As she spoke, Cole opened a leather-bound notepad and wrote. Eddie raised his eyebrows at Rex and nodded to the pad. Rex crinkled his nose.

Cole turned to a fresh page. "When did this start?"

"They've been doing it for weeks."

He nodded. "The kidnappers, was it the same van that normally comes?"

"I don't think they use a regular one."

"Would you be able to describe any of the men?"

"They usually wear grey hoodies and cover their faces. When they came back for the briefcase, a guy wore a T-shirt. He had a snake tattoo wrapped around his right arm."

Rex bit his bottom lip. "Cool."

"Tattoos are not cool," Eddie said.

Ruby glanced at the sun symbol on her inner wrist and gave Eddie an evil look.

"How often are the drop-offs?"

"They came and did it again today. Not been picked up yet."

Cole handed over a business card. "If you can think of anything else."

He walked down the lane towards The Barge Inn. Rex and Eddie attempted to catch up.

"This is exciting," Rex said as they lagged behind Cole.

"The three of us collecting evidence. Filling in the blanks. This partnership with Cole is paying off."

"I guess," Eddie said with a strained throat.

Rex narrowed his eyes at Eddie. "Are you jealous of him or something?"

"I have this niggling feeling, you know? I mean, what do we know about Cole and his case? Only what he's told us. Which could be made up."

"You think he works for someone else? That maybe he's been hired to retrieve the drug money for some gangster kingpin? Or Spin Doctor?"

"It's a little nagging feeling." Eddie furrowed his brow. "It's nothing."

As the pair walked, Rex leaned closer to his partner. "In your gut?"

Eddie gave a tiny nod.

"You have to listen to that. That's your detective instinct."

Cole reached the short brick wall outlining The Barge Inn's property.

"Is it though? Is it not just a general feeling of dread?"

"You do have a pretty high base level dread," Rex replied.

"It might be that. Or Cole's gonna double cross us. Kill us even. Maybe he killed Daryl. I don't know. I just know I don't like this."

"That's good enough for me."

Eddie's face contorted with confusion. "You'd go along with my whim?"

"Your gut instinct, Eddie. Every time."

Cole slowed down and turned back to the pair. "What are you waiting for?" He waved them closer and continued walking.

Eddie stopped. He grabbed Rex's arm. "Why's he beckoning us over to a dark corner?"

Rex shrugged. "Professional courtesy? It's a joint case."

Eddie peered at the electric meter box, a square wooden box embedded in the exterior wall.

"This is a trap."

Rex smiled. "Is that your gut instinct talking?"

Eddie nodded.

The pair darted past Cole and pulled the box open. A leather briefcase fell from the box, landing on the patio. Eddie grabbed the briefcase.

Cole stood with his arms on his hips. "What are you doing?"

Eddie stepped back. "Rex."

"Yes, Eddie."

"Run."

The pair sped down to the river's edge, passing the decking with several boats and yachts moored to it. They reached the old canal lock, a rusty wonky bridge that served as a gate for the mouth of the now filled in canal. A group of teenagers sat on the lock's handrails. They flicked beer bottle caps into the river's marsh as they drank.

Rex and Eddie paused at the lock as the teens gave them dirty looks. The pair ran around the lock to the tarmac path paved over the filled in canal.

Cole barrelled forward. The teens ran off the thin excuse for a bridge to make way for him. One tripped and fell into the tall grass.

Cole jumped over the tripped teen. Rex and Eddie reached a chain-link fence separating the wide alley from an estate of new houses under construction.

Rex clawed his way to the top of the six-foot fence. He rolled over on to the grounds of the construction site. He stood and shouted, "Chuck me the case."

Eddie turned back and saw Cole gaining on them. He threw the case, which hit the top of the fence and bounced back. Eddie covered his head with his arms as it fell back towards him, landing by his feet.

Rex groaned. "Come on, Eddie."

Grabbing the fence, Eddie attempted to climb halfway up the chain-link and pushed the briefcase over the top. Rex caught the case and beckoned his business partner over the fence.

With Cole approaching, Eddie reached the top. His legs stretched over the fence and dangled down the other side. His feet searched for a section of fence to grasp.

"Just jump!"

Eddie pushed his feet into the fence for grip as the chain-link fence swung back and forth. He saw Cole was close. With a defeated sigh, Eddie let go of the fence. He fell to the ground.

Rex hugged the briefcase with one hand and used the other to pull his partner up. The pair ran through the muddy building site as Cole climbed the fence. Eddie's foot wobbled on a loose brick, and he fell. Rex ran straight into Eddie and tripped. They lay on the ground.

Cole sprinted through the building site's uneven surface and past Rex and Eddie. He reached the end of the site which joined a quiet road.

He pulled his Maglite torch from his belt and turned the light on. Cole searched the row of factories and warehouses across the street. Nearby business signs promoted concrete, roof tiles, and digger rentals. Behind him, Rex and Eddie lay in the darkened gutter of the unpaved road.

From across the poorly lit industrial street, an engine purred. A black van's headlights flashed on, momentarily blinding Cole. He turned away from the light and found

Rex and Eddie. The beams spotlighted the pair lying on the dirty ground with an awkward expression on their faces.

Cole ran back across the bumpy building site. "Run."

The van screeched as it drove across the unpaved road. The tyres and metal bumper hit slabs of brick and concrete.

Rex and Eddie scrabbled to their feet and followed Cole, who waited at the fence. The pair slowed, unsure of him. Rex tightened his grip of the briefcase.

"Climb!"

They reached the fence. Cole offered his interlocked hands as a step. The van's front tyres thumped against the paved road, stopping the vehicle. Its back wheels spun in gravel as the engine revved.

Rex landed on the other side with the case. Cole gave Eddie a final push over the fence. He turned back to the roaring van. Its front wheels bounced over the tip of the paved road. With the engine roaring the van zoomed out of the ditch, and charged at Cole.

He took a step away from the fence and jumped. He pulled himself up and over in a flash.

Rex and Eddie ran past the mouth of the canal's lock where one of the resettled teens pointed.

"You've got the eye of the tiger," he shouted with a slur.

The group laughed.

The rest broke into mouth trumpet noises of the Rocky theme. As Eddie gave them the finger, Rex felt inspired by the suggestion and quickened his pace.

Eddie's legs buckled as he ran. "I'm done," Eddie said in a huffed whisper. "I can't do this."

Rex raised a clenched fist. "You can do it, Eddie. Eye of the tiger!"

Behind them the van burst through the chain-link fence's gate, ripping it open. Cole ran past Rex and Eddie, swiping the briefcase from Eddie's hand.

"Run you idiots."

The headlights grew bigger and brighter as the car aimed at Rex and Eddie.

Eddie swallowed. "I think I've got my second wind."

Rex and Eddie sprinted. The teens jumped away from the lock's bridge, diving into the bushes as the van raced past. Following the alley back out to Canal Lane, Rex and Eddie ran towards Cole's vehicle.

Ahead, Cole got in his van. He started the engine and sped off.

Eddie's jaw dropped.

"That's a bit harsh," Rex said. "Guess it's you and me now."

Exhausted, Eddie searched for something to protect them. He caught his breath. "You, me, and the crazy van driver that wants to mow us down."

Rex and Eddie leapt to the side and up the grassy embankment. They reached the top of the raised bank, which stopped the river flooding the road.

The van course corrected, skidding up the wet grass. Both of the back wheels sunk as they ripped through the grass and mud. Losing traction, the front of the van slid down the bank to the pavement and thumped against the street lights. With the front wheels on the pedestrian path, the back wheels skidded against the bank.

Rex raised his fists. "We won."

Eddie shook his head. "Not yet."

The pair jogged away with their eyes on the stuck van. Back on the pavement, the van's engine revved until the back wheels joined the paving slabs. It sped along the concrete and used the momentum to ramp up the bank.

The van reached the top of the grassy area, creating a clear path towards the detectives.

Rex and Eddie picked up their speed as the van rampaged towards them. To their left was the river, a choppy, murky water with a strong current. On their right was the van ready to ram them.

"Perfect." Eddie's lungs and stomach were both ready to quit.

Cole's van zoomed back down Canal Lane. It screeched to a hard stop and waited at the end of the river bank. Cole unwound his window and pushed a button, a clunk noise indicated all the doors had unlocked.

"Get in."

# FIFTEEN

The black van's tyres screeched against the wet asphalt. Cole's foot squeezed down on the accelerator. Rex and Eddie settled into the back seats with a wobble. The van drove towards The Barge Inn and skidded into a handbrake U-turn. The rival van rode down the embankment and bounced off the kerb into the street, blocking the mouth of the road. Pushing the gear shift, Cole drove at the oncoming vehicle.

"Uh, can't we go back through the industrial estate?" Eddie said.

"Relax. We're gonna see what these boys are made of."

Eddie's bottom lip sank. "What if you lose?"

"I'm insured up to my ears."

"What about the rest of your head?" Eddie said. "People always say up to their ears, but that doesn't account for the brain."

"I never lose."

Rex grinned. "That's so cool."

Eddie rubbed his temples. "Surely that means he's overdue a tremendous failure."

Cole revved the engine. "Buckle up."

Eddie searched while Rex bounced around the back. "Uh, there are no seatbelts back here."

Cole checked over his shoulder and turned back to the wheel. "Well, hold on tight I guess."

Eddie grabbed a handlebar above the side door. It broke off in his hand.

The two vans came at each other. The rival van pulled to the right at the last second. The vehicles clipped, which snapped off Cole's wing mirror. The mirror flew through the open driver's window, over Cole's shoulder and into the back. It spun by Rex's feet. Rex's jaw dropped.

Eddie sneered.

Rex pointed at Eddie. "You should see the look on your face."

Rex's back straightened, indicating he had a bright idea. He held up the broken wing mirror. Eddie stared back at himself.

Cole took a sharp turn into the main road. He pulled to the kerb and turned off the van's engine. The lights went out. Cole pulled out a camera on a mini tripod from under the passenger seat. He switched the camera on and pressed record.

"This is Jason Cole's surveillance log. We are in pursuit of the vehicle used in the kidnapping of Daryl Archer."

"Actually," Rex said. "They're behind us."

The rival van turned into the main road, passed the detectives and drove uphill into the neighbourhood. Cole started the engine. His black van followed the kidnapper's vehicle.

Eddie clung to the back of the front passenger seat. He got the Dictaphone out of his jacket pocket and pressed record. "This is Eddie Miles's surveillance log. Chasing after the big van that took Daryl. We are in pursuit of the baddies."

Cole turned to Eddie. "Baddies?"

Eddie shrugged his shoulders.

Cole shook his head. "Subjects are amateur, indicated by the use of the same vehicle used in the kidnapping."

Eddie nodded. "Yes, amateurs, using the same car and stuff. Which is good for us."

"No," Cole barked. "Amateurs are unpredictable." He looked Eddie up and down.

Eddie pursed his lips. "What's that supposed to mean?"

Cole focused on the road ahead. "I've spotted the van at the top of the hill."

"We can see the van ahead of us as the informant drives us up the road."

Cole glared at Eddie. "I'm not your damn informant."

"Informant is getting tetchy."

They followed the kidnappers up a spindly residential street. They couldn't pick up a decent speed because of the speed bumps. Cole braked. The nose of a parallel parking car blocked them from passing.

Cole beeped the horn. "I'll say one thing for Iraq, you never got caught in traffic in the desert."

"Informant is making a point of letting us know he used to be in the forces."

Cole sneered. "Passenger is asking for a smack in the mouth."

The car finished backing into the space. With the road clear, Cole gained on the rival van until it tuned right into a broad, open street. Before Cole reached the intersection, a long bus turned into their road taking up a lane and a half. Cole pulled into a free parking spot to let the bus pass through.

Eddie held the Dictaphone closer. "Driver could have got the space closer for a shorter wait," he muttered.

Cole's free hand waved around trying to grab Eddie. "This is my investigation. You hear me?"

Rex bobbed in his seat as the van pulled out and drove forward. They joined the major road with the kidnappers in sight.

Cole leaned forward. "Licence plate number is Y238 WKW."

Eddie nodded. "Licence plate number is Y238—"

The kidnappers' van turned off into a side street. Cole followed but braked and swerved to avoid hitting an old lady crossing the street. The van thunked against the kerb as the rivals got away.

Eddie turned to Cole. "What was the last part of the licence plate?"

"I'm not telling you."

"Oh come on. Rex, did you catch it?"

Rex opened a can of cola as the mini fridge door closed. "I was busy."

After driving around town for ten minutes, Cole gave up looking for the black van. He drove the pair back to their office in silence as Rex slurped his fizzy drink.

Cole's van pulled up outside Rex and Eddie's office building. Rex and Eddie hopped out of the van's side door.

His arm leaning on the open driver's window, Cole nodded. "I'll research the van's plates and look into the briefcase. We can trade information tomorrow."

"When?" Eddie asked.

"I'll find you when I need you." He pushed a button which automatically closed the side door.

"But the briefcase is ours," Eddie said.

"You know how to pick locks?"

Eddie sighed. "No, but it's ours to do with as we—"

Cole ignored him. "Good night, gentleman."

"Good night, Dad," Rex said.

Cole's van swerved into the road and made a hasty exit.

Rex waved and leaned towards Eddie. "Do you think he noticed I accidentally called him, 'Dad'?"

# SIXTEEN

The ponytailed man unlocked Eddie's old apartment door and waved the detective duo through. He was a tall but somewhat slender man, bulked up by a large blue fleece. A name tag hung from a zipped breast pocket. It was the only form of ID to show he was the High Court Sheriff assigned to Eddie's eviction.

Inside, Eddie pulled the curtains open to let in some daylight. He huffed as he examined the sparse living room. The furnishings belonged to the landlord. All Eddie had to collect was a bin bag of clothes, a few books, and CDs. Eddie left the crockery, as washing them up seemed like too much trouble. He promised himself he would have nice things next time. Even splash out on a frying pan not made of aluminium so he wouldn't get dementia.

*If I don't already have it*, he wondered. *I am in this mess.*

The sheriff took a phone call discussing his evening plans, which he repeatedly guaranteed would be, "Jokes, mate. Utter jokes." Rex hovered nearby staring at the man. The sheriff made eye contact, frowned, and turned his back.

"Rex, can you help."

He joined Eddie at the kitchen doorway. "Sorry, Eddie. I've never met a sheriff before. I thought he'd have a hat or something."

"It's not that kind of sheriff. He's more of a glorified bailiff." Eddie sighed. "I should have brought some boxes."

"Grab the TV," Rex said. "Some clothes, that's all you need." He looked around. "Where is the TV?"

"I sold it the other week as we needed the money." Eddie shifted the dirty dishes in the sink. "I suppose I could do with my bowl, so I can eat cereal in the office."

"Bowl?"

"Bowls, then. I have a spare bowl somewhere." Eddie thought about it. "Either that or I'm using the spare bowl, and something happened to the first one."

"I'm sure it's somewhere." Rex's eyes shifted with possible guilt.

Eddie opened a hallway cupboard which contained a pile of Tesco brand "Bag For Life" reusable bags. He sighed. The collection had grown over the years as he regularly forgot to take them to the supermarket.

"What am I supposed to do with these? I don't need them, but I can't just leave them here, they're for life."

Rex distributed a stack of DVDs and CDs into the various reusable bags.

Eddie slumped into a cross-legged position on the floor. "This is horrible, Rex. I didn't get any notices."

Rex nodded his head towards the busy sheriff. "Did you tell him that?"

"I tried. I've had post go missing before, but the postman says he can only deliver what he receives."

Rex and Eddie lifted the bags and carried them out the flat door. The sheriff locked up and waved them off with a false smile.

Outside, the pair stuffed the bags into the back of the Morris Minor. The postman, a grey-haired man with sideburns and a round belly, passed them. He entered the building.

Rex raised his eyebrows. "Maybe he's been stealing your post?"

Eddie shook his head. "Don't they have to swear some kind of oath?"

"I bet he's the culprit. We should do something about it."

Eddie closed the Morris Minor backdoors.

"I've got a gut feeling about this, Eddie. It's my detective instinct."

"Not that again."

Rex tapped Eddie's shoulder with the back of his hand. "Come on, we listened to your gut instinct. Now it's time to listen to mine."

"But my gut instinct was wrong. Sorry, Rex, we should call it a day."

"What if I'm right? Imagine the other lives he's messed up. The injustice of it all."

Eddie bobbed his head. "We'll follow him around for a bit. If he does anything odd, we can pursue it. But if he's fine, then you drop it."

They followed the postman's van well into mid-afternoon. Rex sat forward the entire time, excited at the idea of catching him. Eddie grew tired but maintained his anger to feel justified in spying on the man.

"We haven't seen him do anything wrong." Eddie turned the key. The engine started. "I think it's time to move on."

The potbellied postman grabbed a cardboard box and some letters from the van and approached a house. He stopped to rattle the box, posted the letters but returned with the package. Entering the front of the vehicle, he took the package with him.

Rex bounced in his seat. "He's taking stuff."

Eddie put his finger on his lips. "Inside voices please."

"I was right," Rex whispered with a sing-song tone. "Me and my gut were right."

"I understand a package might be valuable, but why take warning letters and eviction notices."

At the end of the route, the postman drove to the post office. He parked next to a row of other postal vans. The man got in his own car, a beat-up blue Ford Fiesta. Rex and Eddie tailed him to a four-storey block of flats.

Eddie parked the Morris Minor. The pair joined the path and snuck up behind the postman. Rex peered into the man's plastic bag which contained a couple of packages and letters.

The postman opened the building's front door and caught a glance of the duo. He smiled and held the front entrance door open.

"We've been spotted," Rex whispered.

"Act natural."

Eddie entered, not looking the postman in the eye to avoid recognition. Rex went with intense eye contact and a static grin. The postman reached the second floor of the stairwell. He approached his flat door and put the key in the keyhole. Rex and Eddie slowed, waiting for him to open the door.

He took a breath and withdrew the key. The postman spun around wielding the key like the tiny, blunt, inefficient knife that it was.

"You want some do yah?" he shouted, swaying back and forth in attack pose, ready to pounce.

Rex backed away with his hands in the air. "Actually, keys are better as a knuckleduster than a knife."

Eddie elbowed Rex. "Don't help him."

The postman adjusted the keys between his fingers. He waved his clenched fist about.

Eddie leaned forward. "You've been nicking my post."

"I have not. There's a code of conduct, I'm bound to my code."

"What's in the bag?" Rex asked.

He pushed the shoulder bag of parcels and letters behind him. "I'm in service of my queen and country; a postman is the most trusted government official."

Eddie reached for the bag. "We saw you keep a parcel."

The postman swung his fist of keys at Eddie. Rex threw a handful of coins at the man. Silver and copper sprayed the man as Rex lunged for the bag strap. Stepping away, the postman pulled the bag back. He attempted to swipe Rex with the keys, but Rex swerved to avoid the blunt weapon.

Rex grabbed the bag and rummaged through it. "Lots of names and addresses here."

With a sigh, the postman lowered his weapon. "What are you gonna do, report me?"

"Obviously," Eddie gave a firm head nod. "When we find out how to do it."

"You post a letter to the management. I can drop it off for you."

"Yeah, right. We're not falling for that. What were you going to do with the post?"

"Not open it, that would be illegal."

"Oh, of course. That's where you draw the line."

The postman nodded his head rapidly. "Honest, I don't. I'll show you."

He opened his front door and waved them in. Inside they found wall-to-wall packages and letters of different sizes.

The postman caressed the wall of stolen post. "I'm a kleptomaniac."

Rex's nose crinkled "A what?"

"It means I compulsively take things that belong to others and then stack them into matching categories."

"You're half right," Eddie said.

The postman put his hands on his hips. "What's that mean?"

"Well, kleptomaniac take things, but stacking them into matching categories is different."

"What is it?"

"I don't know, OCD? Being weird?" Eddie looked around. "I guess my multiple eviction notices are somewhere in here?"

The postman slouched. "You were evicted? I'm sorry man." He buried his head in his hands.

Eddie loosened as he patted the man's shoulder. "Don't worry about it." He pulled away when he realised he was comforting the man who put him out on the street.

"It's not organised in postcodes I'm afraid. If you know what size the letter would have been, we could find it. Recent post is near the top."

"Thanks, but I'm already evicted. So the letter wouldn't help much now."

"I'm sorry." The postman turned to the boxes, he narrowed his eyes at them. "These entire walls are— Oh it's a mess. How many other people have been evicted? Families fallen out of contact because of missing Christmas cards? Bushy nostrils because the nasal trimmer didn't show up."

"That's the worst one you could think of?" Eddie asked.

"No one likes bushy nostrils," Rex added.

"Let me make it up to you. I collect stationery as well.

Anything you could want from the post office, I've got it."

"I just want you to stop," Eddie said.

"I'll get help, I swear."

Rex leaned towards Eddie. "We do need some office supplies."

"Come, take it." The postman ushered the pair into the hallway and opened the airing cupboard. He removed two hanging shirts as if they were curtains. Behind them was a middle shelf full of stacked envelopes in various sizes. "I've got stamps too. I leave them in here. The warmth of the water heater preserves them." He removed a pair of hanging underwear to show the lower shelf contained thousands of stamp books. "You can see the queen age as they get newer."

Rex smiled. "Isn't that legal tender?"

The postman crinkled his nose. "I don't think so."

"I'm sure it is. My nan sometimes pays for the bus with stamps."

Eddie looked over the stationery and bobbed his head. "We'll take some pens, envelopes, and a few books of stamps."

"Anything else?" The postman waved his open palm at the cupboard's contents.

"Can I grab some stamps for my nan?" Rex asked.

The postman waved Rex to the airing cupboard. "Be my guest."

Rex tucked a stack of stamp books into his armpit. "She'll love this. That's money in the bank, she'll say."

Eddie pulled his chin in. "I don't think it's legal tender."

Rex tutted. "Of course it is. Bus drivers aren't allowed to turn it down."

Eddie turned to the postman who shrugged his shoulders.

## SEVENTEEN

Grateful for the bounty of stamps, Rex's nan cooked the pair toasted sausage sandwiches. She cut the bread slices into wedges. This meant the toaster burnt the thin end into black dust, while the thickest end became mildly warm bread.

In the dining room decorated with faded flowery wallpaper, Mrs Oats placed the sandwiches on the table. "Here you go, boys."

"Lovely, Nan." Rex took a huge bite.

Eddie nodded. "Thank you, Mrs Oats."

She entered the tiny, yellowed kitchen of her council house; a three bedroom terraced home. Rex's nan was a small woman with curly white hair. She insisted on formalities, so Eddie called her Mrs Oats.

"Would you like another cup of tea, boys?"

"No thanks, Nan."

"I'm fine thanks, Mrs Oats."

"How about a cold drink?"

"No, thanks."

She raised a smile. "We've got orange squash? A glass of water?"

"We're good thanks, Nan."

She nodded. "I thought I'd ask."

The doorbell rang. Mrs Oats tottered down the hallway to the front door.

Eddie persistently chewed away at a bite from the thicker end of the sandwich. Rex lifted the top slice of bread and smothered the sausages in ketchup.

Mrs Oats returned to the dining room. "Rex, you didn't tell me you had another friend coming over."

"I do?" he mumbled through half-chewed food.

"Not with your mouth full, dear."

Jason Cole stepped through the door with the briefcase in his right hand. He towered over the tiny Mrs Oats. Rex's eyebrows raised. Eddie hid his disdain by chewing.

"Take a seat." Mrs Oats fluttered her eyes at Cole and then gave Rex a stern look. "Maybe Jason here can help you with that boy who gave you a black eye." She passed through the kitchen door. "He looks like he can handle himself."

The two beamed hate at him as they chewed their sandwiches. Their cheeks puffed out like little hamsters.

Cole pulled up a chair and leaned forward. "The van's plates belong to a totalled BMW sent to the scrapyard last month—"

Mrs Oats's head popped through the doorway. "Would you like a sausage sandwich, Jason?"

"No thanks," he turned back to Rex and Eddie. "Which means we can't identify the vehicle owner—"

"A cup of tea then?"

"I'm fine, thanks."

"I've got a packet of biscuits for dunking?"

Cole smiled. "It sounds marvellous, but I had a tea before I left. I'm just so full."

Mrs Oats nodded. "I'll put the kettle on for myself then." She wobbled back into the kitchen.

Cole lowered his voice. "I've checked with a few informants, and I believe the gang that took Daryl Archer are The Cloister Posse."

Eddie sniggered. "Posse, do they ride horses into the sunset?"

Cole glowered. "Posse is a regular gang term. They're new. The Cloister Posse broke away from The Massive last month."

"What are they called now, The Extra Large?"

Rex laughed and offered a high five. "Nice one."

Eddie attempted to oblige but went too slow for an actual slap sound. He tried a second time, but Rex recoiled his hand with embarrassment.

"The Massive hired Daryl. It was their drop off so they knew where he'd be. They could've kidnapped him to get money from his family."

"So it was them?" Eddie shrugged. "Case closed."

"I believe The Posse still has connections to The Massive. Someone from inside The Massive could have told The Posse about the drop-off."

Rex tilted his head. "So The Posse did it?"

Cole scratched his stubbly chin. "If they did the ransom could fund their new operation. That way they can compete against The Massive."

"Like a startup?" Rex raised his eyebrows.

"Like drug dealers?" Eddie recoiled. "We don't want to be involved with drugs."

"You two *are* involved. You witnessed a kidnapping, sabotaged my investigation, and stole a briefcase belonging to a gang of drug dealers."

After the kettle whistled on the stove, Mrs Oats popped her head in the door. "Do you want more food? I've got eggs."

Rex and Eddie shook their heads.

"No thanks, Mrs Oats," Eddie said.

"Very well then, just thought I'd ask." She left the room.

Jason turned to Rex and Eddie. "Is it okay to talk about this here?"

Rex nodded. "Yeah, it's Nan. She'll forget it all in five minutes."

"You're sure?"

She returned with a desperate smile. "Now, I know I already asked, but I'm opening a packet of biscuits, does anyone want one?"

Cole raised an open palm. "I'm fine thank you, Mrs Oats."

She patted Cole's shoulder. "Call me Judy."

Mrs Oats hovered over the table, her fingers entwined. The three detectives stalled, waiting for her to leave.

Eddie put a polite smile. "Can we have a cup of tea please, Mrs Oats?"

"A tea? For all three of you?"

He nodded. "We'd love that."

Mrs Oats smiled wide. The three watched her leave. As soon as she entered the kitchen, they leaned around the table.

Cole shifted forward. "There is another possibility."

Rex made an apologetic face. "Nan doesn't make coffee."

Eddie slapped Rex's shoulder. "The case, not the tea."

"This briefcase belongs to The Massive." Cole pinched a half sandwich from Eddie's plate. "My bet is The Posse wants it. They kidnapped Daryl Archer but wore grey hoodies to look like The Massive. He told them about the case, and they went back for it the same night. They've been staking it out to see what happens next. That's why they chased us."

"So they staked it out for another briefcase?"

"Or to follow the pickup. They want to be led to The Massive's secret buyer that only the top members know. We can use this to find Daryl Archer."

Eddie cleared his throat. "From a safe distance, I'm sure."

"We need to go to The Posse as sellers. During the exchange, we'll try to ID the snake tattoo Ruby described. I've set up a drop off through my informants. That's our way to Daryl."

Mrs Oats shuffled in carrying a heavy tray with three mugs of tea, a sugar bowl, a stack of biscuits, and a jug of milk. She was either going to fall forward, or her stick-like arms would snap off.

Cole stood. "Let me help you."

"Oh, I've got it," she said.

"Please, I'll take it," Cole insisted. As she recoiled, Rex and Eddie shook their heads.

"I've got it." Cole grasped the end of the tray.

"Sit down, young man," she barked.

Cole did as he was told. Mrs Oats placed the tray on the table as the three sat in humble silence.

Once poured, the three detectives gave their thanks. Eddie took a sip to show his appreciation.

She returned to her gentle self, smiled, and headed back to the kitchen. At the doorway, she stopped. "How's your mum, Eddie?"

"She's fine."

"Oh good. Got a girlfriend, have you?"

"Not at the moment, Mrs Oats."

"Rex, neither."

"Nan!"

"Well, it's true. You boys should go to a disco. Meet some girls." She passed through the kitchen doorway. "I'm sure Jason can help."

Eddie sipped his tea. "You keep saying us. Why don't you go in as a seller?"

"I crossed paths with the gang before. They know me."

Eddie sighed. "How would we even know it was the right snake tattoo?"

"I viewed the pub's security footage. They don't keep more than a month's cycle. Since it's been icers outside, they've worn their hoodies up, except for one sunny day."

Cole placed a black and white photo of a grainy arm. A thick snake tattoo wound around the arm. The teeth bit into the wrist.

Eddie cringed. "That's unnecessary. Why the wrists?" He put down his sandwich. "Why biting at all?"

"'Cause it's bad ass," Rex said.

"That would be bad arse." Eddie put down his teacup. "Your nan's right, you do watch too much American TV."

Rex grimaced. "Bad arse doesn't sound good. It sounds like an ailment, like dodgy knee."

Cole slapped the table to regain their attention. "Whoever does it will be compensated. Twenty percent of my final fees."

"Done," Rex offered a deal-making handshake.

Cole raised a dismissive palm to Rex. "I think it should be Eddie who goes."

"Done." Rex offered another deal-making handshake.

Eddie raised his hands. "Why me?"

"You think it's a good idea to send Rex in?"

"No." Eddie turned to Rex and mouthed, "Sorry." He turned back to Cole. "Maybe this is getting a bit much. We could possibly pass this information on to the police."

Rex tucked in his chin. "But Maude made up promise not to."

Cole leaned closer. "You could do. And half the police would want to help you. But the others, they work for the gangs. You want that half to take your statement?"

Eddie's shoulders lowered. "I guess not. Why can't we just pay the ransom, isn't that our way to Daryl?"

"You want to help fund a drug gang?"

Eddie huffed. "No."

"The family will pay the ransom if need be, but we have a chance to save Daryl and stop the kidnappers. It's the right thing to do. Are you in?"

Mrs Oats stepped into the dining room. "Have you had enough food? Because I can't let you go home hungry, Eddie. What would your mum think of me?"

"Not now, Nan."

"Thanks, Mrs Oats, but I'm not hungry." Eddie's face tightened. "And my mum won't know. I moved into my own place a few years ago."

"Lovely." She tottered back into the kitchen.

Cole tapped the snake tattoo photo. "Are you in?"

Eddie scratched his chin. "What are we selling exactly?

Cole picked up the briefcase and pushed the lock release. He spun it to face the pair and lifted it open. Inside were bricks of white powder wrapped in clear plastic.

Eddie thought about his options. Save the day, rescue Daryl and earn a payday for a new flat, or sleep on the office floor and hope for a new case. He turned to Rex who nodded eagerly.

"Fine. I'll go into the big scary drug den. It's no trouble. Really it's not."

The aggressive sarcasm went over Rex's head. "Good on you, Eddie."

Cole closed the case and stood. "I've set it up for tonight. We go to the warehouse. You do the drop. The enemy shows their hand."

"But that tattoo is on his forearm?" Rex said.

"Don't we need to network?" Eddie asked, ignoring Rex. "Work our way in? Gain their trust?"

"I have a network. You have an appointment."

Rex jumped in his seat. "That's bad ass."

Eddie turned to Rex with pursed lips.

Rex mouthed, "Sorry."

## EIGHTEEN

The black van drove through the industrial estate behind The Barge Inn. It was 11:22 p.m. Amongst the derelict buildings were actual working factories. At this time of night, they were all closed. Only the street lamps lit the way.

Cole pulled to the kerb and cut the engine. The dashing detective exited the driver's door and yanked the side door open. He beckoned Eddie out of the van with a wave. Eddie stepped out into the street reluctantly. Rex shifted in his seat like a dog annoyed at his owner for going on a walk without him.

"You'll walk from here." Cole placed a baseball cap on Eddie's head. "The drop off is one hundred yards down there. The warehouse on the left with the open gate."

Cole pulled a pair of plain black framed glasses from his coat pocket and placed them on Eddie's face.

"These glasses feature a built-in camera and earpiece. We'll be able to feed information to you."

"No way," Rex said from inside the van. "I'm so jealous."

Rex noticed a video display screwed to a shelf of monitoring equipment. It broadcast footage of Rex from Eddie's point of view.

"Cool." Rex waved at the screen. "Hey Eddie, can you see me?"

Eddie put his hands on his hips. "Yes, you're right in front of me."

Rex turned back to Eddie with folded arms. "Spoilsport."

Cole took Eddie's coat off his shoulders. "Okay, Ed. When you spot the snake tattoo, get footage of the tattoo and his face — in good light. I'll get a positive ID from some police friends of mine." He pulled a hoodie out of a box full of loose clothes. "Got it?"

"Yes, fine." Eddie pushed the sliding glasses up the bridge of his nose.

"Are you sure I shouldn't go?" Rex tapped his round spectacles. "Glasses are kind of my thing."

Eddie tapped his clear lenses. "They're non-prescription, you wouldn't see anything with them on anyway."

Cole clicked his fingers to regain Eddie's focus. "Remember, when you're undercover, you want to put them at ease."

Rex nodded. "We gotta be down with the hood team."

Eddie's eyebrows furrowed, causing the glasses to slide down his nose. "Is that from *Gangster's Paradise* by Coolio?"

Cole clicked his fingers in front of Eddie's face, more forcefully this time. "Focus. As I said, whenever you're undercover, you want to put them at ease. The best way is to appear stupid, but not too stupid."

Eddie stared at Cole.

"That's perfect, Ed."

"I wasn't doing anything."

Cole patted Eddie on the back and handed him the hoodie. "Good luck."

"What's that supposed to mean?"

"It means good luck."

Eddie put the hoodie on. "Because I can't do it without luck?"

He fidgeted with the zip. He pulled it a few inches, but the zip stuck.

"No, I didn't mean it like that."

"Because it's a hopeless situation and I'm likely to get killed?"

Cole tugged the zip and finished it for him. "You'll be fine."

"Well..." Rex hunched one shoulder. "He could get killed."

Eddie waved his arms about. "This is a bloody suicide mission, isn't it?"

"I can come too." Rex pointed at his temple. "Two heads are better than one."

Cole patted Rex's shoulder. "I'm not sure that applies to this situation." He turned to Eddie. "I've done operations like this before. I've got your back. Listen to me, and you'll be fine."

"What about last night, we almost got mowed down by that van."

"Because you didn't listen to me."

Eddie pushed the glasses back up his nose. "What will they do to me if they find out?"

"Whatever it is, remember this: Everyone has a plan until they get punched in the face. That will always buy you time to make your own plan."

"Did you learn that in the military?"

"No, just growing up in Cloisterham. Now, get in there." Cole patted the side of Eddie's arm.

Eddie stomped off towards the warehouse. In his earpiece, Rex's voice whispered, "Psst, Eddie. You forgot the briefcase."

He marched back to the van. The door opened, and Cole chucked the briefcase. It bounced hard on Eddie's chest, but he grabbed the handle as it fell.

"So I go down there?" Eddie asked.

Rex leaned out the van's side door. "Just follow the shoes on the telegraph poles." He pointed above at the dangling, worn Nikes.

As directed by Cole, Eddie walked through an open gate. He approached a warehouse door cut into a giant corrugated entrance and knocked. A slot within the door slid open. Dark brown eyes with a unibrow stared back at him.

Eddie raised the briefcase. "Hi, I'm here for the drop-off."

"Who sent you?"

"Uh…"

"I said, who sent you."

Back at the van, Cole flipped through his notes rigorously. "Bash sent you."

Unsure he heard correct, Eddie wiggled the glasses, shoving the earpiece closer to his ear hole.

"Bash, say Bash."

Eddie smiled. "Bash?"

The slot pushed closed. Bolts clanked, and the door creaked open. A unibrowed teenager in a sleeveless shirt chewed gum while he stood at the doorway. Eddie swallowed, nodded at the boy, and stepped through.

Inside, a skinny boy no older than twenty sat on a table. He had bright blue eyes and a constant sneer. He was decked out in a white tracksuit with gold chains around his neck and wrists. Around him sat his entourage of youthful hoodlums in baseball caps and jewellery. They gravitated towards him, indicating he was the leader.

All the gang smelled of Lynx body spray, which inflamed Eddie's sinuses, even in the big spacious warehouse. The smell of that many youths had created a potent assault on his senses.

The blue-eyed boy closed and re-bolted the door. He patted Eddie down. "Nothing."

"Nothing?" the blue-eyed leader said. "Should I be insulted?"

Sweat beads rolled along Eddie's eyebrows. "I *don't* possess a gun."

The gang members eyed him up and down with sneers. He'd shown weakness.

"I mean," Eddie tapped his nose, "I don't possess a gun."

The blue-eyed leader's tracksuit rustled as he folded his arms. "Why'd you say it like that?"

He stood slack-jawed. "That's what you have to say in case someone's wearing a wire."

Blue Eyes cocked his head. "Why would anyone here be wearing a wire?"

"Uh, no reason."

"You trancing us?"

"What's trancing?"

"You recording on your phone?"

"No." Eddie raised his old Nokia phone. "I don't think it even has a recorder."

The blue-eyed teen inspected Eddie's phone. He strutted to a table surrounded by a gang of young men. They wore tracksuits and baseball caps with the sales sticker still on them. On their necks, wrists, and fingers they wore a variety of gold bling. Not a grey hoodie insight.

"They're all teenagers," Rex muttered over the earpiece.

"Shh," Cole said. "This is for vital information only."

Eddie studied all the teens, hoping to find the snake tattoo.

One of the teens stepped forward. "What you staring at?"

"I, uh, I like your trainers."

"My creps?"

"Your what?"

*The language barrier is killing me*, he thought. *I'm gonna be killed because I can't even talk to a youth.*

"My kicks, you like my sneaks, yeah?… Sneakers?"

"Trainers," Eddie said with a corrective tone. "Why are you using American words? Is this a generational thing?"

"Shoes? Creps, man. You posh or somethin'?"

"Stop talking about shoes," Cole shouted down the earpiece.

"Sorry, I'm getting distracted. Where were we?"

A tubby hoodlum with a cherub face waved his bejewelled hand to beckon Eddie over. "You got somethin' for me, yeah?"

"Yes." Eddie held up the briefcase and gave it a tap. "I've got something for you."

An intense young man with a muscular build and thin sideburns delivered a sports bag to the steel table. His arms were covered by tracksuit sleeves. Eddie noticed some sort of tattoo ink on his wrist, but couldn't make out the design.

"Did you see that?" Cole said over the earpiece. Eddie gave a slight nod for the camera to register.

The muscular youth unzipped a sports bag and took out a plastic-wrapped brick of white powder. He placed it on the table.

A hook-nosed boy took his little knife and cut into the brick. He shovelled a small amount with the knife. He pointed it at Eddie.

Eddie swallowed.

The cherub-faced boy snarled. "You gonna take it?"

"Oh? Me? No, I couldn't."

"You what?"

He searched for the words. "Nah, bruv?"

"Ed," Cole's voice said. "It's a test. Take the drugs."

Eddie shook his head. "I've never taken drugs. If I have kids I want to be able to look them in the eye and tell them 'don't do drugs.'"

The teens gave each other confused looks.

"Why?" Cherub asked.

"So they don't end up like, well, like…"

As Blue Eyes stood from his table his white tracksuit rustled. "You a narc?"

Eddie shook his head vigorously. "No, and again, I think that's an American word."

"You're a narc or a posh git. You think you're better than us?"

"No, no. I'm driving you see."

They all stared.

"Don't drug and drive? That's a thing, right? And I ate before I came here, so I am stuffed."

Eddie rubbed his belly.

The earpiece crackled. "Ed, if you want to make it out alive, take the drugs."

Cherub stood. "Bruv, we be sovereign, yeah?"

Eddie winced. "Yeah?"

"Then we gotta know for sure." He tapped the brick of white powder.

"Perfect," Eddie muttered under his breath. "Bloody perfect."

He livened up, grabbed the knife, and held it below his nose. He studied the muscular youth's arm, wondering if that was a snake tattoo under his sleeve.

"Whatcha staring at?" Muscles said.

"Nothing?"

"You calling me nothing?"

"Oh come on, is there even a correct answer to this?"

"Take it," Cherub said.

"What is this?"

"It's called ASAP."

"A.S.A.P?"

"Yeah. And we want you to take it, now."

The entourage fanned out, blocking any escape Eddie might have had.

Over the earpiece, Rex said: "I think you should take the drugs, it seems really important to them."

"If this is about showing I do illegal things, I can assure you I used LimeWire quite a bit in my day. I used it to download many songs off the Internet, without the permission of the artist or record label."

"Oh, yeah?"

"Yes. I have no remorse, either. From what I understand the FBI would not be happy with me."

"You wanted?" Cherub said.

"Well, those little copyright warnings always mention the FBI, although England isn't in their jurisdiction. I'm sure Interpol would—"

"Shut it." Blue Eyes pointed at the knife. "Take the ASAP."

Eddie blinked at Blue Eyes, over the teen leader's shoulder — amongst the entourage — he saw Jamie, his mugger. Struggling to place Eddie in his glasses and hoodie, the boy glared. Eddie felt lightheaded and wobbly kneed but tried to remain focused.

"I'm not that familiar with drug words, is that like MDF, or MDMA? Is it cocaine, or heroin or pot?"

Over the earpiece, Cole said, "Just take it and get it over with."

"I just feel that if it were a tea form, I'd be much more comfortable."

"Pot?" Hook Nose laughed. "You're well old."

"I'm twenty-eight."

"That is old."

"Well, old," Muscles added.

"Fine, I'm old. I don't know the difference between drugs. In fact, I don't even take headache tablets. Sure, I enjoy the odd beer once in a while, like a few a day sometimes, but it's legal. I even feel guilty about the whole LimeWire thing."

The gang all stared.

Eddie scratched the side of his head. "Is this the type of drug where I want to take lots of water after? Or do I avoid water? One of those could kill me, right?"

No one responded.

Eddie held the blade of white powder to his face. He locked eyes with Jamie in the crowd. The boy's sneer turned to wide eyes. Eddie had been recognised, he could be uncovered any second. Seeing the gang enveloped around him, he felt all the dizzying, heart-pounding fear of the mugging. He dropped the blade and the powder heaped on the floor.

"I'm sorry," Eddie raised his palms. "I'm sorry."

He leant down to pick up the knife, which he wiped on his trousers. "Can I maybe have a fresh one?"

"You can't waste the sample, bruv," Hook Nose said.

The gang grumbled in agreement.

"But it's been on the floor."

Over the earpiece, Cole spoke, "You are seconds away from destroying this case. Take the drugs, find the tattoo."

Blue Eyes cocked his head, he pulled a short revolver from his tracksuit pocket. "Do it, now."

Eddie swallowed. He'd only ever seen a gun with a cylinder chamber in westerns.

"Bottoms up I suppose." Eddie crouched to scoop up the powder. In a panic, he came down a little too fast, and the glasses fell from his face. They landed on the ground upside down, exposing the earpiece.

He grabbed the glasses, sliding them back over his ears and on his face.

Cherub narrowed his eyes. "What was that on the inside of your glasses?"

"Nothing."

"Boss, somethin' fishy is going on."

Blue Eyes stood. As he walked towards Eddie, the gang followed, closing in on the nervous detective.

Eddie swallowed. "Cole?"

"Shut up, Eddie," Cole said over the earpiece.

"Who's Cole?" Cherub asked.

"Jason Cole," Blue Eyes said. "He's coming. Grab that case."

Cherub yanked the briefcase from Eddie and slammed it on the steel table. Hook Nose approached the desk and turned the combination locks.

He opened the case and inspected the bricks of powder.

"All good?" Cherub asked.

The hook-nosed boy inspected the inner lining of the case. His hand stopped at a hard, square bulk. He cut the lining with his pocket knife. The boy pulled out a small plastic device with a blinking red light.

Eddie stepped back with raised hands. Hook Nose pointed the pocket knife at Eddie.

Cherub sneered, revealing several gold-capped teeth. "He's a narc."

# NINETEEN

"He's blown the case." Cole slammed his fist into the side of the van.

Rex threaded his fingers through his hair. "Why did you bug the briefcase?"

"It wasn't me." Cole leaned close to the monitor broadcasting Eddie's view. "It's a transponder."

"We're gonna save Eddie, right?"

Cole took a calming breath. "Let's see if he can get out of this."

The monitor was broadcasting Eddie's point of view. The gang members slowly approached him.

"We can't leave him. He's my friend."

Cole sighed. "If we go in there now, we've lost Daryl."

Rex yanked the van's side door open.

"Hey, wait."

Rex jumped out and sprinted to the warehouse. By the time he got to the corrugated metal door his legs wobbled. Without a plan, he bashed on the door until the unibrowed teen opened it and pulled him in.

"Who are you?" The unibrowed boy held a knife to Rex's throat.

"Ah... Ho..." Rex coughed and spluttered. "I yumana..." He bent down to catch his breath as if there was more oxygen below his knees. Cranking back up, he took a deep nostril breath.

The gang members looked at each other in confusion

Across the room, Eddie stood contorted between the headlock of one hoodlum and two others grabbing both his arms. Muscles hit Eddie in the stomach, knocking the spy glasses off his face.

"Eddie!"

"Where's Jason Cole?" The blue-eyed leader smashed the transponder in his hand. "Where is he?"

"Cole... is... Cole..." Rex growled at the frustration of being so short of breath he couldn't communicate. He raised his hands in defeat and sat on the concrete floor.

The gang members exchanged glances in confusion.

Cherub leaned in close to Eddie. "Cole is a pro. Why'd he hire you?"

Eddie avoided eye contact. "We're the new detectives in town."

"So you're a narc?" Cherub drew his knife's end under Eddie's chin.

"Uh, P.I." Rex waved from the floor.

"What you doin' here?" Cherub shouted.

Eddie winced. "Daryl. We want Daryl Archer."

"Who?"

Muscles thumped Eddie again. His sleeve was slightly pushed up, revealing the edge of a tattoo.

Eddie cranked his neck up. "What's the tattoo?"

Cherub wagged his finger. "I'm doing the talking. He does the hitting."

"I just like tattoos."

"Yeah?" Muscles said. "How many you got?"

"Uh, none."

"You love tattoos, but you ain't even got one. You want me to tattoo you?"

Eddie attempted to jolt out of the three hoodlums' grasp, but they held him down tighter. "No, thank you."

"I can put 'narc' across your forehead." He wrote narc with his finger on Eddie's head, ploughing his finger against Eddie's skull.

Hook Nose picked up the glasses and examined them.

"Boss." He held them up as Cherub turned to him. "These have microchips and crap in them."

Hook Nose chucked the glasses. Blue Eyes grabbed and inspected them.

He held them up to his mouth. "Where's my boy Cole, then? You send in these two comedians to do your dirty work? Yeah?"

A thunderous crack echoed throughout the warehouse. The garage door stretched inwards, splitting the corrugated metal sheets apart. Nuts sprung from their bolts, hitting some gang members. The back of Cole's van tore through the broken door.

Three hoodlums pulled small black pistols and fired at the van. Two of the shooters fired until their bullets ran out.

While they reloaded, the blue-eyed boy approached the van's back doors with his gun in his hand. The van door flew open and knocked the boy in the face. As he held his nose, Cole darted out and grabbed the gun. He pointed at the two reloading shooters. They paused.

The gang waited for their blue-eyed leader's response.

Cole pointed at the van with his head. "Rex, Ed, get in the van."

The gang members let Eddie go. He straightened his

tie and brushed his jacket into place. While passing Jamie the mugger, he narrowed his eyes.

Jamie sneered back.

Rex stood, lowered his hands, and backed up to the van.

"Now, you." Cole waved his newly acquired gun at Muscles. "Show us your tattoo."

He raised his sleeve to reveal images of computer circuits down his arm. "It's a cyborg arm, innit."

Cole backed away. "All of you show me your arms."

They pushed up their tracksuit sleeves. Cole studied the several forearms but found no snake tattoo.

Unobserved, Blue Eyes pulled a revolver and fired at Cole. The bullet whizzed past, hitting the van doors.

Rex and Eddie, halfway between Cole and the van, paused and raised their hands.

Cole grinned. "You fire again I'm likely to fire back. I promise you I'm a better shot."

Rex and Eddie shuffled to the side away from Cole.

Blue Eyes contorted his face, sneering even more than usual. "You got, what? Three bullets? There's ten of us."

"You think three of your men—boys—are interested in dying today?"

The gang looked at each other and then to the blue-eyed leader, their faces solemn and hung low.

"All I want is Daryl Archer. You release him to us, we'll let you carry on with your normal business."

Blue Eyes cocked his head and frowned.

Cole waved the gun. "Where is he?"

In the distance, the sound of police sirens grew. Cole raised his head, alarmed. He turned to Rex and Eddie, they shrugged their shoulders.

"Peg it," Blue Eyes shouted. The gang members ran off in different directions.

Rex opened the van doors, checking the smoking bullet hole as Eddie stepped inside.

Cole passed through the van and climbed into the front seat. He floored it, and they sped away from the warehouse. Pulling up at the river bank, Cole chucked the gun out the driver's window into the water. He put his foot on the gas and drove through the industrial estate.

Ahead, flashing blue lights approached but the sirens were silent. Cole pulled the van to the side of the street and turned off the engine.

Eddie hunched over, breathing loudly.

"You okay, Eddie?"

"I saw the mugger. At least, I think I saw the mugger. I lost my cool when they stood around me. I couldn't help it."

"Shhh," Cole called out from the back.

Police vehicles zoomed past. A few more police vans stopped ahead and created a roadblock.

Cole locked the doors and rolled over the front seats into the back of the van.

He pulled hidden curtains across the equipment and dumped used plastic bottled and food containers across the floor.

"What are you doing?" Rex asked.

"One of those officers is going to approach on foot. I'm disguising us."

Rex's neck straightened. "A disguise?"

Cole unzipped a suitcase and pulled out some old clothes. He handed Rex a dusty poncho and threw Eddie a hoodie covered in mud. "Don't get too excited, we're just a couple of homeless men living in a van. Keep quiet, act calm, and let me do the talking."

Eddie pointed at Cole's thigh. "You're bleeding."

"It's just a flesh wound," Cole said.

Rex's jaw dropped. "That's cool. I've always wanted to say that."

"It's a blatant disregard for his own wellbeing," Eddie barked.

Cole raised a palm. "Stop. Calm down."

Eddie held his chest. "I feel awful. Like I'm gonna die."

Rex nodded. "We probably are gonna die."

Eddie stood in the van which rocked. "I feel hot, I have to get out." He fell to the side, knocking equipment from the mounted shelves behind the curtains.

Cole put on a tattered coat and a furry aviator hat. He reached into the curtain and pulled out a plastic medicine bottle.

"Catch."

Rex caught the bottle. "What is it?"

"Anti-anxiety meds, give one to Eddie."

Rex fidgeted with the childproof cap as Eddie crawled to the backdoors and reached for the handle. Cole pulled him away from the door, knocking him back onto the van floor.

"I need some air." Eddie clawed at the side door.

Rex gave the medicine bottle a solid tug. The cap popped off, spraying the floor with tablets. Rex took one and placed it in Eddie's mouth.

"What's that?" Eddie tried to spit it out but the tablet dissolved in a second.

Rex gave a calming nod. "Anti-anxiety medicine."

Eddie turned to Cole. "You have anxiety?" His words slowed as his vision blurred.

Cole shrugged. "It's a sleeping aid. More for drugging enemies, when the need arises."

Eddie placed his hands on the floor to maintain balance. "You roofied me?"

"You're endangering yourself and others."

Eddie turned to Rex with one twitching eye. "You roofied me!"

"Well, I didn't know, did I?"

"Help," Eddie called out. "I... need a little lie-down."

Overcome with dizziness, Eddie passed out; his face planted on the cold floor.

Rex winced. "He's gonna be angry when he wakes up."

Cole dumped a blanket over Eddie. "Let's delay that until the morning. Shove another tablet in his mouth."

He pulled a spray can from the tatty coat's inner pocket and sprayed it around.

Rex covered his mouth. "What's that?"

"Fart spray from the joke shop. No policeman is gonna want to come in here."

The tap from the back van indicated the police had arrived. Cole put on a twitchy erratic face and opened the door.

"Morning, officer," he said in a croaky voice.

The officer's nostrils flared as the smell wafted towards him.

Outside the van, Cole put on a show as a slightly crazy homeless man. He stepped into the young officer's personal space, causing the man to back away.

The policeman explained they were conducting a raid and ordered them to leave the area.

"You okay to drive?" the policeman asked, his eyes watering from the smell.

Cole assured him he was and re-entered from the driver door.

Rex smiled. "We're safe."

"From them." Cole started the engine and drove towards the blockade, where they were waved through.

"Ed cost us the case. The Posse will be on high alert now."

Rex tucked in his chin. "But they didn't have Daryl or a snake tattoo. You sent Eddie in there for nothing. We got no snake tattoo guy, we nearly got killed, and made some new enemies."

"We know that snake tattoo isn't in The Cloister Posse. Which means it's The Massive that have Daryl Archer. We all need to lay low for the night. I suggest your office. The Posse will likely be waiting outside mine."

"They know you that well?"

"I was involved in a case that put their leader in jail for a long time. They want blood."

"A long time? He only looked twelve."

Cole shifted gears. "Their previous leader. Are we able to hold over at yours?"

"I'm fine with it," Rex said. "But Eddie usually poo-poos that sort of thing. Eddie?"

He turned to Eddie who lay sprawled on the van floor.

Rex smiled at Cole. "I think it's fine."

# TWENTY

The three detectives arrived at 369 High Street in the black van. Cole parked the vehicle around the back by the River Invicta.

Exiting the van, Cole marched to the back and opened the doors. He stepped into the van with a limp.

"You okay?" Rex asked

Cole pulled the curtains back, opened a drawer, and pulled out a small medical kit. "Fine. Maybe Ed could do with your support."

"My name's Eddie," he muttered with his eyes closed.

Rex pulled Eddie towards the van doors. He placed Eddie's arm over his shoulder. Rex guided his drowsy friend out of the vehicle, through the car park, and into their office building.

He ushered Cole in while shuffling Eddie towards the narrow steps. Cole grabbed Eddie's feet and helped carry him.

Up the flight of stairs, Rex dragged Eddie into the Milton Miles Investigations office and lobbed him against the wall.

"You drugged me," Eddie mumbled. "I might as well have taken the RSVP."

Cole sat on the desk, pulled his trousers to his knees and attended to his wound with an antiseptic wipe. "He'll be fine in the morning."

Rex covered Eddie in the unzipped sleeping bag. "He'll be angry."

"If he remembers."

Cole ran a thread through a needle and pierced his skin. He clenched his teeth as he sowed his first stitch.

Rex grimaced and turned away. He noticed Eddie's crooked neck. He took off his blazer, rolled it into a pillow, and placed the blazer under Eddie's head. Eddie dribbled a little. Rex took a paper napkin from the desk. He gently tucked it between the blazer and Eddie's cheek.

Cole put in the last stitch. "You did well today."

"I didn't do much of anything."

"You went after your friend, against all the odds, with no plan. You took control. That's courageous, or stupid."

"Well, which is it?"

Cole cut the thread and pulled his trousers back up. "Both in my books. You've got your work cut out for you, but you're a detective."

Rex smiled for a brief second then pursed his lips.

"What's the matter?"

"I wish Eddie was awake, he asks the good questions."

"What's a good question to you?"

"Like, what happens now? We didn't find the snake tattoo. Do we pay Daryl's ransom?"

"No snake tattoo means no ID. My guess would be Daryl is with The Massive."

"So we go after them?" Rex said.

"We have two more days until the ransom is due. Now, we go to sleep. The unconscious mind works even when we rest. We'll have a better idea of what's going on come morning."

"Yeah, okay." Rex paused.

"What now?"

Rex bit his bottom lip. "How do you punch someone?"

Cole stood tall. He grabbed Rex's hand and moulded it. "You want to make a proper fist. Don't curl the fingers over the thumb. Never let your little finger stick out."

He pushed Rex's shoulder, forcing him to stabilise with a wide stance.

"Use your whole body. The power comes from the legs. Don't draw back to punch, it announces the strike."

Rex nodded.

"You lock your wrist and go for the eyes, nose, or throat. All vulnerable. I like the eyes best. It's a small target, but the socket guides the blow." Cole positioned himself with a broad stance. "Go for my stomach, for practise."

"Really?" Rex's eyes shined.

"Do it."

Rex punched Cole in the stomach, which was firm and resistant.

Cole smiled. "That's alright. Technique is fine. You just need a little confidence. Let's get some sleep."

Rex nodded his happy head, and lay by Eddie. He closed his eyes and tried to sleep.

"Fraternising with the enemy," Eddie grumbled in a slow, quiet voice.

---

The rising sun shone through the window. Eddie woke to the white brightness. His mouth was parched. As he tried to sit up, he wobbled, his balance not quite right. His memory of the night before had been replaced with a hangover and a distinct melancholy. He stood.

Rex entered from the office with a toothbrush in his mouth. "Morning."

"Morning." Eddie cleared his throat. "I need a cup of tea."

"How are you?"

"I feel like an elephant rented my head for the night, with little concern for the deposit. Did you sleep here last night?"

"We all did. Had to lay low."

"You went home to get a toothbrush?" Eddie switched on the electric kettle in the kitchen corner.

"No, I just found it in the desk drawer."

Eddie cringed. "That's my toothbrush. What do you mean by we all did?"

From the hallway door, Cole stepped into the reception. Eddie jumped to his feet and backed up.

"Morning, boys." Cole dropped a paper bag of croissants on the table. "Tuck in."

"Will do." Rex ran over and devoured a pastry.

"Did we catch the snake tattooed man?"

Cole shook his head. "No, which means The Posse didn't kidnap him. We have to infiltrate The Massive."

Eddie rubbed his tight jaw. "My professional opinion would be pay the ransom."

Rex curled his top lip. "That's no fun."

"We could have died last night." Eddie furrowed his brow, trying to recall the night. "Right?"

Rex half-shrugged.

"What exactly did happen last night? Did we get drinks after?"

Rex bit his bottom lip. "We ruled out The Cloister Posse."

"Goodbye, gentlemen." Cole headed out the office door and along the hallway.

His head fuzzy, Eddie lunged into the hallway. "Wait!"

The kettle clicked to indicate the water had boiled. Eddie looked longingly through the doorway at the kettle. At the end of the hallway, Cole turned to the stairs. Eddie sighed and half jogged after Cole. He wobbled on the steps, sliding down a few.

Cole exited the building and crossed the car park. Eddie tottered after him, finally getting the hang of walking again. Rex strolled behind, chewing away at the breakfast foods.

"What about the gang?" Eddie asked. "The one we upset last night?"

Cole reached his van parked at the end of the car park, right against the River Invicta.

"Don't worry about it, The Cloister Posse don't know who you are, or what you drive. They know me, but they have a short-term memory." Cole walked around the van to the driver's side and got in. He lowered the passenger door window. "They were threaders at me last night, but they'll move on to someone else today. They'll forget about us, I can assure you."

"Threaders?" Rex said.

"Angry."

Eddie pursed his lips, unimpressed by Cole's assurance. "So what are we meant to do now?"

Cole turned his key. The engine roared to life. A ball of fire rose from the front. The flames travelled like a hundred tiny orange dominoes across the van. The rest of the vehicle lit up in seconds. Rex dropped the paper bag of croissants as the pair ran to save Cole. The intense heat caused the pair to stop. Eddie raised his arm to cover his stinging eyes. An explosive bang warned them to step back. The twosome pulled back as the van blew up.

The blast shook the pair's ribcages as their feet left the ground. Fire engulfed the entire van.

A wing mirror wrapped in melted plastic landed at their feet. Rex pointed at the cracked port window rolling across the tarmac. Dust rained down on them, covering their skin and drying their lips.

Eddie waved the smoke away from his face. "Bloody hell."

They stood in shock. Eddie expected to fully panic at some point, fret over their own safety, wonder how they'd explain everything to the police, what this meant for Daryl Archer. For now, the whole thing felt unreal.

As the smoke thinned out, Eddie got a clear look at Rex, his fringe was singed and his eyebrows were burnt away.

"Your eyebrows," Eddie said. "They're gone."

Rex felt the bald area above his eyes. His skin wasn't burnt. He peered at the van. "Cole?" he called out.

Eddie grimaced. "I'm pretty sure he didn't make it."

Rex and Eddie were unable to keep their eyes off the burning van.

They stepped backwards, away from it. Rex picked up the bag of croissants. One rolled out of the bag onto the concrete. Rex picked it up.

"You going to eat that?"

Rex held the croissant out towards Eddie. "You want it?"

"No, I just wanted to know if you were going to."

Rex nodded. "Of course."

Eddie swallowed. "I really need a cup of tea."

# TWENTY-ONE

Eddie approached Cole's office door with trepidation. Rex stood in the side alley of the kebab shop with his arms folded tight.

"I still think we should've called the police," Rex said.

Eddie's eyes darted around the street, checking for danger. "Cole said half the police worked with the gangs. For all we know the police blew up the van. We need to find Cole's case file before they do."

Rex folded his arms tight. "You're not gonna get inside. He'll be prepared for a break in."

"Like he prepared for a car bomb?" Eddie put on his cotton winter gloves to avoid leaving fingerprints.

"I needed gloves? You should have told me."

Eddie shrugged. He pressed the buzzer's call button.

Rex's face scrunched up. "I don't know why you're bothering, he's not home."

The intercom went to a message. "Hello, you've reached the office of Jason Cole Investigations. I'm unable to answer your call right now, so please leave a message, and I'll get back to you."

149

Eddie held up his mobile, put it on speaker, and dialled nine. The tone replicated the noise from Cole's office phone. The door unlocked with a buzz. Eddie smiled and put his phone away, like a gun placed in a holster.

"Eddie, that's the coolest thing you've ever done."

After walking up a flight of stairs, Rex and Eddie forced the door open. A black cat ran out and down the stairs.

Rex's jaw dropped. "Oh no."

Eddie shrugged. "It's probably for the best."

Inside, Cole's office was actually a small apartment with the living room acting as an office. Style wise it was a perfect bachelor pad with fancy furniture made from dark stained wood and red leather. The walls were off-white and bare. A single bookshelf displayed the latest gadgets and electronics. Rex dropped crumbs from a croissant as he chewed.

"You're still eating those?"

"You ate your share," Rex said.

"I ate half?"

"No, a third. Cole left his portion."

A robot vacuum rolled past their feet and sucked up the crumbs. Rex and Eddie both scampered back to avoid the machine.

At the desk, Rex picked up a tablet. With a few taps on the screen, he found a video feed of them in the apartment.

"Rex, stop touching things. Fingerprints are gonna confuse the investigators."

"I thought we were the investigators."

"Not of his murder."

Rex picked up a fake moustache from a drawer. "Disguises, cool." As he held it over his top lip, Rex's eyes lit up. "We should investigate his murder."

"No, no murders. Besides, no one's offering to pay us. We have a kidnap victim to find." Eddie sneered. "Put that moustache back."

Rex fiddled with the iPad's settings. Eddie pulled open the filing cabinet drawer and searched for the Daryl Archer case file.

"Found it." Eddie opened the file and read through the documents. "Cole wrote about us."

Rex lifted his chin. "What did he say?"

"I best not repeat it."

Rex grabbed the folder. "Rex Milton, tall, wears glasses. That's true." He scanned through the document. "Childlike? Assuming some kind of mental impairment? Check for medical records?"

"I said it was best not to repeat it."

"Eddie Miles, almost average height, rather anxious, a large, bulbous head—"

Eddie snatched the folder. "I do not have a large, bulbous head. Do I?"

"I don't think he meant it as an insult."

"It's not factually correct." Eddie poked his head forward "Is it?"

"No no, of course not. Maybe he just thinks your head is big because you have small eyes."

Eddie's jaw went slack. "I don't have small eyes."

Rex nodded. "No, of course not. I just mean in comparison to the rest of your head."

The phone rang, Rex reached for the receiver. Eddie blocked him. The answer phone took over. As the answer machine message played, a loud thumping came from the door below.

Eddie gasped. "Someone's trying to break in."

The door took another thump which caused a cracking sound.

Eddie swallowed. "Someone is breaking in. Hide."

They ran around the flat, searching for a spot to hide in. In a minimalist space, there aren't any hiding places. Sparse walls, full cupboards that used every bit of space; even the furniture was too low to crawl under.

The pair ran into the bedroom. Again, the built-in cupboard used every inch of space. They darted into the bathroom and stepped into the bathtub. Rex pulled the grey shower curtain closed.

"This is a mistake," Eddie said. "This is the first place they'll look."

Three young men in grey hoodies barrelled up the stairs and snooped around the flat. Eddie peeked out the shower curtain gap through the bathroom's open door. The first hoodie to enter was the muscular one with the microchip arm tattoo, which made him look like a cyborg. The other was stocky, while the third had a pencil-thin goatee.

"The microchip guy from the warehouse is here," Eddie whispered. "Does that mean The Cloister Posse did kidnap Daryl?"

"Let me see." Rex tugged at Eddie's sleeve. "I've got the right to see too."

Eddie elbowed Rex back, and Rex shoved him. Eddie fell forward through the gap in the curtain. Rex caught him and pulled him back into the tub.

As the curtain settled, Stocky turned to the bathroom and cocked his head. After a brief pause, he shook his head dismissively and went back to searching the flat.

"Saved your life," Rex whispered with a smile.

Eddie frowned.

Rex brushed fluff off Eddie's shoulder. "Sorry."

Eddie put his finger on his lips. "Shush."

"This stuff is wicked," Cyborg said.

Goatee lifted a voice recorder from a shelf. "Yeah man, we got to clear this place out."

"We ain't here for that," Stocky said. "Soon as the fuzz work out he was murdered, they're gonna look for a motive. He'll have papers here on Archer. We don't want no coppers coming for us."

Behind the shower curtain, Eddie clung to the Daryl Archer case file. Goatee and Cyborg rummaged through the desk and filing cabinet. Stocky poked around until he reached the gadgets on the shelves. He picked up a drone with multiple helicopter blades and a mounted camera.

Stocky spun the propeller and held the drone in the air. "Check this out, man. I'm FBI, innit."

Goatee scoffed. "FBI ain't interested in drones, bruv. That's CIA."

"You are both wrong in the head, it's the NRA," Cyborg said. "Look for the papers."

Eddie turned to Rex. "They mean NSA."

Rex nodded, his vacant expression hinting he didn't understand. He rummaged through the file's photos and found a picture of the dreadlocked man taken from a distance.

"It's the guy who took the CD," Rex whispered. "I knew he was involved."

Eddie rolled his eyes.

In the living room, Stocky fidgeted with a remote control until he got the drone's four helicopter blades to spin. He giggled as the drone flew up several feet. The drone spun around the room until it hovered over Microchip.

He tried to swat the device. "Stop it, bruv."

The drone flew into the bathroom and over the shower curtains. Rex and Eddie ducked down into the tub. They lay together huddled, trying to be as thin as a puddle, unsure if the lens's scope revealed their hideout to the gang.

Eddie winced, uncomfortable about the whole thing. Not only was he likely to die, he'd die while being spooned by Rex.

The drone hovered above in suspicious silence and flew through the curtain back into the living space.

"Wicked," Stocky said. "Let's nick it."

Cyborg grunted. "The boss said no stealing. Serial numbers will be listed with insurance. We get nicked with it, they'll connect us to him."

"Let's burn the place," Goatee said. "Can't get nicked for burning it."

Cyborg thumped Goatee. "Yeah, you can."

"Not like nicking though. If it's burnt, there's no evidence. The kebab shop downstairs gets the blame, and we don't have to spend all night looking for that paper."

Stocky nodded with his whole upper body. "Nice one. Let's do it."

Back in the bathtub, Rex and Eddie glanced at each other.

Rex swallowed. "What do we do? Are we going to burn to death?"

Eddie couldn't tell if Rex was more alarmed than usual or if he just looked more so without any eyebrows.

"I believe so," Eddie replied.

"We, we could offer to give them the papers, so they don't need to burn the place down?"

"Then we'll be witnesses. They'll shoot us."

Rex made a sad face. "So our choices are a quick bullet or slowly burn together?"

"I'm sure we'd light up fast, waiting for the fire to reach us, that would be the slow part."

Rex nodded. "I'd still choose the bullet."

From the kitchen area, Stocky called out "I found a lighter for the cooker."

He held the flame to the mid-century sofa in the centre of the room. While Goatee pulled out the fire alarms, the other two threw Cole's files on the couch, creating an indoor bonfire.

The crackling of burning paper, wood, and fabric intensified. The hoodies left laughing.

Rex and Eddie jumped out of the bath and stepped into the living room. Increasing flames burned around the middle of the room.

"Where's the drone?"

"Come on, Eddie. There's no time for picking items to save. We have to run out."

"The drone will have video of the fire-starters. We can identify who killed Cole."

The fire grew bigger and closer. Black smoke covered the ceiling.

Rex grabbed the iPad. "Didn't the video go to the iPad?"

"Yes, you're right."

They headed for the door, but Stocky walked back in.

He pointed at Rex. "Why ain't you got no eyebrows?"

Rex shrugged. "Fashion statement?"

"We're the neighbours. We wanted to check in on Cole, but I see his flat is on fire so we'll be leaving now."

Eddie attempted to pass the hoodie who placed his hand on Eddie's chest.

Stocky pushed Eddie back. "You boys aren't going nowhere."

He snatched the file from Rex's hand.

"Give that back."

Stocky scoffed.

Eddie wagged a finger between him and Rex. "There's

two of us and only one of you."

"Yeah? You think I ain't got maths skills?"

Rex stuck his chin out. "Okay, two against one it is. Ready, Eddie?"

Eddie had goosebumps which he didn't think was possible this close to a deadly fire. He gave a hesitant nod.

Rex made a fist with his right hand, standing in a wide stance.

Stocky laughed and mimed putting his hand over his mouth in shock. "You think I should be scared of you two?"

Rex swung his fist at the hoodie. A little too high, he punched Stocky in the forehead. He retracted his fist and cradled it in his other arm.

Stocky blinked in confusion. "What was that?"

"You just punched him in the skull?"

"I forgot to lock my wrist as well."

Stocky tipped his head side-to-side, cracking his neck. "You two are dead."

Eddie's heart raced. He leapt forward and kneed the hoodie in the groin. As it happened, Eddie felt more like an observer rather than the perpetrator. Stocky fell to his knees.

Eddie snatched the file back. "Sorry."

With his knees on the ground, Stocky bared his teeth and pushed Eddie back. Eddie tripped and fell at the edge of the fire. The file was flung into the air, letting the documents loose. The papers fell into the sofa's flames, crumpling as they burned.

Eddie pulled his legs in as the blaze gained on him. Rex jumped over the smaller fire and helped Eddie up. The growing flames cut off their exit, and the black smoke filled the upper third of the room. The heat intensified and the pair backed up into the bathroom.

Stocky jeered at the pair from the doorway. He exited with a smile.

Rex and Eddie sat on the bathtub's edge with their mouths agape. The bathroom had no windows. Eddie checked his phone. He had no signal bars. Rex's phone was the same. The pair coughed.

"We can't just sit here," Rex said.

Eddie kicked the door closed. He looked back at the bath, rushed to the faucet end, and ran the tub's taps. He put the plug in and splashed the walls with water.

"Oh, great," Rex said. "You've cracked. This is no time for a bath."

"Help me."

"Sure thing," Rex said in a condescending tone. He added some bubble foam into the bath.

"No, you idiot. We need to soak the walls."

Outside sirens wailed.

Eddie grabbed the shower hose and turned it on. He poured it over the walls and the doorway before handing it to Rex. "Keep it pointed at the doorway."

Eddie lifted the heavy lid of the toilet cistern and snapped off the tank float inside. The water filled and spilt out.

"Uh, Eddie. Toilet water?"

"It's the same water."

From across the flat, the sound of boots stomped up the stairs. Firemen ran in and hosed the apartment. The detective duo felt the heat calm down. The tip of an axe burst through the bathroom door.

Rex and Eddie shuffled away from the door, avoiding the black smoke cloud above them. A fireman forced his way through the door and stood over the cowering pair. They were safe from the fire, but they'd have some explaining to do.

## TWENTY-TWO

The two detectives sat in the back of a travelling ambulance while a stout EMT checked them over. The vehicle stopped. As the back doors opened, Detective Inspector Guy Sumner approached with a young officer.

Rex smiled. "Officer Sumner, what are you doing at the hospital?"

"Detective Inspector Sumner," he said with an apologetically corrective tone. "You're not at the hospital."

The pair poked their heads out of the ambulance. They were parked outside the blocky grey Cloisterham Police Station. Rex and Eddie gave each other a look of concern.

"Are they okay?" Sumner asked the EMT. "They're not deprived of oxygen or anything?"

"They'll be fine." The EMT looked at the pair. "You can go."

"Do we get to keep the space blankets?" Rex rustled his silver cover.

The EMT nodded. Rex fist bumped the air.

Sumner and the young officer escorted Rex and Eddie

out of the ambulance and through the station. As they travelled down a corridor, Eddie raised a finger to his lip. Rex nodded and mimed zipping his mouth shut. They were guided into an interview room. The walls were bare and white. A single table flush with the wall had two chairs on either side.

"No mirror?" Rex said. "What if the chief of police wants to secretly watch us?"

"No," Sumner said. "The chief constable has little interest in what you have to say."

Rex's shoulders lowered.

Sumner offered his hand to direct the pair to their seats. All four men sat. Sumner checked through paper notes. The other officer, a tall uniformed man with greased ginger hair stared at Rex and Eddie.

"What were you doing in Jason Cole's flat?" Sumner asked in a mellow tone.

"Uh, we were just visiting, then we saw the fire and wanted to help." Eddie smiled.

The ginger officer, no older than thirty, made notes.

Rex tapped the recording device. "You not recording this?"

Sumner crinkled his nose. "We don't record witness statements, only criminals." He made a neutral expression. "Should I be recording this?"

Rex and Eddie shook their heads in unison.

"What happened to your eyebrows?"

Rex's eyes darted between Sumner and the ginger officer. "Uh, fashion statement."

"And the black eye?" the tall officer said.

Rex sighed. "Walked into a door?"

Sumner interlocked his fingers. "I thought you said it was fighting."

Eddie bit his bottom lip. "As in arguing with me. He

walked off in a rage and hit a… door." Eddie winced hearing his own lie. "Is this gonna be in the witness statement?"

Sumner let out a slow breath from his nostrils. "I guess not, no. I was informed Jason Cole died in an explosion by your office."

Eddie mocked a surprised look. He assumed Rex was doing the same, but no one could tell.

"And now I find you in Jason Cole's flat, as it goes up in flames."

Eddie shrugged. "An unhappy coincidence."

Sumner sighed. "Are you working together on a case?"

"With him?" Eddie scoffed. "No way. We were just visiting."

"So you knew him?" The ginger officer raised one eyebrow.

"Not well."

Rex smiled. "He asked us to water his plants."

Sumner curled his top lip. "Was that before or after he was blown up in your office car park?"

Rex smiled. "Before, obviously."

Sumner pulled his chair in tight.

"What do you know about Jason Cole?"

Rex sat up. "He's the best private detective in Cloisterham."

"Was," Eddie added.

Rex's back straightened. "Did we just become the best private detectives in Cloisterham?"

Eddie grimaced. "The only private detectives."

"Same difference. We should update our newspaper ad."

"Jason Cole was a criminal," Sumner said. "A gun runner."

"Sir," the ginger officer protested.

Sumner waved his hand, "It's okay, Constable."

Eddie sank into his seat. "You can prove that?"

"We have several open cases, criminal activities that Cole was investigating. It's more than a coincidence. He sells illegal guns on the side."

"No way," Rex said. "He's a detective."

Eddie's right cheek twitched. "Why pretend to be a detective?"

"It was a pretext. Cole could use it to get close to the criminals and also find gaps in the black market. When he'd be found at the crime scene, he'd show his detective licence and claim to be on an investigation. It's a way in. Cole rarely ever did what his clients wanted him to do. Many of his cases involved guns. Does yours?"

"He's just a rogue," Rex said with admiration. "Like us."

Eddie shook his head. "We aren't rogues. We're by the book."

"Look, lads. I shouldn't be talking to you about this, but he sabotaged an undercover investigation into a drug gang."

"Sir?" the ginger officer said.

"It's okay, Colin. Rex and Eddie are friends of the force. We've helped each other out in the past. No reason why we can't all remain friends."

Rex leaned his chair back on its two back legs. "Yeah, Colin."

Sumner tapped the table. "Quiet Rex, and don't do that, you'll break the chair."

The ginger officer grinned as he leaned into his chair, which barely supported his tall back.

"Now, lads. We've been collecting evidence for months. We had intel on the gang's drop off points, and have been working out the supply chain."

"You used the trainers, right?" Rex tapped his nose.

Sumner and the ginger officer stared.

"The shoes on the telephone line. That's the intel for the drop off points?"

Sumner ignored the question. "With Cole involved, we're worried the gang is about to arm up."

"He said half the force was corrupt and worked with the gang——"

Eddie nudged Rex into silence.

The ginger officer tsked. "I'm sure he encouraged you to stay away from us. Stop us from disrupting his weapons sale."

Eddie's jaw tightened. Was he aiding an arms dealer by keeping his promise to Maude?

Sumner's gaze returned to his notepad. "A witness that saw you at the site of the van explosion said there were three men in the car park."

"They called us men?" Rex asked.

"We are men," Eddie said.

"I always thought of us more as guys. Men, I like it."

Sumner tapped the table gently to regain their attention. "So you confirm that you witnessed the explosion?"

Eddie shook his head but Rex nodded. Eddie sighed and nodded, by this time Rex was shaking his head.

Sumner leaned his interlocked hands on the table. "Did you see a third man?"

Both shook their heads.

"You were probably in a bit of a daze. Think back. Any hints of a third person watching?"

"Our focus was more on the fire," Eddie said.

"Think. Did Cole turn the ignition when the fire started."

"I think so." Eddie scratched his chin. "Why's that matter?"

"We can determine if the bomb was triggered by the engine ignition, or by radio control."

Rex's neck straightened. "By the third guy. Oh, man."

Eddie thought hard. "It was after—"

"Before," Rex said over Eddie.

The pair glanced at each other.

"It was after."

Rex pursed his lips. "I thought he was just about to turn it."

"But he did turn it. Didn't he?"

"I'm not sure now."

Sumner tapped the table again. "Jason Cole was seen last night on Canal Lane with two other men. Was that you?"

Eddie curled his top lip. "Do we get a lawyer?"

"I can withhold a solicitor for thirty-six hours if I want."

"Bloody hell, Sumner. I thought you were good cop."

"I'm nice cop to nice witnesses. Tell the truth. Did you take a briefcase from The Barge Inn's electric box?"

Eddie's shoulder hunched. "We didn't go to The Barge Inn. We didn't touch any briefcase. We don't know who started the fire."

"Who's Daryl Archer?" Sumner said.

Eddie's heart raced. How did Sumner know about Daryl Archer? "Dunno."

Sumner tapped the ginger officer. "Send in Constable Yates."

He got up and exited the room. A few seconds later he returned with Ruby Trout, the prostitute informant. She entered in a police woman's uniform; a black skirt and vest, a white short sleeve shirt, and a chequered cravat. She wore subtle make-up, which gave her a scowling baby face.

The ginger officer stayed by the door, glaring at the pair.

"Constable Yates works undercover in vice. She spotted The Cloisterham Massive using the Barge Inn as an exchange point."

Eddie swallowed.

"Are these two gentlemen the ones you saw with Cole?"

"Yes." She gave a short, sharp nod.

"We had a GPS in the briefcase you took. It was designed to be taken to the drug dealer's location, as we've been having trouble infiltrating their gang. When the signal stopped and we heard reports of shooting guns, we had to go in sooner."

Rex perked up. "Any arrests?"

"We got a few, but none of them were in The Massive. It was a new gang with little impact. When The Massive hear, they'll be more vigilant than before."

"The whole case is ruined," the ginger officer said.

Yates narrowed her eyes at the duo. "Tell him about the kidnapping."

Eddie feigned shock. "What kidnapping?"

"Daryl Archer."

"We don't know. It wasn't us with Jason Cole, we just have one of those faces." That didn't sound right so Eddie tried again. "Both of those faces." Third time was the charm. "We get mistaken for other people a lot."

Yates crossed her arms. "You introduced yourself as Eddie and him as Rex."

Rex drew in a breath. "We have one of those names."

Eddie buried his head in his hands.

"Both of those names?" Rex tried.

Eddie shook his head inside his buried hands.

164

Sumner sighed. "We know he was taken by the gang. Constable Yates witnessed it. You identified him for us. We just can't work out what's happened to him since. We spoke to his family. They say he's gone on a camping holiday without his phone, and they're sure he's fine."

Eddie looked up out of his hands. "Case solved."

Sumner's mouth twisted. "We want to help the Archers. Come on, lads. Tell me what's going on."

The detective pair gave each other a solemn look.

"I've got all day," Sumner said. "This is my number one priority."

Rex's eyes brightened. "Terrorists."

Sumner, Eddie, and Yates immediately turned their attention to him.

"I beg your pardon?" Sumner tucked his chair closer to the table.

"Cole wasn't working on a drug case. He'd been radicalised." Rex winced at his own words. "He joined this group that is planning a terrorist attack. Here in Cloisterham. I'm sure his cell is still out there."

Sumer furrowed his brow. "That doesn't match anything we've got."

"Is it true?" Yates asked.

Eddie swallowed. "Yes? Cole didn't give us details. After the explosion we, uh, rushed to his office. We hoped to find proof, but it had already been set alight… by the terrorists, I guess. Maybe they blew up Cole's van. Maybe he's selling bombs now."

"You realise that by reporting a terrorist activity you will be putting Cloisterham on high alert."

"Really?" Eddie's voice squeaked.

Rex nodded. "Yeah. Don't you believe us?"

Sumner sighed. "Whether I believe you or not, I'm obliged to take it seriously and report the threat." He turned to Yates. "Get me Counter-Terrorism." Before Yates could fully stand, Sumner pulled her arm and whispered in her ear. He spoke in a hushed, serious tone.

The duo tried to listen. Nothing was obvious but the last word, "CD."

Constable Yates left, passing the ginger officer.

"So, what happens to us?" Rex gave his best puppy dog eyes.

Sumner tilted his head. "Where should I start? Suspicion of arson. You ran away from a murder scene. Am I forgetting anything, Constable?"

"Obstruction of justice?" the ginger officer said.

Sumner sighed. "I'm disappointed, lads. I could keep you busy here for a couple of days. Are you sure you don't want to make a statement about Daryl Archer?"

Rex turned to Eddie.

Eddie put on a fake smile and rested his hands on the table. "I hope he has a safe camping trip."

Sumner's eyes darted between the two. He blew air through his cheeks. "You're free to go."

The ginger officer marched up to the table. "Sir!"

"Colin, be quiet."

"Yeah, Colin." Rex smiled.

Eddie nudged his partner and shook his head.

"The department is stretched thin enough. We can't help the Archers if they don't ask for help." He gave Rex and Eddie a stern expression, even then he looked friendly. "Maybe someone else can help."

---

Outside the police station, Eddie huffed. "What was that in there? You've got the whole force on terror alert now."

Rex gave an innocent shrug. "Maude made us promise

not to tell the police. They were on to us. Now they're busy, and we can find Daryl without interruptions."

Eddie pounded down the pavement, eager to finish the one-mile walk to the car. "This is a huge mess. We have to tell Maude we need to pay the ransom right away. No more delaying."

Rex did a little skip to catch up with his partner. "But what if we can find Daryl first and stop the gang from profiting. We can save the town from armed drug dealers."

"That's if Cole was telling the truth."

Rex bit his bottom lip. "Do you believe what they said about Cole?"

Eddie shrugged.

"If he's a gun runner, why'd he get you to go in the warehouse?"

"I don't know. To get me killed?"

"But he came back for us."

"That's true."

Rex cheered up. "What do you think Sumner said to Ruby?"

"Constable Yates. I couldn't make out much more than CD."

"I heard that. You think it's Daryl's CD?"

"No, but it doesn't matter, we're paying the ransom today. It's our only option. We've got no leads and anything that resembles evidence has ended up on fire."

Rex smiled and raised Cole's iPad from his back pocket.

"You got the iPad. How did you hide that?"

"I stuffed it down the back of my trousers."

"You sat on it this whole time?"

Rex offered it to Eddie. "It was against my back mostly, it was only tucked in."

"Uh, was it tucked inside or outside of your underwear?"

"Inside."

Eddie sneered. "Was that necessary?"

Rex shrugged.

Eddie raised his hands. "I think you should keep hold of it."

Rex played with the home button, but the screen stayed dead. "Ah, it doesn't work."

"So you squashed it?"

"No, it's not bent or anything. It's because of water damage... or fire damage, a bit of both really. You'd have thought they'd cancel each other out."

Eddie shook his head. "Let's take it back to your place and see if we can dry it."

# TWENTY-THREE

The pair entered Rex's house and rushed up the stairs. "Use the mat!" Rex's nan called out from the kitchen.

They hurried back down, wiped their shoes on the mat, and raced upstairs into Rex's bedroom.

The room was a square space with bumpy wallpaper and balding carpet. His shelves were full of books, videos, and collectables, everything else was stacked against the walls. A pile of various game consoles with scratches filled one corner. Next to it was a pyramid of games all out of their cases.

Rex laid his corduroy jacket on a chair covered in clothes, which he liked to call his 'chairdrobe'. Above the unmade bed, a wall shelf held paperback mystery novels inherited from his mother.

Eddie put the iPad on the radiator to dry. Rex's nan always had the heating on so it would warm up fast. The detective duo's office heating was off to save on bills. Whenever a client complained of the cold, Eddie offered them 'the client jumper', a baggy woolly top that had been warped from too many cycles in the tumble dryer.

After thirty minutes the iPad was still dead. Rex wheeled in his nan's hooded hair dryer, the kind that ladies sit under while their hair is slowly cooked. He attempted to hold the iPad under the dryer, but above the wall heater without burning his hands. Rex lowered and raised the iPad between the two.

Eddie crinkled his nose. "What are you doing?"

"It's for curly old lady hair, which is dead and not sensitive to heat. My hands can only take small bursts."

Eddie borrowed oven mitts from the kitchen and held the iPad under the dryer for forty minutes. The tablet was dry but still didn't turn on.

Rex's sister Georgia, a twelve-year-old with puppy fat, leaned on the doorframe. She wore a neon pink tracksuit with matching scrunchies in her otherwise unkempt hair. Georgia tried to look older with eyeshadow, lip gloss, and gold hooped earrings. A light spray of freckles across her nose and cheekbones gave away she was still a pre-teen.

Georgia gave an acknowledging nod. "You know what you need? A hacker. The older kids at school got this hacker to fix up their phones. Take off parental locks and stuff."

"You talk to the older kids?" Rex tucked his chin in. "No way."

"I swear down, the older kids talk to me, 'cause I'm buzzin'."

"Buzzin'?" Eddie's face scrunched up.

Rex leaned to Eddie and lowered his voice. "It's how the younger kids say cool."

"I can hook you up with a hacker. If you say I'm buzzin'."

Rex tutted. "You're buzzin?"

"Not like a question. Like you mean it."

Rex tutted and gave a cheesy smile. "You're buzzin', sis."

"And him."

Eddie wrinkled his nose. "You're buzzin."

"Fine, I'll send a text and arrange a meet. Winky face."

Georgia typed a message into her phone. Immediately following the "whoosh" sound, the phone beeped. She read the message. "Mint. Sirius can meet you tonight."

"Great, we can get to the hacker, open the iPad, and get more information on the case."

"And Spin Doctor's CD."

"No."

"Come on, Eddie. You wanted to speak to him about Daryl's kidnapping anyway."

"Spin Doctor?" Georgia looked at her phone. "I know him."

Eddie cocked his head. "You know Spin Doctor?"

"Yeah." She stuck her neck out. "Not like in person but we follow each other on Twitter."

Rex scrunched up his face. "Why?"

"Follow for follow. I follow loads of peeps." She raised her eyebrows. "He was at The Raggedy Cat Cafe on the high street about half an hour ago."

Eddie smiled. "I bet he's still there. We have to go!"

"Alright, jam your hype, man. He's chillaxing with an almond latte and has decided to try it with the bee pollen. Looks pleased with it an' all."

She showed them the picture of their blond dreadlocked target smiling in a selfie with his hot beverage.

"Props, sis." Rex offered a fist bump. Georgia obliged. After tapping knuckles, they both opened their hands while imitating an explosion noise.

She presented her clenched fist to Eddie. He sheepishly

bumped his hand against hers. Georgia made the explosion noise from the back of her throat. Eddie simply said, "Bang."

"Safe." Eyes on her phone screen, Georgia passed through the doorway. "Sees yah, thumbs up."

Eddie turned to Rex. "What's with the winky face, thumbs up thing?"

"She talks in emojis. Smiley face, frowny face, happy seal. She ends everything that way. Sometimes it's the most understandable part of the sentence. It's how kids talk now."

"You sure that's not just a Georgia thing?"

Rex shrugged. "Dunno. Pretty sure it's all of them."

Eddie sighed "Are we old?"

"I don't think so, Eddie. Old people know stuff about things. When we're old, we'll be wiser."

Eddie gave an unconfident nod. He didn't have Rex's optimism.

---

Rex and Eddie waited outside the Raggedy Cat coffee shop, a three-storey red-bricked Victorian building. The front rose to a point with roofing tiles down the sides. From the cathedral grounds, the pair sat on a park bench watching for Spin Doctor.

The building had tall windows obscured by stuck on sales banners. There was only one entryway, a grand black door in a thick white frame.

Just after five p.m. Spin Doctor exited the building. The giant doorway made the towering man appear average height. He pushed the loose platinum dreads past his shoulders and away from his face as he checked his phone.

He straightened the over-shoulder bag at his side before stepping into the street.

The detective duo followed him along the pedestrianised brick road. The street was lined with Victorian buildings leaning in different directions. Most seemed to bend forward as if they were going to pick the litter off the street.

As the pair followed on foot, Eddie checked the time on his phone. "We have our appointment with the hacker soon. We should probably go."

"I think we're onto something," Rex said.

"What on earth makes you think that?"

"You feel uneasy?"

"Yes, nearly all the time."

"I mean like you're being watched?"

Eddie thought about it. His neck crawled a little. "Now you mention it, yes."

Rex tipped his head towards an alleyway between two wonky buildings. Eddie noticed a silhouetted man.

"The third man," Rex whispered with a grin. "He must be following Spin Doctor too. It means we're on the right trail."

"Unless he's following us."

Spin Doctor reached the end of the pedestrianised brick road where the high street became open to traffic. He crossed at the lights, passing the kebab shop beneath Cole's burnt out home.

As Rex and Eddie reached the crossing, they passed a little girl. She bent her knees to pet the black cat that ran out of Cole's apartment. It snarled at the girl and disappeared down the alley.

Twenty minutes later, Spin Doctor reached the local Safeway, a supermarket with scuffed floors. Missing ceiling panels revealed tubes and electric cables.

They followed him through the aisles to a small little section of gluten-free baked goods. Rex and Eddie watched him read every ingredient of every package as he made his choice.

Spin Doctor stepped aside to allow a family of four to pass by. He did a double take at the aisle corner where Rex and Eddie were spying on him. The pair ran two aisles away to hide.

Through the stack of off-brand bottles of lemonade, Eddie watched Spin Doctor who checked left and right for the detective pair. He shrugged it off and returned to his gluten-free treats.

In their hideout aisle, Rex bent towards the display of photo frames.

Eddie turned red. "This isn't time to do your shopping."

Rex picked up a frame. "Look at this."

"Put it down," Eddie whispered through gritted teeth.

Eddie focused on the gluten-free section. He could make out Spin Doctor's shoulder and a few dreads.

Rex waved the photo frame in Eddie's face. It was a picture of two twin girls with blonde hair.

"Why do I know them?" Eddie grabbed the frame and examined it.

"It's Jason Cole's kids. They all are." Rex waved his hand to the display of picture frames. Each one contained the same picture of two twin girls in jean skirts and red T-shirts sitting on the grass.

"Maybe they're models," Rex said.

Eddie opened up the frame and removed the photo. On the back, it read: Copyright 2003, Stock Imagery LLC.

"The picture is over ten years old. Cole kept a stock photo in his wallet."

Rex's eyes widened. "He did it to get our sympathy when we kidnapped him."

An old lady inspecting a cat ornament peered over her glasses at the pair.

"We didn't kidnap him." Eddie patted his hand down to indicate a lowering of voices. "We interviewed him."

He gave the old lady a smile. She huffed and moved on.

"Cole lied to us," Rex said. "You think Sumner's right about him?"

"Can we focus on this investigation, please?"

Eddie peered past the lemonade stand, Spin Doctor was gone. He dropped the frame and loose picture on the shelf.

The pair dashed to the gluten-free display.

Rex stood on tiptoes for a better view. "You see him?"

Eddie shook his head. "I'll check the aisles to the right, you go left."

They went their separate ways through the horizontal corridor. Eddie turned his head to check each aisle as he passed. At the fruit section, he saw Spin Doctor queue at a five items or less counter. He snuck closer, picked up an apple, and joined the line.

Eddie texted Rex to tell him they were in the five items or less counter near the exit. He would occasionally look over the shoulder of the woman ahead of him to check on Spin Doctor.

She gave him a dirty look, and lowered her open gossip magazine so he couldn't read it.

Spin Doctor placed his gluten-free muffins on the conveyor belt. The cashier, a young man in the red uniform polo shirt, stopped scanning the items. He gawked at Eddie. Spin Doctor turned to see what the boy was looking at. Eddie checked behind him to see what the fuss was about. Nothing. The boy was staring at him.

Rex raced over, joining Eddie in line.

The cashier stepped away from the counter.

Eddie recognised the boy's pointy chin and nose, it was Jamie their mugger, without his baseball cap. Eddie stepped out of the line to get a better look. His heart raced, his skin went clammy.

Jamie jumped over the counter and sprinted for the exit.

"Stick with the target." Eddie ran after Jamie.

A middle-aged man in a white collared shirt and a checked tie lowered his clipboard as Jamie sped by.

"Get back to your counter," the man shouted.

Jamie passed through the automatic doors, shoving customers and their trollies out the way. Eddie attempted to navigate through the crowd, excusing himself with a series of apologies.

Out in the street, Eddie chased after Jamie. His heart raced, not in a panicked way, more of an adrenaline rush. Jamie passed a traffic light, crossing as the lights changed, allowing multiple lanes of traffic to drive again. As Jamie escaped, Eddie watched from the pavement, gaining his breath back.

## TWENTY-FOUR

E ddie returned to the supermarket entrance. Halfway down the street, he saw Rex wave him over. He joined Rex and saw Spin Doctor crossing the road ahead.

"The CD's in his bag," Rex said.

Eddie sized up the over-shoulder bag. "What makes you think that?"

"He keeps patting it, there's something in there of value he's nervous about. We need to find out what it is."

"I don't think that's the best idea."

"Sumner wants the CD, Daryl is involved, and it might even be why Cole was killed. We have to get it if we want to solve this case."

Eddie grumbled. "What do you suppose?"

"We wait for a quiet spot, and we mug him."

"You want to mug him? You know how horrible it is to be attacked like that. I wouldn't wish a mugging upon anyone. Maybe Cole, but I'd bet he'd just have handled it, the git."

"Maude won't let us tell anyone what's going on. You want the people that got Cole to come after us next?"

Eddie sighed. "How would we do it? We don't have any weapons."

"Did you ever see our mugger's weapons?"

"Well no, but—"

"It was all bravado, Eddie. We can do this."

"So what's the plan?"

Rex stepped up his pace. "He's turning into an alleyway."

"But the plan, what's our plan?"

"Think fast."

Rex ran into the alley, Eddie followed.

"Oi," Rex shouted.

Spin Doctor turned around so fast the dreads wiped over his shoulder.

Rex and Eddie paused. Eddie noticed how tall their target was at six foot three.

"Hi," Eddie said.

"This is a mugging," Rex shouted. "Hand over your stuff."

Spin Doctor stood, rigid.

"You hear me?" Rex said.

The man's eyes glazed over. "I don't want any trouble." His voice was crisp and posh.

"Neither do we." Eddie squinted. "Unless you do… then we do, too."

"That's right." Rex's eyes darted between the two in confusion. "Now, hand over the bag."

"Please, not the bag. It's my life's work."

"Shut it," Eddie said. "You don't, uh, want to see my partner, business partner — colleague — angry."

"Yeah," Rex squealed. He cleared his throat. "You wanna make me threaders?"

Spin Doctor cocked his head in confusion.

"Not now," Eddie muttered. He glared at their victim

and pointed to Rex. "He takes his medicine daily, and when he doesn't he's out of control."

Rex nodded, widening his eyes and clenching his jaw.

"But he takes it daily?" Spin Doctor raised an eyebrow.

"I said that, didn't I?" Eddie pursed his lips. "So we're all under control, for now. Hand over the bag."

Spin Doctor reached the bag strap over his head. "It's my life you're taking."

"We will take your life." Eddie snatched the bag.

Spin Doctor sniffled. A tear streamed down his cheek as he reached out to offer the bag.

Eddie softened. "Not like that, I meant the bag. Unless you don't give us the bag. Then, yeah. I guess we're taking your life."

Eddie snatched the satchel.

Spin Doctor took the smartphone from his pocket and offered it to them.

"What's that for?" Eddie asked.

"You want my phone, right?"

Eddie turned to Rex.

Rex shrugged. "It would be weird not to, we are muggers after all."

"Right, okay. Yeah."

Eddie edged closer to their victim and grabbed the phone. It slipped from his hand and landed on the alleyway concrete.

"Sorry." Eddie reached down to pick it up. He brushed the dirt from the screen. "It's fine."

The pair sprinted out of the alley and along the street and hid around a corner.

"That was surprisingly easy," Eddie said.

Rex pulled his shoulders back. "I bet we were right menacing."

Eddie let out a deep breath. "I was a tad scared myself."

"It was intense." Rex opened the bag. It contained a laptop, a couple of cables, and the CD with unreadable handwriting on it. "We have the CD."

"Put it in the computer."

Rex opened the laptop. The screen asked for a password. "Ah, we could take it to Sirius with the iPad?"

Eddie nodded. "Let's go."

---

Rex and Eddie approached the address Georgia had given. It was a skinny terrace house, the kind that lined most streets in this part of town.

Eddie knocked on the door. A bald fat man with a long goatee and a denim waistcoat answered the door.

He swigged his can of lager. "What you want?"

Rex offered an open hand. "Hi, are you Sirius?"

"You what?"

"Sirius the hacker?"

The man smiled with a tucked in top lip. He walked back into the dark living room.

Rex turned to Eddie. "Do we follow?"

Eddie shrugged.

"Susie," the man called out. "Someone at the door for you."

A small fourteen-year-old girl came to the door. She wore a Star Trek captain's shirt, angel wings, and steampunk goggles on her forehead.

Rex raised an eyebrow. "Are you Sirius?"

"I am she."

"We need help reading a soggy tablet."

Her father waved them inside and walked off into the

kitchen. Rex and Eddie followed her to her bedroom. The room was lit by the soft glow of fairy lights thanks to the thick, drawn blackout curtains. Her spacious desk featured a dual monitor set up.

Eddie raised a twenty-pound note. "Georgia said you'd do us a deal at twenty quid."

Sirius crinkled her nose. "I don't accept pound sterling, you got any cryptocurrencies?"

Rex and Eddie gave each other a look of confusion.

"Never mind, just put the twenty on the table."

She clicked the mouse, and her computer display lit up. She unscrewed the iPad like she'd done it a thousand times before.

"I should be able to connect to the tablet's hard drive and run it on my computer."

She unscrewed the case and bashed it against a table to get the hard drive loose. Rex and Eddie winced as the device hit the table top.

Sirius took out the hard drive and plugged in some loose wires. She switched the computer screen to an iPad display.

Sirius smiled. "This what you wanted?"

"Yes, please," Rex said.

Eddie pointed at the screen. "Open the drone app and play the video."

The screen displayed footage of Rex and Eddie in their office arguing and bickering.

Rex crossed his arms. "He spied on us through our window."

"Fast forward," Eddie said.

The video showed Eddie looking through paperwork while Rex played solitaire on the computer.

Eddie's eyes narrowed. "Uh, what's going on here?"

"It was lunch break," Rex said.

"The time says ten a.m."

Rex smiled. "Must be wrong. Fast-forward."

On screen, Eddie made two cups of tea. He sneezed over one, sneered at the cup, and passed it on to Rex.

Watching the monitor, Rex frowned. "Eddie!"

"Sorry."

Sirius shook her head in disbelief and clicked back to the list of video files.

She tapped on the bottom icon. "This was the last recorded video."

On the screen, the hoodies in Cole's flat poked at the gadgets. The drone footage was shot from above, obscuring the hoodies' faces. One of them had his sleeves lightly rolled up revealing a tattoo of computer circuits on his arm.

Eddie pointed. "That's the guy from the warehouse. The one with the cyborg arm tattoo."

"You're right." Rex smiled. "We have a positive ID."

"Zoom in," Eddie asked.

Sirius pushed a few buttons and zoomed in. The quality was blocky and hard to make out.

"That's no good. It's like an old Nintendo game now."

"It's okay, Eddie. Watch this." Rex stood straight. "Enhance," he ordered.

Sirius screwed up her face. "It was recorded at this quality, I can't improve it."

Rex turned up the corner of his lip.

Eddie pointed at the screen. "Play the rest of the video, please."

Sirius played it through, the drone showed the face of another teen.

"That, grab that. He's the one that I kicked in the…" He looked at Sirius and paused. "The groin."

She laughed. "You did what?"

"I'd rather not talk about it. I'm not proud."

"Oh, it was brilliant." Rex's face brightened with pride. "The boy blocked the door, and Eddie said, 'get out of my way.' Then the boy pushed Eddie, so Eddie kneed him, and he flew—"

"He's getting carried away." Eddie cheered up. "It was somewhat brave though."

Sirius sneered at the footage. "What is he? Half your size?"

Eddie's chest deflated. "He pushed me into a fire."

"Must be hard to be bullied by a little sixteen-year-old."

"Can we get an image of him too, please?"

"I'll email you the screenshot, it's called little boy dot jpeg."

Eddie narrowed his eyes as he typed his email address in. "Could you rewind the video, to the other hoodie. The one with the thin goatee."

Sirius tapped a few keys, and the video played back.

He poked at the screen. "Zoom in on him."

She paused the video and blew up the image.

"That," Rex said. "He has a tattoo as well, on his arm."

Eddie squinted at the screen. They could just make out a blocky black bulb on the wrist. Rex pulled out the photo Cole gave them of the Barge Inn's security footage. The snake tattoo in the picture had the same shape and form as the blocky drone footage.

"The Snakebite tattoo?" Eddie said. "But he does The Massive's drop-offs. This doesn't make sense. Who's he working for?"

Sirius unplugged the hard drive. "I've got to stop now. My mum and dad have me turn the computer off from dinner to bedtime."

"Just one more thing." Rex pulled the disc from the bag. "Could you try this CD?"

"We're not sure what it is, but it might be part of the case," Eddie added.

Rex grinned. "It's government secrets—"

"We don't know that," Eddie said.

Sirius sighed as a protest to the extra chore. She put the disc in. The CD drive booted up. Electronic dance music played through wireless speakers, surrounding the room with a loud beat.

Eddie tucked in his chin. "Can you turn that off?"

"This is your CD."

Rex and Eddie glanced at each other as the melody built.

"It's an album," Eddie said. "Daryl's album?"

The track dropped and a bass line kicked in.

Rex nodded to the beat. "He's a musician?"

Eddie winced. "I wouldn't go that far."

He opened the bag and checked out the computer. There were vinyl decals on the back. He unzipped a side pocket and found a stash of flyers with a picture of Spin Doctor behind two mixing decks. The text read, 'Spin Doctor's EDM night, first Fridays in The Loft at the Spout & Bottle pub.'

"Spin Doctor is a DJ," Eddie said with frustration. "The laptop must be his entire music library, his life's work."

Rex's head bounced back and forward to the beat of the song. "You think he'll add Daryl to his playlist?"

"Must you bob your head like that?"

"It's a banging tune," Rex said.

Sirius's Dad approached the open doorway. "Susie, can you turn that down?"

"Sorry, Dad." She ejected the CD and retrieved it.

Rex picked up the disc. "I'll listen to the rest of that later."

"Come on, love," Sirius's dad said. "Supper is ready, and then it's your cool down. You boys are welcome to stay for dinner."

"We're good, thanks," Eddie said.

The pair reached the front door and stepped into the street.

Eddie closed the door. "Did he think we're teenagers?"

"I guess so. I'll take it as a compliment."

"What about being called men? I thought you liked that."

"I'll take that as well. I'm not fussy."

## TWENTY-FIVE

The next morning the Morris Minor pulled up at the office car park. Rex hopped out of the car. He breathed in the crisp morning air before coughing on the river's stench. As Eddie stepped out of the driver's door, he observed the tarmac's blast stains at his feet.

Inside, Maude sat at the top of the narrow stairs waiting for the pair. She no longer wore her bright, bold tights. Instead, she wore autumn brown. Her skin was pale, and her eyes were covered in black eyeshadow to hide her tiredness.

Rex waved as the pair travelled up the steps. "Hi."

Maude gave a nervous smile. "I've not heard from you, but no news is good news, right?" Her smile faded as she fixated on Rex's forehead. "What's up with your eyebrows?"

"He walked into a door," Eddie said, getting his excuses mixed up.

She squinted a little. "And is that a black eye?"

Rex gave a slight nod. "Fashion statement."

Eddie waved towards the office door. "You want an update on the case?"

After unlocking the door, the pair sat behind the desk as Maude rolled her seat closer. She settled into the seat and gave a confused expression. She glimpsed under the seat at Cole's shoes still taped to the base.

"Do you know who kidnapped my brother?"

Eddie cleared his throat. "We believe it's a drug-dealing gang, but we aren't sure which one or where they operate. I'm sorry we couldn't be more helpful."

Rex gave a sympathetic nod.

Maude let out a slow breath. "The ransom is due today. Will you deliver it for us?"

Eddie swallowed. "You want us to do it?"

"My parents wanted a detective called Jason Cole, but they couldn't get a hold of him because—"

"He's dead," Eddie said.

Maude pursed her lips. "You read it in the newspaper as well?"

Eddie gave a theatrical nod. "Uh, yes."

She straightened her skirt. "I don't know what to do. I think he was murdered by the kidnappers, but I can't think why they'd do it."

Rex opened his mouth, "Because—"

Eddie kicked him in the shin. "That's awful."

"I've come to you, you're my only hope." Maude grabbed a tissue from the desk's new tissue box. "Thank God for waterproof makeup." She calmed. "I should go. It's too dangerous. I don't want you to get hurt too."

Rex sat up. "Dangerous is my middle name!"

"Frederick is his middle name." Eddie rested his elbows on the table. "How would we drop off the ransom money?"

"My parents couldn't get all the money together. They aren't cash rich you see."

Eddie rested his elbows on the table. "You want us to do the drop-off?"

"We need a negotiator. Someone to go in and tell them what my parents can offer."

Rex nodded. "We do negotiations."

"My parents would like to meet you. They want assurances. To see you are capable and sensible."

Eddie sighed. "I think we need to pool together all our information. Will your parents be willing to do that?"

"Full cooperation, absolutely."

"Do you know if Jason Cole told them something we don't know?"

"He had two informants that helped on the case. They were autistic or something, but they could possibly identify the people that kidnapped my brother."

"Right." Eddie pursed his lips.

She cocked her head. "Do you know anyone that could fit that description."

"Not that exact description, but I have an idea."

"Who?" Rex asked.

"I'll explain later. Let's meet with our new clients."

---

The pair followed Maude's car to the outskirts of East Rawling village. They arrived at her home, a lavish country house surrounded by green fields.

Eddie admired the red brick farmhouse while Rex waved at a horse in a nearby field.

Maude stood face to face with Rex. "We have a problem."

Rex stuck his bottom lip out. "What?"

She reached into her coat pocket and pulled out a make-up kit. Unzipping the bag, she removed an eyebrow pencil, grabbed Rex's jaw to hold him still, and drew a pair of eyebrows on his face.

"My parents won't hire a man with no eyebrows. They're very traditional."

Within a few minutes, she'd added two curvy eyebrows to Rex's face.

"It looks a little flat," Eddie said.

Maude pulled a second pen from the bag. She bit down on the lid to pull the pen open. "I'm not finished yet."

She added another layer, drawing on individual hairs of a darker colour to add a three-dimensional quality.

Maude inspected her work and nodded. "That'll do. The black eye is mostly faded."

Rex gave a look of disappointment.

As she put away her makeup, she offered Rex a small mirror. He examined his new eyebrows.

"They're a little lighter than normal," Rex said.

"Sorry, I only have the colours that look good on me."

He peered at her forehead. "What happened to your eyebrows?"

"Plucked to oblivion." She paused and eyed both Rex and Eddie. "My father didn't get along with Daryl. Daryl liked to do his own thing, whereas my father had expectations. I'm just telling you because, well, there are some mixed emotions happening."

Eddie nodded.

Maude guided them through the home into the living room where her father awaited them. It was a tall green room with post beams across the ceiling. Drapes and portraits filled the walls. Dark wood furnishings were spread about the place.

Rex and Eddie sat on a puffy royal red sofa opposite

Maude and her father. A glass coffee table lay between them. Mr Archer was a long-faced man with white hair tucked behind his ears. He wore a wool hunting blazer over his buttoned-up shirt.

Eddie wondered if the hunting blazer meant he'd actually been hunting that morning, or if it was countryside fashion. He'd never seen anyone in Cloisterham run in a tracksuit but at least half the population seemed to wear one.

Mr Archer flared his nostrils. "So, you're Milton Miles Investigations?"

Rex pointed at himself. "Rex Milton," and at Eddie, "Eddie Miles."

Mrs Archer entered with a tray of tea and poured it out into five cups. "I'm sorry it took so long."

She sat next to Maude, showing she had the same round head. With friendly eyes and a soft tone, she seemed like a sweet primary school teacher. "I'll suppose you'll be needing to see the ransom note?"

"Yes, that would be useful."

Mrs Archer tottered off and came back with the printed ransom note. It read: We got ure sun. If u want 2 c him again. Bring 400k @ 10PM Friday 2 drop off.

Rex shifted forward on the sofa. "That's tonight."

"I assumed Maude informed you, we aren't cash rich," Mr Archer clenched his teeth as he admitted his financial failing.

Eddie glanced up from the note. "So how do we bring them four hundred grand?"

Mr and Mrs Archer gave each other a look as if there was a bad smell in the air.

"I want you to negotiate," Mr Archer said.

The detective pair gave each other a look and turned back to their clients.

Mr Archer continued, "Bring them a deposit to let them know we are serious but explain that we are cash poor. We'd be happy to settle for a few paintings, an antique or two, even the boat. What are drug dealers into, besides drugs?"

Mrs Archer looked down at the rug, avoiding eye contact.

"I hear they're in the market for guns," Rex offered.

"We could throw in some antique muskets if that's something they'd like. Purely decorative, of course."

Eddie grimaced. "Why don't you sell this stuff and give them the four hundred thousand?"

Mr Archer scoffed. "You don't put a painting on eBay, dear boy. It's a buyer's market, the economy is still recovering. We want the real value, not the market value."

Rex raised a finger. "Isn't the market value the real value?"

Mr Archer gave a dismissive wave. "Try not to think so hard about it. Leave the money to the money experts."

"What does it take to be a money expert?" Rex said.

Mrs Archer took a sip from her dainty teacup. "Why, money, of course."

Eddie curled his top lip. "Aren't you cash poor?"

Mr Archer glanced at the ceiling and sighed. "Cash and money are different things. On completion, we'll give you ten thousand pounds." He looked them up and down. "Are you up to the job?"

Rex and Eddie nodded.

Mr Archer crossed his fingers. "This is our son, we only want the best for him. Unfortunately, Mr Cole let us down."

"By dying," Mrs Archer crinkled her nose.

"We can do it," Rex said. "We're the best."

"These kidnappers aren't well informed," Mr Archer

said. "I assume we can get the upper-end value of any assets they choose. That said, you can negotiate down a little if need be."

Mrs Archer handed them a copy each of a printed spreadsheet.

Eddie curled the right corner of his top lip. "What's this?"

"A shopping list," she said

"These are items we are willing to part with. They can have anything, up to the value of four hundred thousand pounds."

Eddie tucked in his chin. "In exchange for your son?"

The Archer couple didn't blink. Maude winced at the idea.

"I'm sorry, but why would they go for this?"

Mr Archer picked up his tea. "Little other option, I'm afraid. I don't see anyone else willing to foot the bill."

"You must sell it to them, for Daryl's sake." Mrs Archer said. "Make them realise it's better than cash."

Rex's face contorted. "Is it?"

"There are many benefits," Mr Archer said. "Tax avoidance for one. Technically a ransom would need to be registered as either a gift or income."

Eddie cocked his head. "I don't think they bother with their taxes."

Mr Archer scoffed. "What about when they get audited?"

"Again, I think they keep it pretty low key with the Inland Revenue." Eddie tapped the list. "This is a joke, right?"

"Absolutely not. Daryl got himself into this mess, and it's no surprise either. If he'd had the smarts to listen to me, he wouldn't be consorting with hoodlums."

Mrs Archer rubbed Maude's back to calm her nerves.

"As I said, I'm willing to work with the kidnappers within reason. They sent a mobile phone," Mr Archer said. "Wait for it to ring this evening, they will tell you when and where to meet. Don't tell them about the list until you meet. Once they have made their selection, you will come back here to collect."

"Don't forget the ten percent cash deposit." Mrs Archer pushed forward a leather briefcase. "We want them to take us seriously."

Eddie opened the briefcase. Inside, four wedges of bank notes, each a few inches deep, lay at the bottom.

"That's forty grand?" Rex puffed, a little disappointed.

"It's thirty-eight thousand," Mrs Archer said. "All we could muster I'm afraid. The briefcase was worth five hundred pounds new."

Eddie picked at the fraying leather in the corner. "You want us to shortchange them on the deposit?" Rex tucked in his chin. "They'll think we nicked some of it."

"Ten grand of it is mine," Maude said.

Mrs Archer stirred her tea. "It's all we could get our hands on."

Eddie twisted his lips. "Then how will we get paid?"

Mr Archer turned his nose up. "We have a monthly income of dividends and shares. You will have to wait for the beginning of next month. Unless there's something on the list that takes your fancy."

Eddie looked up from the spreadsheet. "Cash will be fine."

---

Mr Archer opened the front door. Rex and Eddie stepped outside with the briefcase of cash. They walked across the pebble driveway to the Morris Minor.

"We're rich," Rex said. "We're gonna be thousandaires once their dividends come through."

"Remember that when they try to flog us their tat. We accept cash only. Okay?"

Rex crunched his new eyebrows. "I never said anything different."

"I saw you eyeing the muskets."

Maude snuck out of the house and followed them to their car.

"I'm so sorry about my parents. They put on a brave face, but they're pretty shaken by the kidnapping."

Eddie put on a pursed smile. "What do you think of the exchange?"

"It's crazy, but we can't go to the police. Father won't borrow from friends as it will raise suspicion. I'm begging you to do whatever it takes to bring Daryl back."

Eddie avoided eye contact. "We'll do our best."

"You're my only hope."

Maude pecked them both on the cheek and returned to her car. Rex grinned. Eddie turned pale.

"Are you okay, Eddie?"

"We're her only hope." Eddie rotated his shoulders.

Rex smiled. "We're the men for the job. How's your neck."

"You know, it's fine, it's almost like it's better. I think it must be from sleeping on the office floor."

"Or you're so anxious, you're now holding your body in a way that aligns your neck upright."

Eddie's jaw clicked and crunched. "I'm not anxious. I mean, no more than usual. I'm base level anxious. We can do this."

"Exactly. We make the deal tonight. Collect the stuff the next day and return Daryl. By the end of next week, we get the cash."

Eddie frowned. "The kidnappers want to get paid. We have to tell them we can trade in a few paintings, old furniture, and some silverware."

Rex cocked his head. "And muskets."

"You think the people that blew up Cole will be happy with that?"

"Muskets, Eddie. Who doesn't want a musket? I've always wanted one."

"You've always wanted a musket?"

"I didn't realise until it was offered, but yes. I've always wanted a musket. Now, let's go to the office and search the internet on how to negotiate. I'm sure there's a wikihow or something."

Eddie huffed. "I can negotiate."

Rex's painted on eyebrows raised. "Like when you tried to get Ruby to talk for ten quid?"

"She was an undercover copper. That wasn't a real trade."

"The muggers? You tried to talk them out of it."

"They were stupid kids?"

"So what are the kidnappers?"

Eddie sighed. "Fine, we'll do a little research to boost your confidence."

## TWENTY-SIX

The phone rang at 10 p.m. telling the pair to travel to the graveyard behind the Octagon Shopping Centre. They got in the Morris Minor and headed into town.

Rex rolled his shoulders. "When the gang gets the ransom, they're gonna buy guns and ramp up drug production. That's not gonna be good for Cloisterham, is it?"

Eddie cleared his throat.

At a red light, the car stalled. Eddie tried to turn the key. The engine was dead, probably from the moist night air.

Both pushed the car to the nearest available street parking. Eddie steered the wheel through the driver's window while Rex pushed from the back.

Realising they would be late for the exchange, they jogged the rest of the way.

Rex stopped and bent forward. "I can't run like this. I've got a full bladder. I need to go."

"Hold it." Eddie crouched, breathless. He gathered enough energy to get back to a brisk walk.

"Eddie," shouted an excited voice from the other side of the road.

His brother Andy crossed the street in a tailored suit.

Eddie slowed to a stop, while Rex hopped on the spot to alleviate his bladder woes.

Andy smiled. "Just got in from London. How are you two?"

"Uh, good thanks." Eddie's eyes darted between Andy and the road ahead.

"You guys out on the town?"

"Something like that."

"Good for you," Andy slapped Eddie's shoulder. "I should get going. I've got tennis, followed by my personal trainer, and then I'm meeting a lady for drinks."

Rex jumped up and down impatiently.

Andy noticed Eddie's tight grip of the case's handle. "What's in the briefcase?"

Eddie paused. "Oh, it's—"

"It's forty grand in cash," Rex barked, still jumping.

Andy gave a quizzical look at Eddie, after a pause he smiled. "Good one. Where'd you get it though? It's vintage, that. Probably worth a few quid."

"You know about briefcases?" Eddie asked.

"My boss has one just like it. Very proud. You don't look well, Eddie. You seem a little pasty, and clammy."

"Fine, fine. Right, Rex?"

"Right."

Andy tucked in his chin. "I'll see you at next week's dinner then."

Eddie nodded. "Sounds great."

The two detectives ran down the street. After gaining some distance, Eddie turned back to see his brother standing in the same spot, confused.

A minute later the flip phone rang while they were still a hundred yards from the point.

"Hello," Eddie said.

"You there?" the disguised voice asked.

Eddie tried running on tiptoes to lower the sound of him running. Out of breath, he gave a wheezy, "Yes?"

"Liar."

"I'm close. We're so close."

Rex pointed ahead at the tied shoes hanging from a telegraph cable. The detectives stopped at the graveyard gates below the hanging shoes.

"Here." Eddie held a stitch in his stomach. "We made it."

"Is he doing the kidnapper accent?" Rex whispered.

Eddie covered the receiver with his hand. "Voice, it's a voice."

"You what?" the kidnapper asked.

"Nothing, we're here. Where are you?"

"Nah, it don't work like that, bruv. You see the bus stop down the street?"

"Ask him if they did the shoes," Rex whispered.

Eddie waved Rex off and peered at the road ahead. Twenty feet away there was a bus stop with a bench.

"Yeah."

"Walk to it."

The pair did as they were told.

"Now what?"

"Now, put the case next to the bench, and walk away."

"What? What about Daryl?"

"Once we've counted the money, we'll release him. He'll be dropped somewhere in Cloisterham town centre with enough bus money to get him home."

"We can't do it that way."

"That's the way it's got to be. Once we've got our money, we let him go."

"About that—"

"You got the money, right?"

"Sort of."

"You sort of got my money? Maybe I sort of kill this Daryl Archer, yeah?"

Rex scanned the area for a decent spot to pee.

Eddie scanned the Octagon's multi-storey car park across the street, hoping to spot the kidnappers watching from above

"You hear this?" A man's scream muffled by fabric, blasted through the phone's earpiece. "If you don't tell me you've got four hundred K in the briefcase, I hang up. You get me, bruv?"

Eddie swallowed. "I've got your four hundred thousand pounds. Okay?"

"Fine, put the case down and walk away, yeah?"

"Yes. Will you call me when you're ready?"

"Ready for what?"

"Nothing, just when you're ready, give me a call."

"Whatever, bruv." The phone hung up.

"I need a pee," Rex said.

Eddie pulled a pen and the spreadsheet from his jacket pocket. He wrote on the back: This is a deposit. Family poor. Willing to offer items up to the ransom price. Call me.

He opened the case, stuffed the note inside and stepped away. "We have to tail whoever picks this up. They'll take us to Daryl's location in case the deal goes sour."

All of Rex's neck muscles were tight. "But I need to use the little boys' room."

"Go find an alleyway or something. Be quick, we have to be ready to follow."

Rex ran off. Eddie walked down the street to the graveyard's corner and jumped over the three-foot wall. He crawled back commando style to the proximity of the bus stop. Concerned that he looked like a zombie escaping a grave, he hoped he would not be seen by any grieving visitors.

Hidden under the shade of a tree, Eddie peeked over the wall at the bus stop. An old lady read the bus schedule and sat down.

*She's not the collector*, he thought. *She can't be. Can she?*

A man in a tall brown coat and a bowler hat joined the bus stop. Could it be him? He does look like he's wearing a disguise. Where do you even buy a bowler hat from these days?

The man questioned the old lady, pointing at the briefcase. She shook her head.

No, this is bad. The kidnappers aren't gonna come until it's quiet. Why'd they pick a bus stop?

A bus came and picked up the old lady. The man continued to wait.

Where the hell is Rex?

Distracted by his missing partner, he glared at the nearby alleyway.

"Rex? Come back out here." Eddie ventured inside where Rex stood with his hands up. "What are you doing?"

"If it isn't Bumfluff, come to join Corduroy."

Jamie stood in the alleyway with his arms wide. He wore his white tracksuit and a new baseball cap.

Eddie leapt at him. He stopped when the three other muggers, Lanky, Bug-eyes, and Podgy, stepped into the spotlight of the nearby lamp post. All three had their hoods up. Jamie smiled, his pointy face looked particularly ghoulish because he'd shaved his eyebrows off.

Eddie tried to step back out the alley. The gang circled

the pair. "Yeah well, you're all cocky with your mates around, aren't you?" He stepped back. "What happened to your eyebrows?"

"Explosion?" Rex asked.

"Na, mate. It's the new trend."

Rex's drawn on eyebrows raised. "Really?"

Jamie tilted his head. "Phones, wallet, you know the rest."

Rex cleared out his pockets. Eddie crossed his arms.

"I don't think so boys, not today."

"You want to get beaten up?"

Eddie gave it a thought. "As a matter of fact, yes. I'd rather be beaten up than have my stuff taken again."

"You don't get it. There are two options. One, you give us your stuff. Two, we beat you up and take your stuff!"

Eddie couldn't let them have the kidnapper's phone. Daryl would be killed.

He nodded. "Fine, but I will need to see some kind of weapon this time."

"Mate, you don't."

Eddie raised his palms. "Sorry, I believe it's standard procedure, and I demand to see it."

"Or what?"

"Or I'll keep my stuff, thank you."

Rex offered a ten-pound note and a handful of coins. "I'll have the usual, thanks."

"No, Rex." Eddie batted Rex's hand back. "This time we take a stand. We can handle ourselves."

Jamie curled his top lip. "Lads, knives."

They all pulled out stabbing weapons. "Hey, Eddie. Remember that time you complained that everyone used guns these days. Looks like that knife crime you were looking for is here. You must be chuffed."

"Chuffed to bits." Eddie's jaw popped from the stress.

He handed over the wallet.

"Phones?"

"We haven't replaced our phones yet."

Jamie thought it over. "Oh, yeah. They were crap anyway."

Eddie's phone beeped.

"You holding out on us?"

It beeped again. Jamie stuck his arm in Eddie's top pocket and pulled out the phone.

"You can't take my work mobile—" Eddie got a glimpse of the device, it was Spin Doctor's smartphone. "I mean, go ahead, take it."

"Well, well, well. That'll fetch a few hundred quid I reckon." Jamie smiled. "So, you got another phone?"

"Uh, no. That's my work phone."

"Nah, mate. Hand it over."

Jamie patted Eddie down until he found the cheap little flip phone in a jacket pocket. "This thing? This ain't worth nothing."

"Can I have it back then?"

"Nah. You cost me my job at Safeway's. Now I'm gonna take this."

Rex grasped his hand full of coins. He swung his arm around and let go, flinging silver and copper at the muggers.

Eddie grabbed the phone out of Jamie's hand. He held it so tight his fingers turned red.

Lanky and Bug-eyes stepped forward to assist. Rex took a deep breath. He stood with his feet apart, clenched his fist, locked the wrist, and swung forward. Rex punched Lanky who dropped the knife. As the teen's eyes welled up, Rex and Eddie were reminded they were around sixteen-years-old.

The gang all puffed out their chests and spread out, ready to fight.

Rex stepped back, closer to Eddie. "Cole said, taking out the tallest one would scare them off."

"You didn't quite take him out."

Lanky grabbed Rex by the hair and shook him about. Rex tried to get another punch in but missed as he was thrown.

Jamie snarled, displaying his long, wonky teeth, he lunged forward and grabbed Eddie's hand clutching the flip phone.

He pried Eddie's hand open, while Podgy punched Eddie in the stomach.

Jamie grabbed the phone and stepped back to the muggers.

"No." Eddie grabbed the dropped knife and waved it about.

Jamie backed away. Eddie swung the knife at Bug-eyes's head, close enough to get them all to back away. Releasing Rex, Lanky stepped back, battered and bruised.

"Give me back the phone. It's worthless to you."

Jamie rolled his shoulders back. "It's the principle."

A distance sound of police sirens grew, the muggers gawped at each other and ran off into the alleyway.

"You all right?" Eddie asked Rex.

"Yeah, you?"

Eddie nodded. "We have to get that phone back to negotiate Daryl's ransom. Otherwise when they get the briefcase— The briefcase! We need to get back to the bus stop."

The pair ran out of the alley and goggled at a police van parked near the bus stop. Two police cars blocked off the road. Police officers, dressed in black bullet-proof armour and helmets with face covers, stacked sandbags around the briefcase. Three more police officers holding submachine guns cleared the area. The bowler hat man and other pedestrians watched from behind yellow tape.

"This is bad," Eddie said.

Rex and Eddie ran to the graveyard wall.

"Stop," a policeman in the armour shouted. "Sirs, stay where you are. This is a controlled explosion."

"Why?" Eddie said, out of breath.

"Cloisterham is on high alert after being tipped off about a terrorist attack. This is a precaution."

A bomb squad robot rolled to the briefcase to deliver the explosives.

"Step back, sirs."

Eddie's jaw quivered as he looked for any excuse that wasn't: that's my suspicious bag of thirty-eight grand which definitely isn't for paying a kidnapping ransom.

A loud yet controlled sound halfway between a pop and a puff echoed in the evacuated street. Smoke shot out of the little sandbag fort as flakes of paper rained down.

The policeman tutted. "I knew it, what a waste of time."

Eddie dropped to the grass and crossed his legs. He was in disbelief.

Rex casually joined him. "What do you want to do now? Pub?"

Eddie nodded. "Pub."

---

Rex walked a shocked Eddie into The Golden Apple pub. The walls were painted a trendy dark grey with chalkboards that described the specials and soup of the day.

He placed Eddie at a table. "You wait there, and I'll get you a pint."

"We don't have any money," Eddie mumbled. He stared into the distance.

Rex took off his left shoe and pulled out a tenner.

"You put money in your shoe?"

"Yeah, after getting mugged I thought no one checks your shoes, so I put an emergency tenner in there. For emergencies. Beer emergencies."

Rex ordered at the bar. When he handed over the foot money, the bartender squirmed a little at the crumpled, sweaty note.

He put the change back in his shoe, picked up the two pints and hobbled towards the table. He paused to jiggle the coins in his foot to a more comfortable spot and continued.

After sitting, Rex lifted his drink. "Two best friends fighting crime. It's what we do best."

"Best?"

"It's what we do."

Eddie downed half his beer and placed it back on the table with a thunk. "What are we doing?"

"Having a break."

"This is madness. It's over."

"You don't want to finish the case?"

"The case? The company."

Rex's jaw went slack. "You're quitting?"

"We've already doomed Daryl. Why get ourselves killed?"

Rex cleared his throat. "Maybe we can talk the kidnappers into releasing Daryl. It's their fault they didn't pick up the bag on time."

"You think they'll apologise and hand him over?" Eddie said. "I don't. No money, no Daryl."

"What do you want to do? Tell Maude we quit? That the money is gone, and so is her brother?"

Eddie grumbled.

Rex's eyes brightened. "It wasn't like the whole ransom was blown up, just the deposit. We still have the list of assets. Let them pick four hundred grand's worth of stuff. We'll tell the Archers they took the money as interest."

Eddie took a big gulp of his beer. "If we meet them empty handed they might kill us on sight."

Rex nodded. "The ones we hurt are you and me."

Eddie glared. "Is that Coolio again?"

"A prophet of our times."

"Isn't he from the nineties?"

Rex clicked his fingers. "Spin Doctor's over-the-shoulder bag."

Eddie gave a dismissive wave. "We'll return it to him later."

"I mean if we take Spin Doctor's bag we won't be empty-handed."

"An empty bag will get us killed."

Rex took a sip of his drink. "What if we put my copy of the asset list inside? Would that make you feel better? It's either this or tell Maude how you lost the money."

Eddie opened his jaw and it clicked. "That's on you. The money was only blown up because you put the police on terror alert."

"You left the bag on the street."

"Yeah to find out what was taking you so long."

"Well pardon me for getting mugged."

Eddie sighed. "It's over."

Rex nodded. "You're right. It's over now. Let's push forward."

"No, I mean we're not real detectives. I can't handle this."

"We've just hit a little snag. We have to push on."

"I'm gonna move in with my parents. I'll get a job at Andy's firm." Eddie made a face like he'd tasted his own burp. "I'll be fine."

Rex's bottom lip wobbled. "We have to finish the case."

"Why? Why would I do that?"

Rex hunched his shoulders. "Because no one else can do it."

"We have no ransom and no phone. What makes you think we can do it?"

Rex screwed his face up like he was really concentrating. He smiled slowly.

"What? What is it?"

Rex swigged his beer. "What if I can get the phone back?"

# TWENTY-SEVEN

Rex and Eddie arrived at the Safeway supermarket at 10:50 p.m., ten minutes before closing. They marched straight to the customer service desk.

"Excuse me," Eddie smiled. "Can I speak to the manager please?"

The young woman with bleach blonde hair and a permanent scowl glared at the pair.

"What for?"

Eddie leaned in, lowering his voice. "We need to uh, make a complaint about a worker, Jamie."

"He's been fired. Problem solved."

"Jamie?" Rex asked. "With the long face?"

"Yeah, that's him. Got fired." The girl looked over the pair's shoulders to the next customer in line. She put on a higher voice with a bit of a spring in it. "Can I help you?"

Eddie stepped back into her view, blocking the person approaching. "I guessed that, but we're private investigators, and we're currently pursuing him for theft."

"What kind of private detectives go after a little thief like Jamie?"

"The kind he thieved from." Rex gave a sharp nod.

"What'd he nick? Your gun? Your badge?"

Rex gazed down at his shoes. "We don't have those things."

She rolled her eyes. "Nah, you ain't detectives. What are you? You like a secret shopper? I bet you were sent by corporate to test me on giving out employee information?"

"No, we're here to speak to a manager."

"Well, you can't, Mr Secret Shopper."

"That's it. I'm making a complaint."

She handed Eddie a clipboard with a form on it. "You can fill this out. I'll make sure the manager sees it."

"Please madam, this is a life or death situation."

She held up a microphone console and pushed the red button. In a light singsong voice she said: "Hello shoppers, this is a quick announcement to remind you we close in five minutes. Please take your items to the cash register. Thank you."

Rex pulled at Eddie's blazer. "I got an idea."

The pair travelled to a refrigerated section. Rex opened a jar of pickled eggs. He sniffed it and smiled.

Eddie gave him an odd look. "What are you doing?"

Rex peeked down the corridor where a worker on a step ladder was restocking the top shelf. He poured the pickle juice on the ground.

"Rex?"

He stepped forward and skidded in the juice, his backside smacked on the laminated ground.

"Ouch, oh, I slipped. What careless person left this spillage here."

The worker, an acne-ridden skinny boy, jumped from the step ladder. "Are you okay?"

Rex wriggled in a pantomime of pain. "I don't know? I might need a trip to the hospital."

The boy looked at Eddie, deferring to him.

"Maybe you should get the manager?"

He nodded and ran off.

Rex held his back and scrunched up his face.

"Did you really hurt yourself?"

He calmed and grinned. "Nope. We'll have that phone in an hour tops."

Behind Eddie, someone cleared their throat. The boy had returned with the blonde from customer services.

He smiled. "Sirs, this is Chevy, she's the night manager."

Chevy folded her arms.

Eddie turned to Rex. "How you doing now? You alright?"

Rex mimed patting his lower back. "You know I feel a lot better. I think I'll be okay." He crawled to one knee and stood. "Yeah, I think I'll be fine. I mean. Maybe a complimentary jar of eggs would tide me over."

Rex picked up a jar and raised his eyebrows.

Chevy retained her blank expression.

Defeated, Rex put the jar back. "Or maybe not. Maybe go home and sleep it off."

---

Eddie was delighted to see the Cloisterham Police Station was open that late in the evening. The pair stepped through the automatic doors and approached the reception desk.

The ginger officer stood behind the bulletproof glass. When Rex and Eddie reached the counter, his top lip thinned.

"Can I help you, gentlemen?"

"We'd like to speak to Detective Inspector Guy Sumner," Eddie said.

The man's brow drew together. "He's unavailable."

Rex leaned towards the aluminium speak-thru. "What about Ruby. She owes us one."

"Who?"

Eddie put on a polite smile. "Constable Yates, is she available?"

"She's off duty. Is there anything I can help you with?"

Eddie locked his jaw.

"Anything you'd like to report?" The officer sneered. "Maybe a missing person?"

Eddie sighed. "Yes."

A smile crept on the officer's face.

Rex nudged Eddie and whispered, "We promised Maude."

"I'd like to report a stolen phone. I was mugged in the alleyway by the railway bridge on the high street."

The officer's smile faded.

"The boy who stole it, his name is Jamie, and he used to work at Safeway until yesterday."

"You could probably get his address from the manager," Rex added.

"I need the phone back tonight, it's really important. I'm, uh, expecting a call."

The officer made notes with a pencil almost worn to a nub. "What kind of a call?"

"An important one."

He finished taking notes. "Thanks for reporting the incident. Would you like to leave a phone number so we can call if we have any further questions?"

Eddie gave the office number. "Anything else?"

"That should do it. Thank you." The ginger officer turned his attention to a computer screen.

Rex and Eddie glanced at each other.

Eddie tapped the glass. "What happens next?"

"I'll file the incident report later."

"And then a unit will go to Safeway?"

The ginger officer grimaced. "Have you been watching the news?"

Rex and Eddie eyed each other.

"No," Eddie said.

He pointed at the silent TV screen mounted on a wall in the corner. The screen displayed footage of police officers including Sumner in a forest. Behind caution tape, people in disposable white body suits and purple rubber gloves took samples with tweezers.

Eddie stepped closer to the TV. "What's going on here?"

"They found a terrorist cell's camp. Bomb-making equipment and camping gear. They've been training in Cloisterham Woods this whole time."

"All because of our tip?" Rex said, bright-eyed.

"A jogger called it in, he was shaken after the controlled explosions we've been doing all day. We're too busy to deal with one mugging."

"It was two muggings actually. They robbed us a couple of days ago as well."

The ginger officer flared his nostrils. "You want me to fill in another form?"

"No, I want you to help me get my phone back."

"Losing your expensive smartphone might feel like the end of the world to you—"

"Flip phone," Rex said.

"One of those thirty quid ones?"

Rex nodded.

Eddie held his hands in prayer pose. "We're expecting a very important phone call."

"Get out of here before I book you for wasting police time. Go on, clear off."

Outside the police station, Eddie buttoned up his suit jacket to protect himself from the cold night air.

Rex grinned.

"What are you happy about?"

"They found a terrorist cell because of us?"

"Because of a jogger?"

"Yeah, but we put everyone on high alert in the first place. We did a good thing for the community."

Eddie's eyebrows pulled together. "By accident. What do we do now?"

Rex stroked his chin. "What would Jason Cole do?"

"Apparently, rip off his clients and sell guns to criminals."

Rex's smile disappeared for a second. "What would the version of Jason Cole we knew do?" He brightened. "Eddie, we're gonna need a disguise."

# TWENTY-EIGHT

E ddie stared at himself in the mirror. He wore a weathered brown cardigan, a pair of rectangular glasses, and overly high trousers.

"I don't see Jason Cole doing this."

Rex stuffed a folded handkerchief into Eddie's top pocket. "They're my granddad's old clothes. Nan kept them all."

"I know that. Why am I wearing them?"

Eddie had spent the night sleeping on Rex's floor, a decision he regretted. To make himself comfortable, Eddie shoved the clutter along the floor to create a six foot by two-foot pit. This had a grave-like effect, which had Eddie up all night contemplating death.

"Because you're gonna be my dad," Rex said. "Here's a map of Cloisterham. We were mugged at these two spots, and we saw Jamie at Safeway." He'd drawn a red circle which encapsulated the three spots. "The only secondary school in the area is Richard Watts Academy. My bet is one of the muggers goes there. We're gonna go to the local school. You'll say I'm being bullied and we'll identify the muggers."

Eddie nodded reluctantly. Rex was dressed in his old school uniform, grey trousers, white shirt, a red tie, and a green V-neck jumper with the school shield embroidered on the right breast. Usually, the logo went on the left, but Rex and Eddie's school used the cheapest uniform designer in England. They got what they paid for.

At the front door, Rex's nan commented on how handsome Eddie looked in his new clothes.

The pair collected the dried out Morris Minor and drove to Richard Watts Academy. They drove through a gate past the tall metal fence with spikes on top. Eddie parked in the visitor parking spot. He scoped out the yellow brick building. The school seemed more like a juvenile detention centre than a school.

Rex pulled a fake moustache from his jacket pocket. "Here, put this on."

"I'll look ridiculous."

"You look too young. You need it."

"Maybe I shouldn't have shaved this morning and kept the stubble. That would have done the trick."

Rex winced, too polite to say his patchy facial hair actually made Eddie look younger.

Eddie knew what the silence meant. He peeled the back paper off and applied the moustache.

The pair exited the car and headed toward the reception entrance. A group of underage teens were openly smoking in their black blazers. They glared at Rex and Eddie as the detectives approached the front door.

Inside the reception area, the secretary sat with a permanent scowl while Eddie signed them in.

A tall woman in her late forties with a short grey pixie

haircut approached the pair. She wore a sleeveless purple dress and thick gold bracelets.

"You're Mr Milton?" the tall teacher asked.

"Yes," Rex said.

The teacher observed Rex's school uniform and gave a smile. "That's adorable." She offered her hand to Eddie. "Mr Milton?"

"Uh, yes that's me."

Eddie put his hand out, but his hand was still a foot away from hers. Rex's granddad's glasses were particularly thick, and Eddie was having a hard time judging distances.

She stepped forward to shake his hand. "I'm Miss Donavon."

"Yes, Miss," Eddie said, having regressed in the school environment. "Uh, sorry."

"Please come with me, and I'll be sure to get to the bottom of this bullying. If it is one of our students, I'll make sure he is punished."

She walked with purpose to her office, and the pair followed. Rex gave Eddie a sly thumbs up and pinched his school jumper. "It's working."

They followed her through a door. Motivational phrases on plaques covered the white walls of Miss Donovan's office. Plastic plants bookended her desk.

Eddie straightened his cap as he read a sign that said: Forget the mistake, remember the lesson.

The duo took a seat as Miss Donovan removed a thick three-ring binder from a cabinet and sat.

"Now, how old do you think the students would be?"

"Oh, eighteen, easily," Eddie said.

She sat with a confused expression. "Sorry, I didn't realise you were there during the incident."

"Uh, I wasn't," Eddie said. "But my Rex can hold his own. They'd be eighteen. Sixteen at the youngest."

She opened the binder. Coloured divider tabs had each school year written on it. Miss Donovan turned the pages to the last tab, year 13. Each page featured rows of school photos. She placed a card border over the pictures to cover the student's names.

Rex scanned through every page of sneering teenagers. They found no photos of the muggers. The year 12 section had the same outcome.

Rex shook his head.

She winced. "Do you want to go to the year elevens or a bit younger?"

Eddie leaned in. "He didn't get bullied by kids, it has to be year eleven. That's sixteen years old right?"

Miss Donovan bobbed her head. "Fifteen to sixteen."

Rex rummaged through the year eleven photos and found a picture of Jamie in a tie and blazer. He had a round blond step haircut.

"That's one of them." Rex pointed at the picture.

Miss Donovan studied the photos. "Ah, I'm afraid he was expelled some time ago."

"Crap," Rex said.

Eddie's disappointed sigh was interrupted by Miss Donovan clearing her throat. She raised her eyebrow and nodded at Rex.

"Right, uh, watch your language, Rex. Why was he expelled?"

"I believe his grandmother became poorly and needed to be moved to a retirement home. His mother took a second job to pay for the care. Then his grades dropped, he misbehaved, began stealing from other students."

Rex and Eddie nodded.

"Do you have his address?" Eddie asked.

She gave a polite smile. "I can't give you his address."

217

Eddie folded his arms. "Right, but you can't punish him?"

"He's already been punished. Have you tried the police?"

"Come on, Rex. Let's go."

"Mr Milton, please. If Rex continues, I'm sure we'll find the other teens bullying him. I will have a word with them."

They searched through the year eleven and year ten photos but found none of the muggers.

"Year nine?" Miss Donovan offered.

Eddie grimaced. "What's that? Fourteen years old?"

"Thirteen to fourteen."

"This is a waste of time," Eddie said.

"Would you, Rex?" Miss Donovan asked.

Rex nodded. A third of the way through the year nine photos Rex found a familiar face.

"That's the boy who gave us the finger."

"While bullying you?" Miss Donovan said.

"No, while we were driving."

Eddie peered at the photo and nodded.

"I'll make a note of it, can you see anyone from the incident?"

"No."

Miss Donovan turned the page. Rex pointed at a photo of the tallest member of the muggers.

"He's one of them."

She checked the picture. "That's a girl."

"Oh sorry, I meant that one," He repointed at the tall mugger.

Miss Donovan frowned. "Yes, that's a girl."

"A girl?" Eddie barked.

"A fourteen-year-old girl." Miss Donovan sat up straight. "Are you being bullied by a girl?"

"No," Eddie said.

"Yes." Rex pointed to the picture of the tall girl. "I punched that one."

A corner of Miss Donovan's mouth lifted. "You punched a girl?"

"Yeah, well I was told to punch the biggest one, so I did."

Miss Donovan checked the picture. "She's big?"

"Well, tall. I guess." Rex bobbed his shoulders. "Tall is a better word. She's not big. More like a crane. As in the bird, not the industrial lifting equipment."

"I think we need to get both her parents and your mother here and talk this out. We can't have you punching my students."

Eddie grabbed the binder. "This can't be right." He brushed aside the name covering border and flicked through the photos.

"Mr Milton, please give that back."

Eddie slammed the binder on the table. "What about that one?" He pointed to the bug-eyed mugger. "That's a boy, right?"

"I'm confused Mr Milton, were you there?"

"No, Miss. I mean— No. I'm sticking with no."

Miss Donovan folded her arms. "Something is going on here."

Eddie flicked to the page with Jamie.

"Mr Milton!" Miss Donovan attempted to tug the book back.

He pulled at the book and caught the name: Jamie Weber.

The sweat on Eddie's face loosened his moustache. He pushed the corner back on this face.

Miss Donovan tucked in her chin. "What's going on here?"

"We have to go," Eddie said.

Rex and Eddie speed-walked down the corridor towards the exit.

Eddie pulled the moustache off. "I can't believe you had me wear this stupid thing."

"Cole used disguises without a problem. I stole it from his office."

"Does the man not sweat?"

Rex pushed the door open as they ran out. "No, he was too cool."

"Oh shut up."

They sprinted to the Morris Minor and got in. Miss Donovan stood at the building entrance. She pointed out Rex and Eddie to a pair of men in tracksuit trousers and polo shirts. The men marched towards the Morris Minor.

"Uh oh," Rex said. "She's set the PE teachers on us."

Eddie turned the ignition. "What are they gonna do? Give us ten press-ups."

The Morris Minor screeched off out the car park, leaving skid marks on the concrete. The car barrelled over the street's speed bumps. Eddie pulled off the granddad cap and swung it into the back.

"We have a name. Jamie Weber. What now?"

Rex smiled. "I could see if my sister knows him?"

# TWENTY-NINE

Rex and Eddie walked past the halls of residence towards the halfway house by the River Invicta.

"Are you sure about this, Eddie? We've never bought drugs before."

"We aren't buying drugs. We go up and tell them we want to speak to Jamie Weber."

Rex twisted his mouth. "Then Jamie will run away like last time."

"No, because thanks to your sister — and us sending her multiple messages of praise in keeping with her emoji etiquette — we know what old people's home his nan is staying at."

Rex's jaw dropped. "You're gonna threaten his nan?"

Eddie rolled his eyes. "Let's get this over with. Remember, we're a couple of druggies hoping to score some drugs. We don't want to scare them off before we've got the information."

"And if they recognise us?"

"No one's going to remember us."

In the distance, the halls of residence door opened.

Karl stepped out with newly dyed red hair. He caught a glimpse of the pair, turned around, and went back inside.

Rex waved a palm at the halls of residence door.

"Okay, fine. Some people remember us. We never bothered the dealer so we should be good."

The pair approached the drug dealer's ground floor window. It was an awning window which only opened out a few inches from the bottom. This gave the dealer a sense of professionalism, like a bank teller's screen.

Behind the glass, a young man with fuzzy brown hair covering his eyes looked up. He had a big, thick nose and a weak chin.

"You like to paint?" he asked.

Eddie put on a toothy smile. "I'd, uh, like to score some drugs, please."

The dealer sneered. "What's score?"

Rex and Eddie glanced at each other in a panic.

Eddie turned back to the dealer. "As in to get, purchase? Do people not say score anymore?"

"Nah, fam. It's pick up. You pick up." He pulled a face like he'd detected a bad smell. "Not score."

"Pick up?" Eddie grimaced. "That doesn't sound right. You pick up laundry."

Rex shrugged having never washed his own clothes.

"I haven't tried laundry," the dealer said. "What's that like?"

Eddie tucked in his chin. "You haven't done laundry?"

"Do you smoke it or snort it?"

"You wash it."

"Sounds weird. I'd try it."

Eddie tried looking over the dealer at the dark room, hoping for a clue.

"You two want to pick up some paint or what? You're acting well bait."

Eddie's shoulders dropped. "I want to speak with Jamie Weber."

The dealer sniggered. "Don't know what you're talking about."

"You tell him we want our phone back. If he doesn't return it in the next hour, I'm going to Grizdale House Nursing Home to see his nan. I'll tell her he was expelled from school, he works for drug dealers, and mugs people on the side."

The young man blew air. "Harsh."

Rex nodded.

Jamie stepped into view at the window, he'd been in the room the whole time. "You leave my nan out of this."

"Where's the phone?"

"I ain't got it."

"You better have it. It doesn't belong to me, it belongs to The Cloisterham Massive, or The Cloister Posse — one of the two — and they want to call us. If you don't give me the phone, I'll tell them you've got it, and where your nan lives."

Rex mouthed, "Sorry," to Jamie.

"We need the phone, now. It's a life or death situation."

Jamie's upper lip tightened. "You're the contact for the kidnapping, aren't you?"

"Phone, now."

"Give me a minute." He unzipped a duffel bag of phones and wallets."

Rex peered into the bag. "I'll have my phone and wallet as well."

"Mate, I can't be going through this whole bag."

"You want to explain that to your nan?"

Jamie sighed. He poured the bag contents on the bed and spread them out. "You can have any two phones you want. One wallet as well."

Eddie pointed out his mobile and wallet. He lengthened his neck to get a better look.

"That's the flip phone."

He took the items through the gap in the open window. Eddie opened the flip phone. The display said 8 missed calls, no messages.

"Thank you very much," Eddie said in the most insincere way possible.

The pair turned and walked away.

"Oi," Jamie said.

Rex and Eddie turned back.

"Without the phone, how were you gonna tell the kidnappers about my nan?"

Eddie shrugged. "I hadn't thought that far ahead."

---

The flip phone lay on their desk as the detectives waited for the kidnappers to call. The office phone had eleven messages, all from the Archers no doubt.

Eddie checked the mobile again, no new calls. He made sure the ringer was on, and the volume was high. On average, he'd done this every three minutes for the last half hour.

"Watched sausages never boil," Rex said.

"You boil sausages?"

Rex's forehead wrinkled. "A watched pot never boils?"

"A watched pot never stews?" Eddie offered. "I don't know what the saying is now. We've talked about it too long, and they all sound weird."

"Do you want to listen to Daryl's music CD while we wait? Some of the tracks are quite good."

"I'm not a fan of electro."

"One of them has this lyric where he talks about

wanting to disappear and having a secret. You think it might be a message?"

"This isn't some *I am the Walrus*, Paul is dead, hidden meaning nonsense."

Rex sighed. "You're right. I haven't tried playing the track backwards yet. Maybe there's a clue in that."

Eddie groaned.

A ringing alerted the pair. Eddie picked up the office phone in a panic.

"Hello?"

The ringing continued. Eddie hung up the receiver

Rex grabbed the flip phone and answered. "Hello?"

Eddie waved his hands, calling for the phone to be handed to him. Rex shook his head.

"This is the kidnappers," the voice was disguised. "If you want to see your son—"

"This is the detective," Rex said.

"What?"

"He's not my son, he's my client. Well, my client's son... or brother."

"You what?"

"It's not an incest thing, we have clients who are both parents and a sibling. Separate people."

Eddie tried to grab the phone, but Rex ducked and dodged each attempt.

"Where's the money?" the voice asked.

"It's gone because you chose a bad place, and didn't pick it up in time."

"We said no police."

"Then don't ask us to leave a suspicious package in a public place. That's on you. We didn't call the police."

Eddie snatched the phone. Rex attempted to grab it back, but Eddie kicked his leg out repeatedly to keep Rex away.

"Where is the ransom now?" the voice said.

"You don't know?"

"We left when the feds arrived."

"You mean the police? They blew it up like it was a terrorist threat. Controlled explosion."

The voice fell silent. Eddie worried they'd hung up.

"Hello? Where's Daryl now? Is he still alive?"

"We still have him. Alive."

"Can I speak to him? To know he's alive?"

"No."

"Please?"

"No."

Rex waved. He puffed his chest out. "Act tough."

Eddie shooed him away. "So we brought the money to the drop off location. When do we get Daryl?"

"We still need money. Why would I give you Archer for nothing?"

"Because… it's the right thing to do?"

Rex whispered. "Tell them about the ransom."

Eddie put his finger to his lip, telling Rex to be quiet.

The kidnapper sighed. "We didn't see no explosion. We want the ransom."

Eddie smiled. "I can give you jewellery and stuff. Silverware. Paintings. Do you like boats?"

"Cash, we need cash for a deal, pronto."

Eddie winced. "I mean, it's just… all the cash got blown up so—"

"Bring the gold and stuff, but you come with cash — Fifty K — or Archer is dead. You get me?"

"Fifty grand in cash, and we pay the rest in valuable items. What if we can't get the money? This is a bit short notice."

"No money and we kill Daryl. The drop is at midnight. Meet us at—"

With Eddie's guard down, Rex grabbed the phone.

"No." Eddie threw his hands in the air. "What are you doing?"

"Taking control," Rex whispered. He returned to his normal volume, but did a voice-disguiser impression, "We'll meet at the Cloisterham Football Stadium at nine p.m."

"You messing with me?"

"I'm calling the shots. We need to meet somewhere neutral. We tried it your way, and the money got destroyed. You want your ransom, then you'll do as I say."

Eddie raised his eyebrows, Rex was entirely convincing.

"There's a game on tonight," the kidnapper said. "I'm not sure it will be empty by nine."

"Okay, midnight, but because I said so. Because that's the way I want it. Your comments were taken into consideration, but I'm in charge."

"Midnight, Cloisterham Football Stadium. No feds."

The phone clicked and buzzed.

"He's hung up," Rex said.

"You can stop doing the kidnapper voice, now. In fact, you never have to do it again."

---

The Morris Minor pulled up on the gravel driveway of the Archer's country home.

Eddie sighed. "We're gonna get caught. First, we told the kidnappers we'll have cash, which we don't. Now, we have to tell the Archers the kidnappers picked their stuff, which they didn't."

Rex unbuckled his seatbelt. "Relax, Eddie. We made it this far. We're the best detectives in town, remember?"

"You keep pointing that out like it's a good thing."

"Well, isn't it?"

"Not when the previous best detective got blown into itty bitty pieces it's not."

Rex shrugged. "Need help picking the items?"

"No, it's fine. I highlighted all the small valuable stuff, that way we can fit it all in the Morris Minor. No boats or any of that nonsense."

"Muskets?"

Eddie highlighted another line. "Fine, but only so you won't be tempted to barter for them when the job's done."

Rex's smile dropped. He'd blown his chance of owning them.

The pair exited the car and stepped across the gravel to the Archer residence. Eddie raised his hand to knock on the thick wood door. It creaked open before he could touch the wood.

"You're here," Maude said. "Thank, God. Mother and Father have been worried sick."

She beckoned them in and closed the door. The detective duo followed her to the living room and sat.

For a brief second, Eddie felt comfortable in the soft red sofa. It was a short holiday compared to sleeping in camping gear or sitting in the car. He wished he could take a two-day nap on the thing, but Mr and Mrs Archer arrived.

"We've been trying to ring you all day," Mr Archer said. "What happened?"

"We gave the deposit to the kidnapper." Eddie cleared his throat. "Sorry we couldn't get back to you sooner, we basically negotiated all night. Right, Rex?"

Rex shifted in his seat, uncomfortable with the lie. "Yes?" he said in a soft voice.

Mr Archer leaned in. "And?"

"They picked out some things, mostly for their metal value. Gold, silver, crystal, that kind of stuff."

"They weren't interested in any of the paintings?" Mrs Archer wrinkled her nose.

"Just the ones with frames made of gold?"

Mr Archer took the spreadsheet and put on his reading glasses. "The paintings are the most valuable. I think you should have pushed the paintings a little more. They didn't want the boat?"

He breathed a sigh of relief. His wife nudged him in disgust.

"The boat can be traced," Maude said. "They only want what can be melted down."

"Right, yeah." Eddie nodded rapidly. "All metals. Jewellery, that necklace." He pointed at Mrs Archer's neck.

"But that wasn't on the list."

Eddie gestured with a beckoning palm. "Still we promised them gold, all the gold and precious metals you have. It's the kidnapping equivalent of the cash for gold shops."

Mrs Archer handed over the necklace.

"You know how there's cash for gold shops," Rex said. "How come jewellery shops aren't called gold for cash? That's essentially what they are?"

"Not now, Rex." Eddie sighed. "Also, they want more cash. Fifty grand."

Mr Archer pointed his chin up. "It's not like we didn't already give them thirty-eight thousand, is it?"

Eddie cleared his throat. "Good... good point."

"They can sell the items themselves. It's all the correct value."

"We have the insurance value papers to prove it," Mrs Archer said.

"Still, if you have any cash, any friends that will lend to you?"

Mr Archer leaned back in his leather armchair. "You'll have to work with what you've got."

---

The detective pair loaded up the car boot with the various bartered items for the exchange. They placed the paintings on top of the rest of the car's contents. Rex rammed the back doors closed with a clash of precious metal and the tear of something valuable.

"You'll be a bit more careful with our son, I'd hope," Mr Archer said.

The Archer couple turned their noses up and headed indoors. Maude stepped along the gravel driveway and gave a pitiful smile.

"My parents do care about Daryl," she said. "They really are broke. It's been a tough year."

Rex tilted his head. "We still get paid though, right?"

"Not now," Eddie whispered. He smiled at Maude. "It'll be okay. We'll get your brother back." He put his hand on Maude's shoulder. "I can assure you, Daryl is in safe hands, we are professional."

Maude's eyes welled up a little. "Thanks."

Rex and Eddie got in the car, and Eddie tried to start the engine. The car engine was flat.

Eddie wound down the window. "I'm sorry, can you give us a push?"

She let out a laugh that also cleared her eyes of the tears.

Rex got out and pushed with Maude while Eddie pushed from the front and controlled the steering wheel.

As they got the car rolling, he turned the ignition, and the engine started.

"Sorry, Maude," Eddie called out as he jumped into the car.

"Sorry," Rex added as he ran to catch up and get in the passenger door.

The Morris Minor tottered down the country lane.

Eddie huffed. "They aren't gonna accept this. They want cash. We're gonna die tonight."

"We've got eleven hours until the drop-off. We could open a jewellery shop and sell the stuff."

Eddie perked up. "Of course."

"Really? Can we call it Gold for Cash?"

"I've got a better idea."

# THIRTY

"This is a lot of jewellery." The Pakistani shop owner placed the necklaces on a scale.

He was short and round with grey hair parted to the side and a thick, black moustache.

Rex and Eddie were at the Cash for Gold shop, a dozen doors down from Cole's burnt office. The windows were opaque, letting nothing but the shadow of the bars come through. The dull grey room had security cameras in every corner.

"You do silver too, right?" Eddie said.

"We do all precious metals, diamonds as well."

"Great," Rex dumped another bag of items on the counter.

"What do we need to do?" Eddie asked.

The man held his palm to his forehead. "Why are you selling so much?"

"Death in the family." Eddie gave an inappropriate smile.

"So sad," the shopkeeper said.

Eddie turned solemn and nodded a little too long. "Yes,

very much so." After giving an appropriate moment of silence, he lightened. "What do you think we can get?"

"Oh, well I'll need to examine and weigh it all. This could be thirty thousand. Maybe even forty grand."

"That sounds fine," Eddie said.

Rex leaned to Eddie's ear. "Doesn't it have to be fifty?"

"We give them what we can. Cash in a bag will at least get them talking to us."

The shop owner handed over a clipboard. "You just sign this form with your name and address—"

A corner of Eddie's top lip rose. "Is that necessary?"

"It's the law."

Eddie's shoulders hunched.

Rex clicked his fingers. "What if you lost that piece of paper and maybe we absentmindedly left a grand on the table. Right here?"

Eddie's heartbeat rose, worried about the reaction.

The man smiled, turning his thick moustache into a second furry smile. He looked twice as happy.

Eddie calmed.

"I can be clumsy," he said. "I'll work out the price, we'll get the transaction started, and you'll have your money tomorrow."

"Tomorrow?" Eddie stuttered. "Not today?"

"I can't have that amount of money today, I have to test the metal's quality and give you a final offer. It's a twenty-four hour waiting period."

Distraught, Eddie searched around for something, a kind of hope. Behind the glass windows, between the bars stood the silhouette of a tall man.

Eddie grabbed his partner's arm. "It's the third man. He's here."

Rex and Eddie quietly poured the goods back into the bags.

"Come on, gentlemen. You can wait a day, can't you? I'll give you a good price."

Eddie watched the silhouette fade as the person stepped away. "Sorry," he whispered to the shopkeeper. "We have to go."

---

Rex and Eddie darted out of the Cash for Gold shop. The tall man rushed away from the window into a side alley.

At the corner of the alleyway, Cole's black cat sat and cleaned its front paws. Rex stepped closer. The cat hissed at him. It backed up into the shadowy alley and calmed at the feet of the tall man. Rex and Eddie looked up to see a clean-shaven Jason Cole. He wore a black leather jacket instead of his usual brown coat. Other than a little red shaving nick on his chin, Cole was unscathed. He smirked.

Rex and Eddie stared, slack-jawed.

"Cole?" Eddie said.

"Evening, gentlemen." He nodded to the parked Morris Minor. "Get in the car. Pull it into the alleyway, and leave the back door unlocked. I'll explain everything on the way."

The pair got into the car, buckled their seat belts, and drove to the alleyway. Cole got in the back seat. With all the items in the back, it was a bit of a squeeze. He sat forward to avoid the corners of the painting frames stabbing his shoulder.

Eddie put his foot on the accelerator. "So, you're not dead then."

Rex gawked. "How did you survive?"

"I had to go black."

The detective duo glanced at each other, confused.

"As in, free of surveillance."

Rex's nose crinkled. "I don't get it."

"He means he faked his death," Eddie said.

"I was being watched by the gangs, I knew they'd find me and possibly be led to you. By taking myself out of the picture I allowed you to continue the investigation while I went covert."

Rex nodded. "Cool."

"It's not cool. It means he spent this whole time watching us do his dirty work."

"I've not been anywhere near you. I've been with my sources."

Eddie narrowed his eyes at the rear-view mirror reflection of Cole.

"How'd you do that?" Rex smiled. "Did you go under disguise? Costumes and make-up and stuff?"

"It's a bit more complicated than that."

"You mean, voices too?"

"Come on Rex, if he could do voices do you think he'd stick to that monotonous tone."

Cole didn't react. "I used my informants to gather intel. If the gangs thought I was alive, I'd never get that information."

"But now you don't have a van or any of the kit."

"My contract covers unlimited expenses."

"Really? How much are you getting paid?" Eddie asked.

"That's not necessary information."

"Because the Archers are broke. Did you collect that intel? They're trading in heirlooms for ransom. You think they're going to pay you?"

"We retrieve Daryl and the ransom money, take our fees, and return the rest to the Archers."

Eddie sneered. "What money?"

"The Archers made many withdrawals this week. It's my understanding they had fifty grand."

Eddie peered into the rear-view mirror. "You see, the money's gone."

"You already gave it to the kidnappers?"

Rex slouched. "No. It was blown up."

"Why?" Cole asked, looking lost for the first time.

"The gang made us leave it on the street. It got mistaken for a suspicious package, so the police came by and—"

Cole's shoulders stiffened. "You idiots. You total morons."

"It's not our fault the whole town's on terror alert," Rex said.

Eddie cleared his throat, knowing full well it was their fault.

"Me and Eddie have another idea for the ransom."

"It's Rex's idea."

"What is it?" Cole said with resignation.

Rex pulled the over-the-shoulder bag from under his seat and tapped it. "Plan B. We called in a favour with a friend."

Eddie shifted in his seat. "Forget it. We're not doing it."

The Morris Minor entered a roundabout and joined the highway.

Cole looked out the window. "Where's the drop off happening?"

Rex grinned. "Cloisterham Football Stadium."

"Smart choice on their part. We'd only have one way out, and they can hide extra men in the stands."

Rex's grin faded. "Do we have any advantages?"

Cole nodded. "Me."

Eddie eyed Cole in the rear-view mirror. "Why should we work with you? D.I. Sumner says you're a gun runner."

Cole's eyebrows furrowed. "That's what they think of me? You've seen the way I operate. I don't do guns."

"He said you've been involved in lots of cases involving gun sales."

"Because I'm trying to keep guns out of Cloisterham."

The Morris Minor turned into a roundabout and joined a four-lane A-road. Eddie kept in the slow lane as he preferred not to go over fifty miles-per-hour. The speed limit was seventy, but that made the car chatter.

"How'd you fake your death?" Rex asked. "Rigged the van for explosives while we slept? I bet you brought us down to witness it." He clicked his fingers. "And jumped in the river as the fire distracted us?"

Eddie tutted. "Don't be so ridiculous."

Cole nodded. "He got it right."

Rex smiled. "What? Exactly that?"

"Yep."

Eddie recoiled. "But the River Invicta isn't suitable for humans, it's barely suitable for fish." He frowned. " Wait, so you got us to stand by your van, and you set up our side to blow up first."

"Yeah."

Rex stuck his jaw out. "What if we got hurt?"

"Or blown up?" Eddie added.

"The risk was minimal compared to your driving."

Eddie turned to Cole to give an evil stare. The Morris Minor veered into the hard shoulder.

Rex recoiled. "Uh, Eddie. Eyes on the road."

Eddie straightened up but kept an evil eye on the rear-view mirror.

Cole stared back. "I believe The Cloister Posse has re-joined The Massive."

Rex faced the backseat. "That's why we saw the guys

with the snake and cyborg tattoos at Cole's flat." Rex turned back to the windscreen "Pick a lane."

"Yeah." Eddie shook his head. "In and out of gangs every week, it's ridiculous."

"He means you're swerving over the road markings." Cole pointed at the road ahead.

Eddie adjusted the steering wheel. "Sorry, it's not every day I have a dead man in my car."

"We'll all be dead if you don't watch your driving. The Massive has a new drug called paint, they plan to launch it wide."

Eddie's eyebrows narrowed. "A new one? Like in a lab?"

"None of them are technically new. They mix two drugs together with other stuff: pancake flour, arrowroot, one even uses ground ginger. So many are mixed with flour now they even offer a gluten-free option."

"Snorting ginger sounds uncomfortable," Rex squirmed in his seat.

Eddie straightened his neck, setting off a series of tiny cracks. "It sounds unnecessary."

"In my investigation, I discovered Daryl Archer sold the drugs he found to a rival gang called Wainsbury Boyz. That's boys with a z."

Eddie crinkled his nose. "Another gang?"

"When The Massive and The Posse split, The Boyz tried to move into their territory."

"So The Massive killed the gang member Daryl found?" Eddie said.

"That's right. The Boyz broke the rules, so The Massive retaliated."

Rex tucked in his chin. "Who makes the rules?"

"Nowhere is where it gets complicated. These gangs

are affiliates of The Palmer gang, who have run the whole south-east since the sixties. You heard of them?"

Rex bobbed his head. "Kind of."

"All the little gangs, they're like affiliate gangs, that pay a percentage to the Palmers."

Eddie furrowed his brow. "How is this important to us?"

"The Palmers protect the gangs. If one gang fights another, the Palmers punish the instigator. It rarely happens because the gangs have different specialities: sharking, smuggling, counterfeiting, that sort of thing.

"But The Boyz and The Massive both deal in drugs?" Eddie said.

Cole nodded. "There's always been tension."

"So why would The Boyz enter The Massive's territory? They knew The Palmer gang would come down on them."

"Because The Palmer gang is having a succession crisis. Their leader was jailed, so they've turned a blind eye. Plus no-one can prove The Boyz did anything."

A corner of Eddie's mouth turned up. "Except you?"

"It's a working theory. Which leads to my other theory: when The Massive split into two they appeared weak. The Boyz saw this as an easy fight."

"They're using the split as a chance to do a land grab?" Rex said.

Cole nodded. "I believe the split was a ruse to rile up The Boyz. So The Boyz would publicly attack."

Eddie tightened his grip on the steering wheel. "When we saw snake tattoo and cyborg tattoo working together, it was because they were always in the same gang. It was The Massive the whole time."

Rex pressed his lips together. "So The Boyz broke the

code of conduct, which allows The Massive to retaliate in self-defence."

"Once The Palmer gang have reorganised they'll give The Massive a slap on the wrist."

Eddie's right eye twitched. "So why did you make me human bait for The Massive?"

"I needed to see their new operation. I couldn't get close myself, so I sent you, for the good of Cloisterham. I'm sorry I wasn't more honest."

"What's Daryl got to do with this power struggle?" Eddie asked.

"Nothing really. Daryl found a dead member of The Massive, who was shot by the Wainsbury Boyz. He took the drugs on the body and sold them to The Boyz. The Massive considered the drugs stolen and Daryl owed them a debt."

"How'd they know about it?"

"Security camera footage and a dodgy police officer who tipped them off. The Massive wanted their money back. When they learnt Daryl's parents were rich, they knew they could get a lot more from him."

"They want a war chest to use against The Wainsbury Boyz," Eddie said.

"They buy weapons. Under price their new drug, which would cut The Boyz' profits. They can then recruit the disloyal Boyz, and kill the rest."

Rex's eyes widened. "A takeover?"

Eddie looked at the car ahead. "I'm going the speed limit."

"No not that kind of takeover. A corporate takeover."

"With a death toll," Cole said.

Eddie scrunched up his face. "So? Let them get on with it. They can kill each other off and let the rest of us continue with our lives."

"It'll be a massacre with innocent victims. Not including the overdoses from having a highly potent and cheap drug everywhere. Cloisterham ends up with one large, confident gang running the town."

Eddie frowned. "A couple of insecure gangs doesn't sound any better."

"As long as they're afraid of each other, it keeps them in check. I've reason to believe they've arranged to purchase fifty grand's worth of guns tomorrow."

"That's what the ransom is for." Rex's jaw went slack. "We're helping them buy weapons."

"By doing our job and paying the ransom?" Eddie said.

Cole raised an eyebrow. "The job is to return Daryl. How we do that is up for debate."

Eddie scoffed. "Alive, I think are the parameters set up by the employer."

"Alive doesn't mean we have to hand over the ransom."

"So why did you take the case, if you think it's so bad for Cloisterham?"

"I had to control the situation, not let some idiots ruin it." Cole paused. "No offence."

"None taken." Rex smiled, oblivious that Cole was referring to them.

"We need to maintain balance and stop The Massive from arming up. We try to get Daryl back, alive, for the Archers. We return the ransom, arrange payment for our services, everyone goes home happy."

Rex raised his eyebrows. "Except the kidnappers."

Eddie shook his head. "This sounds like a lot of assumptions. We don't have all the facts."

"You never have all the facts," Cole said. "You have to fill in the blanks."

"With your gut?" Rex asked.

"Exactly."

Rex raised a fist in celebration.

Eddie rolled his jaw to loosen it. "And what if Daryl gets killed?"

"We don't get paid, but we save the town a lot of trouble."

Eddie winced. "And what if one of us gets killed?"

"Don't worry boys, I've got a plan."

# THIRTY-ONE

E ddie pulled the Morris Minor to the kerb outside Cloisterham Football Stadium. The stadium was a short walk from East Cloisterham Train Station, at the edge of the town.

There used to be pubs along the route. Too many fights between the Cloisterham supporters and the rival fans led to the landlords selling up.

Now the stadium was only surrounded by residential houses. After each game, petrified homeowners would watch through the window's netting, expecting the football fans to kick off and burn a car.

Close to midnight, the street was quiet, and the nearby house lights were off. Eddie parked on the double yellow lines near the front corner. The stadium had covered stands down both of the long sides. The metal covers were painted blue to match the team's home kit.

"Let's go," Rex said.

"I can't leave it here, we might get towed."

"Don't worry about it." Cole leaned forward between

the two front seats. He pulled a disabled badge from his top coat pocket.

Eddie twisted his face. "How many things you got in that coat?"

"It's his utility coat," Rex said.

Cole hung the disabled badge from the rear-view mirror.

"During the exchange make sure they're in the middle of the pitch. I'll throw on the north stadium lights, and when they're blinded, you extract Daryl and run for it."

"Perfect." Eddie sneered. "We stand in front of the men with guns while you provoke them, and hopefully we'll get out alive. That's the plan."

"If they bring handguns don't panic. A decent hit requires a non-moving close target. The light will give you the brief seconds you need to get out of range."

"What if they bring sunglasses?" Rex asked.

Cole tightened his lips. "Why would they bring sunglasses?"

Eddie furrowed his brow and turned to Rex. "Yeah, why would they bring sunglasses?"

"To look cool."

Eddie turned to Cole. "What if they wear sunglasses?"

"The odds of getting shot are minimal."

"But not zero?"

"Is anything ever zero?"

Eddie's lips tightened. "My enthusiasm for this plan is fast approaching zero."

"Come on, Eddie," Rex said. "We have to do it. Gang warfare will hurt people who can't protect themselves, like my nan and sister."

Eddie sighed. "Fine, I'm doing this for Rex's nan and sister, and other innocent people." He pointed at Cole. "Not because you told me to."

Rex picked up the over-shoulder bag they stole from Spin Doctor. "Best not forget the fifty k."

"I thought the money was gone," Cole said. "You have fifty thousand pounds?"

Eddie pursed his lips. "Kind of."

Rex and Eddie left Cole at the car and walked along the stadium.

"How do we get in?" Eddie asked.

Rex pointed ahead. "When I was a teenager I volunteered as a ball boy, we entered over there. It's a doorway to under the stands. The door is so battered, you whack it a little and it unlocks."

They walked around the stadium to a doorway covered by a steel fence with pointed tips.

"Ah, this is new," Rex tried to wriggle an unmoving post. "Must have upgraded when they went up a division."

"Right, so what's Plan B?"

Rex scratched his head as he studied the fence's pointed posts. "Climb?"

"What about motion detectors? Security cameras? That sort of thing?"

"They aren't in the premier league, Eddie. It's a fence. That's all."

"Let's go back to the car."

After explaining the situation to Cole, he parked the Morris Minor close to the fence. Rex clambered up on the car and clutched the top of the steel fence. He raised his leg to the top, placing it between two spikes. Eddie climbed up on the car and gave Rex a push to the other side of the fence.

As Eddie climbed over, the fear of getting attached to the spike distracted Eddie from the fear of falling. He climbed forward but slipped. He fell head first towards the concrete ground but stopped mid-air. His laces had looped one of the steel spikes.

Braced for a fall, Eddie held out his hands and froze. A few seconds later he opened his eyes and crossed his arms in annoyance. He quickly calmed as the blood flowing to his head had a therapeutic effect.

Rex lifted Eddie up, nestling Eddie's face in his armpit. Eddie shook his foot away from the spike. His foot loosened out of the shoe. He fell forward, knocking Rex back and using him to cushion the fall.

The pair got up and dusted themselves off.

Eddie attempted to get his shoe by jumping at the spike. He accidentally pushed the shoe over the other side of the fence.

Despite squeezing his hand between the bars, the shoe was just out of reach.

Rex beckoned Eddie over. They walked down a corridor under the stadium seating and entered the pitch. Eddie's exposed sock soaked up the wet grass with each step. They reached the middle of the field.

"Cole said the middle," Eddie spun around to the north, "facing the north lights."

Rex frowned. "But he's turning on the north lights isn't he?"

"No, he's turning on the north facing lights—"

"Oi," a gravelly voice said from the rafters. "Whatcha think you're doing 'ere."

A single light bounced to and fro down the steps towards the pitch. Under the moonlight stepped a short old man in a security uniform holding a Maglite. He marched along the grass towards the detectives.

"This is private property."

Eddie put on a polite smile. "Sorry, it's just, we can't go."

"I think you can."

"No, you see. We have an appointment."

The security guard reached the pair and put his hands on his hips. "Let me guess. Another scattering of the ashes, is it?"

"Is that allowed?" Eddie thought ashes scattering was more likely to allow them to stay than a kidnapping exchange.

"It ain't food for the grass. It's against 'ealth and safety."

"Please, it's just this one time."

"One time, he says. You know 'ow many times I've 'eard that? If we let everyone that wanted to be buried 'ere 'ave their wish, you wouldn't see the grass. It would be the world's biggest ashtray. You think people would come to see that?"

"I would," Rex said. "Could even be in the Guinness Book of Records."

"Funny man are you?"

"I'm serious. Is Cloisterham in the Guinness Book of Records?"

"Not that I know of." The old man lost his steam. "Now get out of 'ere."

He escorted them both by the arm to the main entrance.

"This doesn't happen in the movies," Rex muttered. "You can go to any stadium at any time and pay a kidnapping ransom, buy a nuclear warhead, or whatever."

The security guard unlocked the entrance gate. "No ashes, no ransoms, and definitely no warheads."

He shoved them to the pavement where Snakebite and Cyborg stood with Hook Nose and Stocky behind them. Cyborg and Hook Nose pulled modified starter pistols on the detectives and security guard.

# THIRTY-TWO

R ex and Eddie took a step back towards the stadium's main gate, leaving the old guard out in front.

Cyborg and Hook Nose pointed their modified starter pistols on the detectives, neither concerned by the security guard.

Snakebite sneered at the old man. Stocky, who had received a knee to the crotch in Cole's flat, glared at Eddie.

Eddie mouthed, "Sorry." He backed away, hitting his back against the stadium's turnstiles.

At the sight of the gang, the security guard's head had lowered into a hunch. He straightened his neck and stuck out his chest. "You're a bit late for the game, fellas. Best come back Saturday."

Snakebite glared. "Nah bruv, don't think so."

The guard turned to Rex and Eddie. "This your appointment, is it?"

They nodded.

"As I told your friends. This ain't no place to 'old a funeral."

"Take a break, old man," Snakebite said. "Unless you want to be early for your funeral."

The guard's Adam's apple bounced up and down. "Well, uh, I think I'm due a break. Maybe get myself a cuppa."

Eddie gulped at the idea of being left alone as if the old man security guard could have actually protected them. The guard walked down the street past a black BMW. A pale Daryl sat in the back seat, his once bouncy hair now flat and thin. After six days of being held captive, he was shaken and stared into the distance. Another gang member leaned on the car's hood with his arms crossed. Rex elbowed Eddie and nodded to the car.

Eddie attempted to give Daryl a confident smile to let him know he was safe. Instead, he bared his teeth. Daryl leaned away from the window and avoided eye contact.

In the dim light, Eddie strained to get a better look at Snakebite. The gang member tipped his chin up, allowing more streetlight on his face. He had no eyebrows, just like Rex.

The anxious detective studied the others. All of them had different eyebrow shaves. Stocky had shaved his off completely. Hook Nose cut his into vertical stripes. Cyborg had shaved the right eyebrow off leaving the other alone.

"What you staring at?" Cyborg popped his shoulders back.

"I was just… admiring your eyebrows?"

"It's a gang thing," the Hook Nose said. "It was Pete's idea."

He nodded his head towards Stocky, the one Rex had told his missing eyebrows were a style choice.

Rex leaned towards Eddie. "Looks like I picked a good time to lose my eyebrows, it's fashionable. What a coincidence."

"Because you started it," Eddie whispered back through gritted teeth.

"I'm a trendsetter?" Rex raised his painted on eyebrows. "How do I remove these?"

"Not now, Rex."

Cyborg waved his gun, pointing the pair back onto the pitch. Rex and Eddie raised their hands higher as they walked backwards. The Massive entered the stadium, Stocky closed the gate behind him. The whole gang sneered as they followed the detective duo to the middle of the pitch.

Cyborg eyed the bag at Eddie's side. "You got the fifty k and the gold?"

"Yeah, well I mean it's not like gold bullion or anything. It's jewellery, and antiques, and—"

"Muskets," Rex added. "You got Daryl?"

"Yeah."

Eddie tapped Rex's shoulder. "We saw him in their car, remember."

"Just following protocol." Rex adjusted his collar.

Snakebite stepped forward and held out his hand for the bag. "You show me the money, I show you Daryl. We swap and my man brings you the hostage."

Snakebite pointed at Rex. "Your man brings the money."

"His man?" Rex asked. "I'm my own man. At the very least I'm our man."

Eddie raised a finger. "About the ransom—"

"Ace. Show it."

"It's in assets."

"What's that mean?"

"Since the original ransom was blown up we can't pay with cash."

We have valuable items instead."

"Nah, bruv, we want money. Mulla. You get me?"

"I get you."

"'Cause you don't be acting like you get me. You hear me?"

Eddie grimaced. "I hear you. The assets are all I can do. They'd need to sell this stuff to get the cash. You'd have to keep Daryl longer. That's bed and board, that's eating into your profits. This way, you can sell on the stuff yourself."

"We know you like money," Rex said. "So we picked up something a little extra for you. I think you'll like it."

"Is it money?"

Eddie shook his head. "No."

Snakebite huffed. "Chuck it to me."

Eddie dropped the bag towards the gang. Cyborg reached down and picked it up.

"The thing about the bag is—"

"Shut up." Cyborg opened it up, the inside was full of pages of postage stamps. "Bro, what's this?"

"Those are postage stamps to the value of fifty grand."

"What am I gonna do with those?"

Rex raised a hand. "That's legal tender. You can pay for things with it. It's money in the bank."

Snake Tattoo shook his head. "This is a joke, right? Where do you even get this?"

Eddie swallowed. "We have a friend at the post office."

Rex gave a stern look. "It's legal tender, you're not allowed to turn it down."

Eddie leaned to Rex and whispered. "You're not allowed to kidnap people either, I'm not sure you're gonna win them over."

"Or you can send a letter," Rex said.

"I got an email address, bruv. I don't think I've ever sent a letter. For real."

"It's a deposit," Eddie said. "It's still of value. When you bring Daryl to us, we bring in the assets. It's a sign of goodwill. Like leaving a credit card at the hotel lobby, or a watch."

"A watch?" Snakebite asked. "You want to leave a watch? Is it Rolex?"

"I think we have a watch in the car if that's something you want."

"Nah, bruv, because I got a phone. A watch is useless, like your stamps."

Cyborg slammed the bag closed. "Pshhh, stamps. You're jokers." Infuriated, he stepped forward and pointed the modified starter pistol at Eddie's head.

"Four hundred thousand in gold," Eddie blurted out. "I mean it's not all gold — jewellery, silverware, paintings, and the watch—"

"I don't want no watch."

"Precious metals," Eddie said. "Lots of those."

Cyborg narrowed one eye, targeting the gun at Eddie's skull. "Where is this ransom?"

Eddie's eye darted to the stadium entrance and back. He needed Daryl brought in so they could grab him when the stadium lights turned on.

"When you bring in Daryl, we'll call in our guy."

"You brought someone?" Snakebite said as he marched to the front of the gang.

"Well, I brought our guy. We needed to have a guy."

"I said come alone, just you two."

"Come on, there's four of you. I can't rightly leave a car full of valuables on the street. It would get nicked."

Snakebite thought it over and nodded. "Fine." He turned to Hook Nose. "Check out the stands. Make sure they ain't got no help waiting."

Hook Nose swaggered into the unlit stands.

"Bring in Daryl and my man will come," Eddie said.

Cyborg nodded at the stocky hoodie. He nodded back and headed to the entryway to collect Daryl.

Eddie glanced up at the lights on their side. The duo faced east while the gang faced west. For Cole's plan to work, he needed to manoeuvre the gang to face the floodlights.

Snakebite turned up the corner of his top lip. "Where's your shoe?"

Eddie put on a half-smile. "Let's keep the talk to business."

"We hung it up on the telegraph pole," Rex said. "You know. To let you know we were here."

"Why would that tell me you were here?"

The detectives made small, sideways steps. The gang moved to maintain distance, unknowingly being positioned in front of the lights.

"You know, because drug gangs use shoes to mark territories and drop-offs and stuff." Rex sniggered and pointed his thumb at Snakebite "I thought you were a bad boy drug dealer."

Rex and Eddie navigated the circling gang beyond the stopping point and moved back to get it right.

Snakebite stepped forward. "I am a bad boy drug dealer."

Rex tucked in his chin. "So, no shoes as a sign?"

They all shook their heads.

"How would that even work?" Cyborg asked. "You stand under the shoes all day and wait for the dealer to show up? What kind of idiot would do that?"

"No, you're right," Rex mumbled.

As Stocky brought in a distressed Daryl, the hostage had a skittish walk. Rex and Eddie stopped circling. The gang stood south, and Rex and Eddie faced the north.

"Are you okay?" Eddie asked.

Daryl flared his nostrils. "Who are you?"

"We're your hostage negotiators, Maude hired us."

"You're a day late."

Eddie drew his eyebrows together. "Sorry about that, we had a bit of a mix-up."

Cyborg threw his hands in the air. "Now you get your man to bring me my loot."

Eddie nodded. "Well, I guess now we do it. We make the exchange."

*We didn't communicate a signal*, Eddie thought. *Cole could have driven off with all the ransom stuff. And my car.*

Cyborg sneered. "Yeah, bring out the ransom."

"Right now?"

"Yeah now."

Eddie gave an awkward smile. "'Cause now is the time to do it."

"Yeah."

Rex nodded. His knees wobbling with nerves. "Right this second."

Cyborg waved his gun. "Yeah, man. Do it."

"Do it." Eddie looked around, waiting for the lights but nothing happened.

"Boss," came a voice in the seats. "Boss, I got him."

They turned to the southern stands. Hook Nose dragged the person down the stairs.

"Looks like we found your man."

*Perfect*, Eddie thought. *Cole's been captured.*

Hook Nose kicked the captive onto the pitch, he shone a torch in the man's face. It was Eddie's brother, Andy. His face was pale, and his eyes blinked rapidly.

For a brief second Eddie relaxed knowing he wasn't the only nervous family member, then returned to being terrified.

"That's not our man," Eddie said. "Just a fan."

Snakebite sneered. "A fan?"

"Of the football team, not us. We don't have fans."

Rex cocked his head in disappointment. "Not yet anyway."

"You're saying you don't know him."

"No," Eddie said.

Andy gave Eddie a desperate look.

"So you don't mind if I pop a cap in his ass."

Eddie winced. "Arse."

"You what?"

"Nothing, but yes I would mind."

"You do know him?"

"Well, I wouldn't want him shot whether I knew him or not. He's still a human—"

"If he's not yours, then you'd still be able to call in your man, right?"

"Our man will show up, and you'll see this guy has nothing to do with us." Eddie cleared his throat and shouted, "We're ready."

The echo faded. No sign of Cole.

Rex leaned in for a whisper, his hands still raised. "Eddie, I'm not sure we can grab Daryl and your brother in the short time we have?"

"We'll do our best. You get Daryl. I'll get Andy."

"Cool," Rex said. Fully assured.

Eddie gave Rex a sour expression, annoyed that Rex could so easily be calmed by Eddie's false confidence. Part of it was jealousy. Eddie would love to be duped into comfort, in what was increasingly likely their last moments.

Hook Nose pushed the gun towards Andy's temple.

Eddie scratched his head. "Our man is running a little late."

The gang stared back at him.

He muttered to Rex, "He must be having trouble finding the light switch."

"You sure?" Snakebite called out. "'Cause I think this is your man. And you know what I'm gonna do? I'm gonna surprise you."

Eddie's forehead wrinkled. "You're gonna do the opposite of putting a cap in his... rear?"

"No, that's what I'm gonna do?"

"Seems unnecessary," Eddie said.

"And not very surprising," Rex added.

Andy whimpered. "I'm his brother, okay. I'm Eddie's brother." He checked the gang members' faces, not sure if it would annoy them or not.

Cyborg sneered. "Who's Eddie?"

Since his hands were already raised, Eddie waved. "That's me. Sorry, we were never formally introduced. I'm Eddie."

"And I'm Rex, his partner."

"Business partner."

Cyborg eyeballed Eddie. "He's your man."

"He's a man, of which I hold partial ownership, in a brotherly sense. He's not our man. He's not part of the plan. I assume he followed me here."

Andy nodded his head rapidly, informing the gang Eddie was right.

The main entrance gate creaked open, drawing the attention of everyone.

Snakebite smiled. "Here comes your man now."

A gangly man with a mullet of dirty blonde hair stepped out of the dark entryway and onto the grass. He wore a baggy Cloisterham F.C. football shirt. He chewed gum and gave a disdainful look.

Eddie frowned. "He's definitely not our man."

Cyborg rolled his eyes. "Not this again."

"No, really," Rex said. "We don't know him."

Behind the mulleted hoodlum, four other men stepped onto the pitch. They were older than The Massive, mid-to-late twenties, with a few extra scars and tattoos. They all wore Cloisterham F.C. shirts and held black, compact pistols targeting The Massive.

"What you all doing?" Mullet shouted. "This stadium is Wainsbury Boyz territory."

## THIRTY-THREE

The hooligan with a mullet stepped to the middle of the football pitch. The rest of The Wainsbury Boyz followed: a giant brute, a skinhead, a man baring his gold teeth, and one with a large silver nose ring.

Daryl, Maude, and Andy looked to the detectives for comfort. Rex and Eddie clenched up.

Although The Massive gave each other nervous glances, Snakebite and Cyborg took confident stances.

Mullet glared at The Massive. "I said, this is our territory."

Cyborg patted his chest. "Cloisterham FC is our team."

"Guys, it's just a football team," Eddie said.

The Boyz member with a skinhead sneered. "Why, what team do you support?"

Neither Rex nor Eddie paid much attention to football, Eddie grumbled.

"We, uh, don't support anyone," Eddie said.

Both gangs pulled disapproving faces.

Rex smiled. "Except Cloisterham, of course."

The gangs calmed.

Mullet sucked his teeth. "Who are these jokers?"

"Rex Milton. This is my partner Eddie."

"Now, other than for a beating, why you all on my turf?"

Rex's jaw dropped. "We're actually on turf. It's literally your turf."

"It's not their turf," Snakebite said. "It's ours."

"I'm sure the team owner disagrees," Eddie muttered.

Wide-eyed, Rex turned to Eddie and whispered. "Is this an actual turf war?"

Mullet straightened his shoulders. "Whatever's happenin' here, we get half."

Cyborg shrugged. "Just talking, bruv."

"Nah, man. This is an exchange. What is it?"

"Kidnapping ransom," Rex said.

Eddie punched him in the arm.

"Crisp." Mullet gave a satisfied nod. "I'll allow it. Half is ours."

Mullet glared at Daryl, who hunched and cowered next to a red-faced Hook Nose.

"Ain't that Daryl Archer? He killed one of The Boyz." Mullet pulled a gun and pointed it at Daryl.

"He found your man dead already." Eddie dismissed Daryl with a wave of the hand. "He's a trustafarian with poor decision-making skills. At this rate of bad life decisions, he'll get himself killed soon enough. If he makes it past tonight."

Daryl scowled at Eddie.

Mullet pointed his chin out at Eddie. "He won't make it past tonight with me around. It's a matter of principle."

"How about I do you a deal?" Eddie's voice raised in a desperate, please don't say no, way.

"What kind of a deal?"

"You punch him, you can say you taught him a lesson. Justice is restored. Everyone goes home happy."

Daryl looked up. "Everyone?"

The Wainsbury Boy with gold teeth poked Daryl with his handgun to silence him. Hook Nose stepped away from Daryl, giving up the hostage.

Mullet turned to his fellow gang members and offered a shrug. He turned back. "What about retribution for all of yah trespassing on this hallowed ground?"

Eddie sighed. "Right, well. I think you need to sort that out with The Massive. That's not our department."

Mullet stroked his chin. A naughty grin grew on his face. "We get to stab one of The Massive. In a thigh or something."

Cyborg puffed out his chest. "I ain't letting no-one get stabbed. You're mad."

Eddie raised his hand with a nervous wobble. "Can we please consider how this could be a good thing? The Massive get their ransom, everyone leaves alive, it's just a little stabbing."

Snakebite sneered at Eddie. "You get stabbed."

Mullet cocked his head. "Who picked the location?"

Rex frowned.

Eddie glanced at his pale partner and back to the gang. "I don't think that's relevant. As we aren't gang members, we shouldn't be included. We are — I'm not sure what you'd call a non-gang member — civilians?"

"I think you're involved. Enough to punish yah." Mullet clicked his fingers. "We found someone outside that I think yah know."

*Oh crap,* Eddie thought. *Cole has been caught.*

A Boyz member with a toothpick in his mouth entered the pitch pulling Maude by the arm. Toothpick dumped her on her knees.

Maude looked up. "Sorry, guys."

She gave Daryl a pursed smile, and he gave her a little nod.

Eddie blew his cheeks out. "This is getting a bit much."

"What do we do now?" Rex whispered. "You save your brother, I save Maude? Who's gonna save Daryl?"

Eddie shrugged. "Cole?"

"Yeah. He'll fix this. Where is Cole? Do you think he was a gun runner after all and nicked the ransom?"

"I do now."

"This is your man, is it?" Snakebite gave a half-smile. "You brought a woman?"

"No, but a woman could be our man if she wanted. You're being a bit sexist—" Eddie noticed Snakebite's fixed stare. "Our man is still out there. I think."

The gangs raised their eyes over the detectives' heads.

"What's that?" Mullet said.

Rex and Eddie looked back. Above them, the scoreboard counted down: four, three, two, one.

The detectives turned to the rival gangs.

Flash! The stadium lights behind the gang lit up, blinding Rex and Eddie for a few seconds.

Startled, gang members raised their fists ready to fight. Those with guns pointed them at each other, while a couple targeted the rafters in case of attack.

During the confusion, Rex and Eddie tried to run and grab Maude and Andy but wobbled about the place. Disorientated by the bright white lights, pink spots danced around Eddie's vision.

"I told you it was the north lights," Rex said.

"No you didn't, that's what I said."

Eddie tripped over Andy, who helped Eddie up and pulled him through the crowd. Maude yanked Rex's hand and followed Andy towards the stadium entrance.

Toothpick grabbed Maude. Disorientated, Rex swung a punch but missed. He lunged forward and accidentally head-butted the man. The thug dropped to his rear and swallowed the toothpick. While he held his throat in shock, Rex and Maude ran.

Eddie and Andy ran towards the exit, but the wet mud suctioned Eddie's shoeless foot and he fell. Andy tried to pull Eddie back on his feet.

The gangs settled while Mullet pointed his gun at Eddie and Andy. Snakebite's pistol aimed at Rex and Maude. Gold Teeth held Daryl in an armlock and held his gun to the hostage's temple.

Mullet marched toward Eddie and held the gun at Eddie's forehead. The cold touch of the muzzle gave Eddie goosebumps.

"Don't try anything."

Eddie blinked away the last of his vision's pink spots. Eddie gave an apologetic smile to Rex. Rex returned the gesture.

"Get up."

Eddie and Andy arose.

Mullet stepped back and waved his gun. "The four of yah, hands in the air. Now, one of yah has to be punished. Who's it gonna be?"

Eddie's shoulders dropped. "My vote is Cole."

"Are you sick, man? Jason Cole is dead." Mullet tipped his head at Cyborg. "The Massive blew him up."

"Nah, bruv," Cyborg said. "You did."

"We don't blow people up, that ain't our style."

The gangs shouting intensified and those with guns waved their weapons.

"Excuse me," Eddie tried. "Hello?" No one listened. "Cole blew himself up," he shouted.

The gangs quietened.

"At least, he made it look that way. Cole's our man. He has the ransom." Eddie turned to Snakebite. "If you want to share with The Wainsbury Boyz, that's up to you. If you want to stab or shoot yourselves, that's your business."

Eddie stepped back, joining Maude and Rex. Andy followed.

"But I'll be leaving with my business partner, my kidnappee, and I'll take these two as well."

Eddie pointed at Andy and Maude.

Snakebite raised the corner of his top lip. "You ain't got no bargaining chips."

Eddie slumped. "Right, um. No."

Mullet stepped nose to nose with Eddie. "So why we gonna do what yah say?"

Eddie took a step back. "I hoped if I showed enough bravado you'd mistake me for a leader and… and do as I say?"

Mullet held the gun at Eddie's forehead.

"Please?" Eddie tried.

Mullet drew closer, staring into Eddie's eyes.

Daryl looked at his sister. "You hired these guys?"

Gold Teeth tightened his grip of Daryl and grinned, displaying his full metal mouth.

Maude gave a shrug. "Sorry, I didn't know who to turn to. This is my first kidnapping."

"Ours too," Rex whispered.

Right then the roar, or asthmatic cough, of the Morris Minor engine came from the entryway. The headlights beamed across the pitch. It spluttered along the grass. All the gang members watched with suspicious eyes.

The car stopped and Cole got out.

"Hands up," Mullet ordered.

"This is my kidnapping," Snakebite said. "I say hands up."

Cole did as he was ordered, keeping one hand closed. "I'm unarmed."

Mullet bared his teeth. "What's in your hand, man?"

The detective stepped away from the car slowly.

"Show me what's in your hand."

Cole opened up his palm and revealed a little device with a red button. He smiled and pushed it.

Eddie grimaced. "Oh no. Not the car."

Cole ran and ducked. Rex and Eddie followed his lead and dived into the damp grass. They pulled Andy and Maude down with them.

After a moment of silence, the car crackled and fizzed as smoke rose from below the Morris Minor. It had a burnt smell, but the car was fine.

Eddie looked up. "Thank goodness."

Andy and Maude crawled away from the smoking car while Cole stood, brushing dirt from his jacket.

Mullet narrowed his eyes. "Lil', Cue. Grab him."

The giant and the skinhead grabbed Cole's arms, holding him in place.

"Take your half," Snakebite said. "But we're gonna deal with Cole."

"Yeah." Stocky stepped close to Snakebite. "He's ours."

Mullet aimed his gun at Stocky and shot him in the chest. He fell to the ground, dead.

The Wainsbury Boyz pointed their pistols at The Massive.

Mullet cocked his head side-to-side, cracking his neck. "This is a hostile takeover. Either yah join The Wainsbury Boyz, or yah dead."

"Does that include us?" Rex said.

Mullet looked Rex up and down and scoffed. "Nah, bruv."

Eddie sighed in relief.

Snakebite raised his hands to his side, protecting his gang. "We don't scare so easy."

Cyborg passed Snakebite, reluctantly walking over to The Wainsbury Boys. He handed his starter pistol to Mullet. Mullet passed the starter pistol to one of his subordinates.

Snakebite's face flushed. Other members of The Massive walked around the Morris Minor to join The Wainsbury Boyz.

"Watcha doin'?" Snakebite said. "This ain't how we do things."

"Sorry, bruv." Mullet sucked his teeth. "It's just business."

He fired his gun. Snakebite fell back into the wet ground with a hard splat; he was dead. The remaining members of The Massive lined up with The Wainsbury Boyz and handed over their weapons.

Eddie backed away. "So, the ransom is yours now, and we can go?" He waved his fingers at Rex, Andy, Maude, and Daryl.

"Be on your merry way, yeah?" He waved his gun to the exit.

Gold Teeth let Daryl go. He hobbled towards the group and Maude hugged him.

"I'm so glad you're safe," she said.

Eddie turned to Andy. "What are you doing here?"

"I thought you were acting weird, so I wanted to check on you." Andy smiled. "Looks like you can handle yourself pretty well."

Eddie smirked. He turned to Mullet and raised his hand. "And the car?"

Mullet stuck out his chin. "We'll leave it on the street when we're done with it. Yah can pick it up later."

As they approached the stadium entrance, Rex peeked back at Cole. "What about him?"

Eddie pursed his lips. "I'm sure he'll find a way out."

"Shouldn't we save him?"

Eddie pointed with his eyes at the dozen gang members, several with guns. "How are we going to do that?"

"I don't know, but he saved us at the warehouse that time. And when that van was trying to run us over."

Eddie's head hung a little lower as the five of them continued to cross the pitch.

Back at the centre of the field, Nose Ring got into the Morris Minor and turned the key. The engine sputtered — Bang! An explosion consumed the car with smoke and fire.

Mullet screamed, "Nooo!" as the paintings curled in the flames.

Rex, Eddie and the others turned to see what had happened. The inside of the car burned in an intense fire.

Eddie sighed. "Figures."

Hook Nose tried to open the back door but burnt his hand. Cyborg covered his hand with his hoodie sleeve and opened it. They managed to kick some silver candle holders and gold necklaces out of the back. The fire was too hot to grab anything else.

The flames crackled. A second explosion pushed the gang members away. Bits of silverware flew out like shrapnel.

In the commotion, Cole ran from the car. He passed the confused detective duo and Archer siblings.

"Run," he said. "Handguns don't have this range."

Rex, Eddie and the others ran. Cole led them through the stadium entrance. They passed the stiles and ticket office.

Outside of the gate, four Wainsbury Boyz waited on

266

the street next to their van. They all had pointed pistols, ready to shoot.

Cole stopped and raised his hands. The rest followed suit.

"Perfect." Eddie browsed the desperate faces of Maude, Daryl, Andy, and Rex. He turned back to his burning car. He hated that thing, but it was his thing. "Bloody perfect."

## THIRTY-FOUR

The six hostages were all tied to pillars in pairs, back to back with each other. Even though Eddie only saw Cole in his peripheral vision, he managed to sneer at his pillar partner. Rex seemed quite pleased to be paired with Maude. Meanwhile Daryl and Andy, not knowing each other, shared a pillar awkwardly. Daryl looked the most at home, having become accustomed to being held hostage.

The room was a dimly lit area of an old draughty warehouse.

"Their zip ties are excellent," Rex said. "We need to keep some of these in the car."

Eddie clicked his jaw. "The bomb site you mean?"

"I'm sorry." Cole stared into the distance.

"Is blowing up modes of transport your solution to everything?"

"I hoped to create a big enough distraction to get you two and Daryl out, but five people were too many."

"We got them to accept the ransom. We were all set to go."

The rest all turned to Cole.

Cole sighed. "If they got the ransom we'd have helped fund gang wars and drug pushing. It would destroy Cloisterham."

Andy blinked rapidly, taking in all the information.

Eddie huffed. "They still have the ransom, it's still gold and silver that can be melted down."

Cole fidgeted with the cable ties around his wrists. "The metal's lost its antique value, the painting was completely destroyed. They don't have the cash for their gun runner meeting. We hindered them."

Daryl screwed up his face. "My parents don't have gold and silver."

"Sure they do," Rex said. "They have loads of it. Silverware and crystal ornaments and stuff."

"No, they swapped that out after the recession. They sold it on the quiet and bought a bunch of knock-offs. Same with the paintings."

Cole straightened up. "You're saying the whole ransom was a bunch of fakes?"

One corner of Eddie's top lip turned up. "No, he's saying you blew up our car for nothing."

"My parents are broke, they put off bankruptcy to save face."

"But they offered boats?"

"It's a lease. Which they are months past due."

Maude blinked in astonishment. "They're broke?"

"Mother and father sold it all while you were in college. They've been pretending ever since."

The sound of footsteps grew from the outside corridor.

"We're in danger." Cole twisted his torso to see as many other hostages as possible. "It's best to solicit their sympathy, remind them we are all human. I recommend singing hymns. People don't like to hurt the religious."

Eddie scoffed. "I'm not pretending to be religious, I've got some self-respect."

A rolling door in a dark corner pulled open. Three men in balaclavas, backlit by the corridor lighting, stepped inside. An armed hoodie closed the door behind him.

The tallest of the three walked around the pillars. Although his face was covered, the microchip tattoo on his wrist poked out of his sleeve. It was Cyborg.

"We want money today, or you're all dead. So the question is, how much are you all worth?" Cyborg stood between the pillars where Daryl and Maude were tied. "Your parents have got twenty-four hours to pay us, or you're both dead."

"I keep telling you, they don't have money," Daryl stuttered.

"Well, someone here better have a family member willing to part with their cash."

Cyborg approached Cole and patted his jacket. "You got any loved ones, Mister?"

Cole stared silently.

Cyborg pulled out Cole's wallet. He flipped the wallet over to show the stock photo of two little blonde girls.

"These yours?"

Cole nodded.

"Be a shame for them to grow up without their daddy. Who do I call?"

Cole remained silent. He looked away, uninterested.

"I'm talking to you. Who's gonna pay me for your life?"

Cole just grinned. "I'd like a copy of the Bible."

"Me too," Eddie said. "A copy of the good book." He began to sing. "Kumbaya my Lord—"

"Shut it." Cyborg leaned towards Cole. "You give me a number to call, or you'll never see your girls again."

He walked around the pillars, as he passed Maude she cried. Cyborg stepped around the post and stopped at Rex.

"You, what you worth?"

Rex's eyes jigged about, he wasn't sure where to look. "I got five quid in my shoe. You can have it. "

"You what?"

"There's two quid in stamps too."

"What are you worth to someone else?"

"Um. I don't know. I like to think I'm good company. I do the dishes when I can—"

"What they gonna pay for your life?"

"My nan says she wouldn't trade me for all the tea in China. Is— Is that what you mean?"

Daryl leaned back to get closer to his sister. He muttered, "Seriously, you hired these guys?"

Maude hung her head. "They were very… affordable."

Searching Rex's pockets, Cyborg found the bulldog clip of club cards. He reached in again and pulled out the stock photo of the blonde girls. Rex had taken it from the photo display at the supermarket.

Cyborg curled the top of his lip. "Why you got a picture of his kids? That's weird, bruv."

From the other pillar, Eddie leaned to the side to see the photo past Cyborg's shoulder. He rolled his jaw.

"They're my kids," Rex said. "Are you saying Cole has a picture of my daughters in his wallet?" He mimed distressed. "That is odd."

Cyborg glared at Cole. "What's going on here?"

Cole studied the scruffy photo. He turned to Rex. "You idiot. You got the exact same photo as me?"

"I didn't expect to be captured with you."

Cyborg waved the gun between Cole and Rex. "One of you tell me what's going on?"

"I'll tell you if you do me a favour," Eddie said.

Cyborg marched up to Eddie and pointed the gun at him. "Talk."

"It's a tactic," Eddie blurted. "You start to have empathy when you think of them as a parent. Means you treat them nicer. Now, can I have a copy of the Bible, please? I seek comfort in My Lord and Saviour, Jesus Christ."

Cyborg narrowed his eyes at Eddie. He walked back to Rex.

"What's your nan's number?"

Rex winced. "She's not very good at the phone."

"Number. Now."

As Rex read out the number, Cyborg dialled.

"Hello?" came the tiny voice of the little old lady.

Cyborg held a voice changer over the receiver. "Your grandson has been kidnapped. If you want to see him again, you'll have to pay fifty-thousand pounds."

"Sorry, dear. You sound muffled."

"Your grandson, Rex Milton, has been kidnapped."

"Rex? He's gone out."

"No, I have Rex Milton."

"Well, what you ringing me for? Speak to him yourself."

"Fifty-thousand pounds or you'll never see your grandson again."

"Fifty-thousand? What's this for again? Windows? I had the double glazing done ten years ago. Can you take me off your list?"

"This ain't no sales call."

"Is this billing? You'll have to talk to my Rex, he deals with the bills. Rex!" She continued to call out for him. "I'm afraid he's not in."

Cyborg grasped the phone in frustration. "I know he's not in. He's here with me."

"Then what you calling me for?" The phone went dead.

"Hello? Hello?" Cyborg hung up and glowered at Rex. "You're brown bread."

"I'm what?"

"Brown bread." He ran a finger across this throat. "Dead."

Rex's jaw dropped. "It's not my fault."

Cyborg stepped over to Andy. "You, what are you worth?"

"I can get you the fifty grand."

"Who's gonna pay it?"

"I am. I'll pay it."

"Fifty grand?" Eddie's pitch rose as he spoke.

"You take us all to the bank," Andy stammered. "I'll pay you, and you walk away with the money. Leave us there."

Cyborg stood back. "Fifty k. For all of you?" He pointed at Rex. "Even him?"

Rex huffed at the insult.

Andy nodded.

Cyborg grinned. "It's a deal. We go in the morning."

He signalled to the other hoodies, and all three exited through the rolling door.

Rex smiled. "That's bought us time until the banks open."

"You have fifty grand?" Eddie said.

"Yeah. It's my life savings. I've got it in an ISA. They should let me withdraw it if I show up in person."

"You wouldn't go halves on Mum and Dad's theatre tickets for their anniversary."

"I have a budget."

Eddie tutted. "Obviously."

"I will not feel pressured to overpay."

"Unless there's a gun to your head."

"Leave it out, Eddie," Rex said. "He's paying top dollar to get us free."

Cole shook his head. "There is a way out of here without paying a ransom."

Daryl went limp. "I just want to go home."

Maude leaned forward to better see Cole. "What's that mean?"

Eddie scoffed. "Don't listen to him. We'd have all been home in bed by now if it wasn't for him. Cole is just a madman with a stick of dynamite, and he's all out of dynamite."

"Don't be so over the top," Cole said.

"Did you spend the last couple of days in Cloisterham Woods making a bomb?" Eddie narrowed his eyes.

Cole clenched his jaw. "What is your problem with me?"

"I'm sick of the way you act like you're so brave and never scared of anything."

"You think I'm not scared?" Cole pulled at the zip ties. "Of course I am. I put on a bit of a show to make others feel safe."

"You're not just trying to show us up?"

"No. I didn't mean to do that."

Eddie sighed.

Rex tilted his head. "If you're scared how'd you do this all the time?"

"Bravery is choosing to do something that scares you. If I feel scared I know I'm doing the right thing. At this moment, the right thing is to not give these guys fifty grand."

The other five gave each other looks.

The rolling door flung open, inside marched the two gang members wearing balaclavas. The tall one in a football shirt gave his identity away with a toothpick in his mouth. The shorter one wore a grey hoodie.

"Oi," Toothpick said. "No nattering. You all keep it down." He snarled at Rex.

Cole coughed, loud and hoarse.

"What's up with him?"

Eddie shrugged.

Cole turned red as the coughing fit increased.

Toothpick approached Cole while Hoodie pointed a gun at the coughing detective. Hoodie's hands shook.

*That kind of nervousness could be enough to affect his aim and get me shot*, Eddie thought.

He leaned away from Cole. "Watch where you point that thing, yeah?"

Annoyed, the hoodie's eyes widened, filling the balaclava eye holes. He pointed the gun steadily at Eddie.

"That's not quite what I meant."

Once Toothpick got close to Cole, the detective launched his legs up, kicking the hoodie in the head. Unconscious, he dropped to the ground. As Cole's legs and body fell back against the pillar, his back smacked against the zip ties. With his arms pulled as wide as possible, the pressure of his back landing snapped the zip tie. Cole was free.

"Ah, cool," Rex said.

Eddie's head bounced left and right, trying to see what was happening on the other side of his pillar. "What is it? What's happening?"

Cole raced to the fallen gang member and took his weapon.

The hoodie aimed his gun at Cole. "Don't move."

Cole straightened his knees, raising to a standing position. His hands were up with the stolen gun held by the barrel.

"You're not a killer," Cole said. "I can see it in your eyes."

The hoodie squeezed the gun tight, his hand turning red.

"You're one of The Massive, right? Got brought into The Wainsbury Boyz."

"Shut up," the young hoodie said.

Eddie tilted his head. There was something familiar about him.

Cole calmly stepped forward. "The one with the mullet, he's already killed tonight, and I bet that's got you worried."

"Do I know you?" Eddie asked.

The hoodie shook his head. "Nah, mate."

"Jamie Weber?"

He paused. "So what if I am? What you want to do about it?"

"Who's Jamie Weber?" Cole asked.

"He mugged us," Rex said. "Twice."

Cole widened his raised arms. "Put down the gun, Jamie. You don't want to be here. We can get you out."

Jamie ripped off the balaclava, revealing his eyebrowless, pointy face. "You can't leave The Wainsbury Boyz." His voice cracked as he spoke.

Eddie pursed his lips, he felt sorry for Jamie. "You're gonna get us out of here."

"Or what?"

"Or we'll get out of here without your help, and then I'm gonna tell your nan."

"You can't use that one again."

"And I'll get her to tell your mum."

Jamie's face dropped. While he thought about the prospect, Cole dived forward and grabbed the gun. The teen raised his hands in defeat.

With Jamie no longer a threat, Cole freed the others from the pillar. Rex attempted to free himself by copying Cole. He flipped his legs up but bruised his back as they came back down.

Cole leaned to Eddie. "How'd you know the mum thing would shake him?"

Eddie shrugged. "All mums are scary, right?"

Cole winced. Eddie turned to the rest of the hostages. Andy nodded in agreement. Daryl, Maude, and Rex were confused.

With no eyes on Jamie, the teen ran out of the door.

"You can't leave The Wainsbury Boyz," he shouted down the corridor.

Cole dashed to the doorway, but Jamie had disappeared down the hallway.

Maude crossed her arms. "That can't be good."

## THIRTY-FIVE

C ole stepped out into the corridor. He waved the others out of the holding cell in a straightforward, military fashion.

"Cole is so cool," Rex whispered.

"What has he done that's cool?" Eddie said. "He's used us as cannon fodder and lied to us. Name one cool thing?"

The detective duo, Andy, and the Archer siblings all rushed down the corridor to catch up with Cole. Cole stepped around the corner and jumped back. A sideburned hoodlum ran towards them. Cole flung his arm forward. The gang member ran into his fist. As the hoodlum fell, Cole grabbed the goon's gun and checked the loaded magazine.

Rex raised his eyebrows. "That was rather cool."

Cole pulled back his shoulders. "We've got a mutual enemy that needs to know we are dangerous. We go in with a display of confidence. That means we go in and attack the biggest baddest one."

"And then get shot by the rest?" Eddie said.

"If it means they don't take us alive, that we die free and with bravery, then so be it."

Rex raised his eyebrows. "That was cooler than the first thing."

Eddie pursed his lips.

"You got a better idea?" Cole said.

"Maybe we can negotiate with them, they were gonna take Andy's money."

Rex grimaced, concerned about Eddie's previous negotiating techniques.

Cole turned to the rest of the group. "We're gonna get out without funding their war chest. You with me?"

Maude cleared her throat. "We have their balaclavas. Could you wear them and disguise yourselves as The Wainsbury Boyz?"

Rex and Eddie nodded.

Cole thought it over. "We don't have enough for all of us. The rest will have to be hostages being moved."

"We have two balaclavas." Rex pulled the balaclava and threw it at Eddie. "That's enough for two of us to pass as gang members."

Maude removed a cosmetics kit from her bag. "We could make it three with my makeup remover."

She grabbed Rex's chin forcefully and applied some remover to his forehead, washing away his drawn on eyebrows. Maude showed Rex her travel mirror.

He grinned. "Look, Eddie. I'm in The Massive."

Eddie and Cole put on the two balaclavas as Rex took the unconscious teen's tracksuit top.

They headed down the corridor towards some scuffed white double doors. Daryl, Andy and Maude walked in front pretending to hold their arms back like they were tied up. Cole and Eddie wore balaclavas and stood behind Andy and Maude, pretending to move the hostages.

Behind Daryl, Rex put on a swagger in his new tracksuit top and baseball cap. Rex pushed the double doors open, and the group walked through.

Two bulked up young men with guns walked towards them.

"What's going on 'ere?" the heavier one asked.

"Moving the hostages, innit, fam," Rex said.

Cole and Eddie nodded, appearing calm and collected.

"Boss wants the hostages moved? No one told us."

"Jam your hype, yeah, bruv." Rex dismissed them with a puff of air. "You boys are being well moist. We gonna pick up the ransom this morning. We all be buzzin." He turned to Eddie and Cole. "Right?"

"Buzzin," the pair repeated.

The heavier hoodie narrowed his eyes and inspected the hostages. "What about the other three?"

"Psst, there's only three of us, so we're moving them in two goes. We could use a few more peeps if you want?"

The other hoodie nodded.

"Yeah, alright, bruv."

The two muscular hoodies passed through the group towards the holding cell door.

Rex nodded. "Winky face."

The pair frowned at Rex's odd reply but shook it off. After gaining some space between them, Eddie tapped Rex's shoulder.

"They're gonna alert everyone when they find we're not there."

"I got rid of them didn't I, bruv?"

Eddie cocked his head. "Don't you bruv, me——"

"Gentlemen." Cole nodded at the double doors with an exit sign above.

The group passed a side door on their way to the exit.

"Fam," the heavier teen called from down the corridor.

"You don't want to be going that way. Boss is in there." He pointed to the side door.

Rex looked at the others in a panic, then back to the door.

"I got it, bruv." He raised his thumb. "Thumbs up."

Cole muttered to Eddie, "What's with the emoticon speak?"

"He says they all do it," Eddie whispered back.

The heavier teen stared at Cole and noticed his suit, "What's with your threads?"

The other heavy looked Eddie up and down. "Why you only got one shoe?"

"It's cool, bruv." Rex quickened his pace.

The two heavies marched back towards the group.

"Uh, run?" Rex offered.

Cole nodded. "Run. Everyone."

The group raced towards the exit door as the two heavies pulled guns and pointed. "Stop."

Cole kicked the doors wide open. On the other side was a hanger full of gang members surrounded by empty assembly lines. They partied with drinks and various drugs on the tables.

As the group stormed in everyone turned to the doorway, except Jamie who skulked along the back wall looking for an escape.

Cole walked in with a bold step. Rex made a superhero pose, Eddie slowed down, confused. He compared himself to Rex and adjusted to a more heroic stance.

Mullet rolled his eyes. "Who let you out?"

At the back wall, Jamie looked down at the concrete floor.

Cole marched up to the biggest brute and punched him in the face. The brute fell back. Various gang members pulled guns and pointed at the escaping hostages.

Cole raised his arms. "Okay, you can take me down. You can take us all down, but I promise to take as many of you to the morgue with me as I can."

Rex mouthed "Cool" at Eddie.

Cole clenched his fists and bent his knees, firmly grounding himself.

The rest of the gang pulled out their knives.

"There you go Eddie, more knife crime, just like you wanted."

Eddie glared at Rex as he raised his hands.

"I think we can work this out," Eddie said.

Cole kept his eyes on the gang. "Quiet. You're showing weakness."

"Perhaps I am showing weakness," Eddie projected at the crowd. "But isn't it our weakness that becomes our strength?"

The gang looked at each other and shook their heads.

"I'm sure I read that in a book once." Eddie tried to read his audience; they were various levels of bored, annoyed, or high. "The stubborn man who doesn't listen, also doesn't listen to the naysayers? Does he not?"

Cole leaned to Rex and spoke in a hushed tone, "What's he doing?"

"I think he's negotiating," Rex whispered back.

"Does not the person with the weak back, become the better yoga student because of that initial weakness? Maybe my weakness is negotiating? Or standing up for myself?" His voice cracked. "Or... or speaking in public. But am I not doing those things anyway? Does that not make me something more? More of a negotiator, a public speaker?"

"Stop saying 'does it not'." Rex tucked in his chin with embarrassment.

Mullet pointed his gun at Eddie. "What you want, nonce?"

"I want to go home. Can't we work out our differences? Like the Wainsbury Boyz and The Massive did? You've proven that you can open dialogue and create understanding. That's all I want, understanding and dialogue, and to make it out of here alive."

Daryl raised his arms. "You realise they worked out their differences with guns and death threats."

Eddie slumped.

The hoodlum with gold teeth snuck close to Cole and made a lunge for him. Cole grabbed the man's knife-wielding arm. He took the knife as he threw Gold Teeth against a table. Cole planted the knife into Gold Teeth's hand, pinning him to the table top.

"He's got to pay for that." Mullet turned his gun on Cole. "Out of respect."

Eddie stepped between the pair. "Come on now, that's just another difference for us to work out. We can do that, right? I mean The Massive never took it to heart that you killed their leader, or that you forced them into this arrangement."

The eyebrowless youths, all previous members of The Massive, began to murmur to each other.

"Or that you managed to take the ransom off them, which would have made them more powerful than you."

Mutterings grew into vocal groaning and complaining.

"Shut up," Mullet said.

"Or that you managed to take over their territory. They hold no hard feelings. Happy to serve in the place that they once owned. Not bitter that they took a beating." He paused to think. "They didn't even take a beating really, they just did what you said, and you still respect them."

"I said shut up, okay?"

The gangs backed away, separating into their original two groups. Jamie's eyes darted between the gangs. He stepped behind the old machinery.

Rex nudged Andy. "It's turned all West Side Story. My nan loves that film."

The Massive and The Wainsbury Boyz eyed each other with suspicion. They turned their guns and knives on each other.

"Can't we all just get along?" Eddie said.

Mullet turned to the gang, his mouth agape. "Settle down."

A nervous unibrowed hoodie moved his shaking gun to his other hand so he could wipe his sweaty palm on his clothes. Squeezing a little too hard, he fired at a former rival.

The Boyz fired at The Massive. Those armed with a gun shot back, while others retaliated with knives. Some threw factory equipment or grabbed pipes to use as weapons. When a gun ran out of bullets, it too was used as a hitting implement.

Daryl pulled Maude down behind old warehouse equipment. He held her in a tight hug.

Cole pushed Andy to the ground.

A stray bullet clipped Rex's right forearm. Eddie pulled him down behind a crate of drugs. They all stayed down, their ears ringing from the loud bangs. Maude, Daryl and Andy all closed their eyes and covered their ears. Rex and Eddie flinched at every bang, while Cole fended off any gang members that came their way. He punched a thug with neon red hair unconscious for coming close.

"You okay?" Eddie said.

Rex prodded his bleeding arm in disbelief. He turned

to Eddie. "It's just a flesh wound." As soon as he heard himself a smile grew on his face.

Mullet crawled around the crate, his face red with rage. He grabbed Eddie by the collar and stood, pulling Eddie up with him.

"I'm gonna gut you—"

Eddie kneed Mullet in the groin and stood back in shock. Eddie's forehead creased. He turned to Rex. Rex nodded at him. Eddie placed his feet hip distance apart, and bent his knees, grounding himself. While taking several punches from Mullet, he clenched his right fist. He locked his wrist and threw a punch. His knuckles hit Mullet square on the nose. The gang leader spun as he dropped to the floor.

"Yes!" Rex offered a high-five.

Eddie released his fist into an open palm. The pair high-fived. Both shouted "ouch," realising they'd used Eddie's newly minted punching hand and Rex's injured right arm.

Eddie leaned his hands on his knees. "I feel wrong like I have vertigo. Ground level vertigo. Is that a thing?" He puked.

Cole threw a hoodlum over the crates "It's normal to heave after your first big fight."

A giant brute lunged at Cole. He punched hoodlum who stumbled backwards and tripped over Andy lying on the floor.

Andy looked up and saw a smiling Cole.

"Cheers, fella."

Andy put on a smile. "You're welcome."

A stray bullet zipped over Eddie's shoulder. He dropped into a crouched position behind the crate, as bullets tore holes in the wall behind Rex. He kneeled to stay out of the way.

While the hostages stayed hidden, the fighting petered out. By the end, every gang member was either dead or too wounded to get up.

The detective duo peeked over the crate. Bodies lay across the factory floor. Some squirmed in pain, while most lay dead.

Andy got to his feet and joined the duo.

Rex smiled at Eddie. "You did that."

Eddie swallowed as he took in the sprawl of casualties. "I did?"

Cole slapped him on the shoulder. "You set them against each other. What was that, reverse psychology?"

"I'm not sure what to call it. Is there such a thing as anti-psychology?"

"Anti-psychology?" Cole mused as he kicked weapons out of reach from the wounded gang members. "I'll have to use that someday. Save me grazing my knuckles."

Maude helped her brother up to his feet. Daryl leaned on a stack of boxes. "If everyone is done, I'd quite like to go home and take a shower."

# THIRTY-SIX

R ex and Eddie stepped out of the old warehouse, they were close to the river by huge silos. The morning sun hung low over Cloisterham while birds sang from nearby trees.

"I can see our office from here." Rex pointed across the water with his unwounded arm.

Daryl and Maude stepped out. Daryl protected his eyes from the daylight. Maude approached Rex and Eddie and hugged them both.

"Thank you so much."

"You're welcome." Eddie basked in her cherry fragrance.

Rex winced from her squeezing his shot arm.

She let go and stepped back. "Are you okay?"

Rex took a deep breath, taking in the moment. "It's fine, it's just a flesh wound." He grinned.

Maude gave a confused smile back.

"Thank you," Daryl said with some hesitation. "I was wrong to doubt you. I mean, you did nearly get us all killed a couple of times, but other than that you came through for me."

"You're welcome." Eddie cleared his throat. "Maude, now the case is over, would you maybe like to get a drink sometime?"

Her smile faded. "Sorry, I like Cole."

Eddie's face screwed up. "Why?"

"He's rugged, and manly."

"I'm not manly?"

"No, of course you are. It's just he's more *Bourne Identity*, you guys are more, born yesterday. You know?"

The faint sound of police sirens grew.

A black motorbike sped down the sloped street towards them. The rider, decked out in black leather, removed his helmet and revealed a bald, square-jawed, middle-aged man with sky blue eyes and laughter lines. He smiled.

"You took your sweet time." Cole passed through the doorway, patting Rex and Eddie on the back.

"Who's that?" Eddie said.

Cole walked towards the biker. "My partner."

"His partner?" Rex said.

Eddie raised his eyebrows. "Cole had a business partner this whole time?"

The biker chucked Cole a helmet. He caught it without taking his eyes off the rider, reached the bike, and shared a passionate kiss with his partner. With a smile, Cole got on the back of the bike and strapped on the helmet.

"See you fellas around." Cole winked.

The biker put his own helmet back on and revved the engine.

"Goodbye, Rex. Goodbye Ed. It's been… a pleasure."

"Cole has a partner, partner." As the bike drove towards the sunrise, Eddie straightened his neck. "He was the third man, wasn't he?"

Rex shrugged.

Police cars and vans arrived. Officers exited the vehicles and pointed guns at Rex and Eddie. Other police pulled the warehouse barn doors open to find the mess of sprawled bodies inside.

D.I. Sumner got out of a car and told the police to holster their weapons. He joined the detective pair.

"Had quite an evening, have we?" He winced at Rex's arm.

Before Sumner could ask, Rex proclaimed, "It's fine, it's just a flesh wound."

Eddie rolled his eyes. "Yes, we get it." He turned to Sumner. "We can explain."

"We can?" Rex said.

"It's okay, we had one of our top people on it." Sumner waved their attention to inside the warehouse.

Inside, a tall, slim hoodie stood. Unzipping the hoodie revealed a bulletproof jacket. With short buzzed hair and no eyebrows, the pale hoodie stared at Rex and Eddie.

"Is that Ruby?" Rex asked.

"Officer Yates, and yes," Sumner said.

It was hard to tell how annoyed she was without eyebrows, but Eddie guessed pretty annoyed.

He gave an apologetic wave. "You had her undercover this whole time?"

"The last couple of days. We were trying to bust the gang for buying illegal weapons. I don't think that will be happening now."

Eddie winced. "Sorry, about that."

Officer Yates glared at Rex and Eddie as she walked past the pair. She entered the nearby ambulance.

"She was playing a boy?" Rex laughed. "So what about the tall mugger? She was an undercover policewoman as well, right?"

Sumner frowned, but Rex didn't notice.

"Eddie, I didn't hit a girl."

"I don't know why you'd be so pleased," Eddie replied. "You'd still have hit a woman."

Rex huffed. "Why can't you just be happy for me?"

"You punched a teenage girl?" Sumner got out his notebook.

Noticing the paper pad, Rex lowered his excitement. "Uh, it was more a kerfuffle really."

Eddie shook his head, he was exhausted.

"Cheer up, Eddie. We beat the baddies, we saved the girl, we got the hostage, we made it out alive. We won."

"Yeah?"

"Definitely." Rex's grin faded. "Except, what was the deal with the CD?"

Sumner grimaced. "What CD?"

"When you interviewed us, you whispered something to Ruby, uh Officer Yates, about a CD?"

The detective inspector scratched the side of his head. "CID? I sent her to the Criminal Investigation Department."

Rex giggled as Eddie shook his head.

"What's a CD got to do with this?" Sumner asked.

"Uh, nothing. Daryl gave a music CD he gave to a DJ. It's unrelated."

"We better give him back that bag we…" Rex stopped as he looked at Sumner. "Borrowed."

Andy and Jamie walked out the barn door with their hands bound behind them. They were escorted by two police officers.

"Uh, D.I. Sumner, that's my brother."

Sumner waved the officer to release a dazed Andy. Once his hands were free, he joined Rex and Eddie.

Eddie smiled. "This is Detective Inspector Sumner. We've worked together on a couple of cases."

Andy shook Sumner's hand. He turned to Eddie. "You really are a real detective."

"Yeah." Eddie grinned at Rex. "We are."

"And the other one?" Sumner nodded his head at Jamie being escorted by an officer. "Is he one of yours?"

Eddie looked Jamie in the eyes. He was tired, scared, and lost.

"Yeah, he's with us as well." Eddie put his hand on Jamie's shoulder. "Let's get you home to your mum."

Jamie hung his head. "You're not gonna tell her?"

Eddie let out a long sigh. "No. I'm not gonna tell."

---

The group were checked over by the paramedics and gave their statements at the police station. Jamie and Andy headed to their homes while Rex and Eddie sat at the nearby bus stop. It was time for the detective pair to visit the Archers' country home.

Rex removed the sock money, a sweaty and wrinkled five-pound note, and three stamps. A bus arrived, and the duo stepped on.

Rex greeted the driver. "Two returns to Maidenstone, please."

"That'll be six pound, forty."

Rex placed down the note and the stamps.

"What's that?"

"Stamps. You know, to pay the rest."

The driver scoffed. "It's cash only."

Rex pouted. "Stamps are legal tender."

"No, they aren't." The driver shook his head.

"But my nan says she gets a bus with stamps."

The bus driver leaned in. "That's just a driver being nice to an old lady."

Eddie peeked past Rex's shoulder. "We've had a hard day, could you let us get away with it too?"

The bus driver grumbled. "It's five pounds for two singles."

Eddie huffed. "Singles would be great."

The bus drove them to Maidenstone town centre, and they walked the additional mile into the countryside.

When Rex and Eddie arrived outside the Archer's home, they saw Daryl, Maude, and D.I. Sumner waiting at the front door.

Mr and Mrs Archer opened the door as Rex and Eddie approached the gravel driveway.

The couple hugged their son and squeezed him tight.

Mrs Archer smiled. "You're here. You made it."

"Yeah, no thanks to you two," Daryl said.

Mr and Mrs Archer let go and backed away into the doorway.

"Officer, we're so glad you found him."

"Actually it was Miles Milton Investigations."

The detective duo waved as they arrived at the door.

Rex pointed at his bulky sleeve covering a bandaged bicep. "If you're wondering about my arm, it's just a flesh wound."

Sumner's tone lowered. "They also alerted us to a pile of gold-plated brass and other metals in possession of the kidnappers. We believe them to be destroyed replicas of the items you reported stolen this morning."

Mr and Mrs Archers turned pale. When Rex and Eddie didn't return with Daryl the previous night, they assumed the pair had failed. Mr Archer had reported the replicas and fakes as stolen. Once processed they could have claimed hundreds of thousands of pounds from the insurance policy.

Daryl and Maude corroborated Rex and Eddie's story, much to the dismay of their parents.

Sumner sighed with disappointment as if he never liked to arrest anyone. "Mr and Mrs Archer, I'll need you to come with me to answer some questions at the station."

He took the couple to his car and drove off.

"So no payday then?" Rex asked.

Eddie nodded. "It would seem that way."

Maude buried her hands in her pockets. "I'm sorry. I put everything I had into the ransom."

Daryl scratched his chin. "What did my parents offer you?"

"Ten grand," Rex said.

Eddie stepped forward. "We have expenses as well, like a blown up car."

Daryl glanced to the large detached garage. "Maybe we could make an arrangement to keep you on the road."

He guided the pair to the garage and opened the door. The garage contained three cars.

Eddie had his eyes on the silver Mercedes, but Rex hovered to the red Audi. Daryl briskly passed those, he waved the pair over to a 1981 Escort Hatchback. It was banana yellow, and the slight rust at the bottom made it appear ripe.

"It has a sunroof, and electric windows," Daryl said.

Rex practically bobbed with excitement. "And headrests, oh it's brilliant."

Daryl's face contorted as if he'd never realised there were cars on the road without headrests.

Eddie grimaced. "I'd prefer the cash."

"I got about five hundred quid I could pay you as well, I know it's not a lot," Daryl said. "But I'm not sure my parents are gonna pay you anytime soon. The car is in my name, and I can give it to you."

"Are any of the other cars in your name?" Eddie said.

Daryl shook his head.

Rex surveyed the other vehicles. "Got any vans? Maybe one with a porthole?"

Daryl's brows tightened.

With his face close to the passenger window, Eddie inspected the inside. "You think we could fit your parents' puffy red sofa in here?"

"I think so," Daryl said. "Why'd you ask?"

The detectives agreed to take the car and sofa in addition to the five hundred pounds. The vehicle registration was signed over to Eddie, and the pair carried the couch into the back.

Rex and Eddie got into the front seats. Eddie prodded at the yellow foam sticking out of a hole in the driver's seat.

"It's okay, Eddie. Nan's got some duct tape at home. I bet she'll make us a victory bacon sandwich too."

---

After Rex's nan served them a sandwich, two rounds of tea, and a slice of marble cake each, the pair drove back towards the office.

Eddie braked at the stop sign. While he checked left and right, Rex leaned towards the dashboard.

Rex pushed his glasses up on his nose. "Is that Georgia?"

Eddie squinted at the intersection ahead. Rex's sister carried two pairs of worn out shoes with the strings tied. She lobbed them up at the telephone wire above. The shoes wrapped around on her first try.

Rex pushed the window button. It made a satisfying "vush" sound. He popped his head out.

"Oi, Georgia, what you doing?"

She saw Rex and ran off into Elizabeth Gardens Park.

"Another mystery solved," Eddie said.

Rex gave a satisfied nod, oblivious to Eddie's sarcasm.

Once they arrived at their office, the pair carried the puffy red sofa up the narrow stairs. With a bit of wriggling, they made it into their office and placed it against the bare wall.

Rex glanced around. "What work do we have to do?"

Eddie checked the phone's messages. Zero. "We should give Spin Doctor back his stuff, but that can wait until tomorrow. Now we can catch up on sleep and wait for a new case."

"So we are gonna do another case."

"I guess we handled the last one pretty well." Eddie looked around at the walls and furniture. "And since I now live in a detective's office, I guess I'll have to keep calling myself a detective."

"That's great, Eddie. Anything else I can do today?"

"Well, someone needs to wash the mugs."

Rex scrunched up his face.

"I'll take care of it," Eddie said. "I guess I should be a little more house proud. Right now, I could do with a rest."

Eddie pulled an unzipped sleeping bag and pillow from the bottom filing cabinet drawer. He sat on the red sofa. His fingers stroked the velvet cushions.

"Hey, Eddie. Remember when we used to have sleepovers?"

"Yeah?"

"Can we do that here?"

"There's no bedding for you."

"That's fine." Rex gave a closed smile.

"No spare pillows," Eddie said.

"I don't need them."

"I've not got anything, it would be the hard wood floors."

Rex shrugged. "It's good enough for me."

"Well, yeah, if you want to."

After brushing his teeth in the communal toilet's sink, Eddie switched off the office lights. The orange hue from the street leaked though the window's blinds.

Eddie fluffed the pillow, settled on the sofa, and closed his eyes.

Rex lay down on the floor and wiggled into comfort.

"Hey Eddie, is a koala bear the only bear that lives in Australia?"

"I don't think it's a real bear. It's a marsupial."

"So it's more like a cross between a kangaroo and a monkey."

Eddie opened one eye. "Not sure that's accurate."

"What came first? The dinosaur or the egg?"

"I don't know."

"Do crocodiles laugh at chickens?"

Eddie screwed up his face. "Why?"

"Because if birds evolved from dinosaurs, do you think they're the butts of the jokes to crocodiles?"

"I don't think crocodiles think about it. They don't remember dinosaur times. They just get on with their day."

"Should you never smile at an alligator?"

"Please, no more animal questions."

Rex took a deep breath. "Sorry. Goodnight, Eddie."

"Goodnight, Rex."

Rex & Eddie return in

**WHEN IT RAINS**

## GET A FREE BOOK!

One of the best things about writing is building a relationship with my readers. I occasionally send newsletters with details on new releases, special offers, and other news related to the Rex & Eddie Mysteries series.

When you sign up to my newsletter I'll send you **Rebels Without A Claus: A Rex & Eddie Mystery**, a novelette set between book 1 and book 2!

Get your freebie today by signing up at

WWW.SEAN-CAMERON.COM/FREEBOOK

## ENJOY THIS BOOK?
### YOU CAN MAKE A BIG DIFFERENCE!

Book reviews are an excellent tool for getting the attention of new readers. If you've enjoyed *The Third Banana* I would be very grateful if you could spend just five minutes leaving an honest review (it can be as short as you like) on the book's Amazon page.

Thank you very much.

# ABOUT THE AUTHOR

Sean Cameron is from Rochester, England and currently lives in Los Angeles, California. When not laughing at the British weather report, he finds time to write the comedy book series *Rex & Eddie Mysteries*.

He likes carrot cake, dinosaurs, and hiking; although not much hiking happens as he fears being eaten by a mountain lion. He dislikes squash soup, traffic, and mountain lions.

You can drop him an email at sean@sean-cameron.com or visit his online home at www.sean-cameron.com.

facebook.com/seancameronauthor

twitter.com/seancameronuk

instagram.com/seancameronuk

amazon.com/author/seancameron

## ALSO BY SEAN CAMERON

### *Catchee Monkey: A Rex & Eddie Mystery (Book 1)*

Amateur sleuths Rex and Eddie stumble upon a murder mystery that sees them outnumbered, outgunned, and outwitted. They'll have to solve the case before it kills them or before they end up killing each other. *Catchee Monkey* is a hilarious detective novella that's equal parts British Comedy and gripping thriller.

### **Feline Fatale: A Rex & Eddie Mystery (Book 2)**

Rex and Eddie accept a case to find the missing cat of their old school teacher and first crush, Mrs Nerdlinger. The duo are pitted against a creepy stalker, a nosey neighbour, and a rude old woman claiming to be the cat's real owner. *Feline Fatale* is a fun and farcical thriller full of sharp dialogue, clever twists, and silly antics.

### **The Office Spy: A Rex & Eddie Mystery (Book 3)**

Spies, sleuths, and sandwich thieves — For Rex and Eddie, it's just another day in the office. Hired to find a corporate spy, Rex and Eddie go undercover as pest exterminators. Their spy hunting antics entangle the pair in office politics, employee secrets, and the search for the kitchen's sandwich thief. *The Office Spy* is a fun novella packed with silly hijinks, clever jokes, and crazy thrills.

**The Third Banana: A Rex & Eddie Mystery (Book 4)**

After a routine surveillance job ends in witnessing a kidnapping, dimwitted detectives Rex and Eddie get on the wrong side of super sleuth Jason Cole. He's special forces, they're just… special. Now the detective duo must prove their worth against the best, solve the kidnapping case, and stop a gang turf war that could destroy their hometown. Full of witty mayhem, *The Third Banana* is a comedy thriller with appeal.

## ACKNOWLEDGMENTS

I'd like to thank the following for their help with this book: Sam Whittam, Eleanor Hoal, Sherry Holthe, Wesley Farrow, and John Atkins.